PRIVATE PRACTICE

PRIVATE PRACTICE

Steven Mollov

authorHOUSE®

AuthorHouse™
1663 Liberty Drive
Bloomington, IN 47403
www.authorhouse.com
Phone: 1-800-839-8640

The names and accounts of these characters are fictional. Furthermore, there is no association between the title of this novel and any other similarly titled media event.

First published by AuthorHouse   07/20/2011

ISBN: 978-1-4634-2185-4 (sc)
ISBN: 978-1-4634-2184-7 (dj)
ISBN: 978-1-4634-2183-0 (ebk)

Library of Congress Control Number: 2011909757

Printed in the United States of America

Any people depicted in stock imagery provided by Thinkstock are models, and such images are being used for illustrative purposes only.
Certain stock imagery © Thinkstock.

This book is printed on acid-free paper.

Dedication

To Mark and Liam, who make me smile every day.

ACKNOWLEDGMENTS

I would first like to thank my wife, Paula, for her encouragement in finally bringing this story to fruition.

I would also like to thank my daughter-in-law, Sarah Green Mollov, for her significant efforts in editing the final version, a task which no author should have the responsibility of performing!

To my cousin, Elaine Rosenkranz, for her invaluable contributions to the manuscript.

And finally, to the labor floor nurses at Anna Jaques Hospital for their enthusiasm with its content and generating the excitement in me to make this a reality.

CHAPTER ONE

FEBRUARY 1988 HAD BEEN a particularly heavy month for snow, even for the town of Breedville, New Hampshire. Its residents were used to five or six big storms each winter, and this year was no exception. The grass on the town mall hadn't seen daylight since Thanksgiving, and the white crust on George Washington's cap as he sat astride his mount in the square was beginning to look commonplace. Of course, snow was no problem for the folks of northern New England. The town budget always managed to have enough money to keep the streets clean, and a four-wheel drive could be found parked outside most homes.

The snow was just beginning to slow when the phone rang in the Barron home. Joshua Barron, deep into a dream, was just sinking a 20-foot birdie in the Pebble Beach Pro-Am Tournament. The roar of the crowd blended in with the noise of the phone, and it took four rings before reality interrupted his flawless round of golf.

"Hello," Joshua sputtered. A pause. "Ah-hah, I'll be right there."

With the perfect putt a distant memory, the tired obstetrician trudged to the bathroom. He glanced in the mirror. The graying, tussled hair and unshaven face did not bespeak the impeccable professional who would show up at the hospital a mere thirty minutes later. Would you let this man deliver your baby? With this thought in mind, a grin slowly crept across Joshua's face. He knew that force of habit would transform his tired, middle-aged self into the confident obstetrician he was known to be. In less than ten minutes, Joshua was in the garage, warming up his '83 Jeep Cherokee. The cold blast of frigid air was the last stimulus he needed to jump-start his body. He backed the car out into the snow and headed down his quiet cul-de-sac towards Main Street and Breed General Hospital.

The call had come from Casandra Robinson, who worked the eleven to seven shift on the labor floor at Breed General. Sandy, as she liked to be called, was in her twelfth year at Breed, having spent all of her professional career on the maternity floor. She was a native of Breedville, leaving for only two of her thirty-two years to earn her nursing degree at the old Boston Lying-In Hospital. She eagerly returned to the familiar surroundings of her hometown following graduation. The city had been too hectic for Sandy, and though she appreciated the instruction and experience she felt she could only get in a big city hospital, she longed for the more peaceful pace of her quiet, rustic town.

Sandy felt badly waking Dr. Barron at home for the third straight night. He'd seemed so tired recently and had lost that sparkle in his eyes he used to get each time he welcomed another child into the world. Sandy liked working with Dr. Barron—he was so warm and upbeat, with the quiet confidence of a seasoned professional. She also knew that her feelings for him ran a lot deeper, but that had been discouraged years ago. Nonetheless, her calls to Dr. Barron these last few nights gave her the juvenile satisfaction of bringing him in to spend time with her.

Ellen Landry felt like she had been pregnant forever. Her actual due date was not for another week, but she was grateful for the bloody discharge and the intense, persistent cramping in her stomach. This was her second pregnancy, the first culminating in a seven-pound girl two weeks overdue. Ellen was a regular of Dr. Barron's, a loyal patient for six years now. She still found it astonishing that she'd picked him out of the yellow pages during the second month of her previous pregnancy—not exactly the most discerning method. She should have requested a referral from her former physician, the local medical society, or even a neighbor over the back fence. But at the time, Ellen had been new in town. She let her fingers do the walking and never once regretted her decision. Her first pregnancy had been complicated by a variety of problems: first trimester bleeding, gestational diabetes, and then, the eternity of waiting two weeks past her due date. Throughout it all, Dr. Barron had been there for her, and she found his presence entirely comforting and reassuring. To Ellen's way of thinking, he could do no wrong, and she had since referred many of her friends.

Ellen's thoughts were interrupted by another tremendous spasm in her mid-abdomen, requiring her to lean against the kitchen wall for support. Her husband Jack was asleep. He had just gone to bed an hour before, insistent on seeing the end of Johnny Carson. Although he had been very supportive during her pregnancies and was a wonderful husband and father, Ellen knew that Jack was not one to get wrapped up in the minute-to-minute details of her labor. He was also not terribly fond of blood, pain or hospitals, and it had taken all of Ellen's powers of persuasion to get him to go through labor by her side. She had in turn felt terribly guilty when he hit the floor of the delivery suite like a felled tree as his baby daughter's head entered the world. Fortunately, the fall had been broken by a hapless student nurse witnessing her first delivery. The poor girl suddenly found herself sprawled on the floor, a limp 210-pound new father atop her. It had been a scene right out of a sitcom. As with the make-believe of television, no one was hurt, a little dignity was lost and everyone had a good laugh at Jack's expense. Since then, Ellen agreed that Jack could be in the waiting room for their next encounter with childbirth.

As the spasm of this latest contraction faded, she heard her mother's car enter the driveway. She had called her fifteen minutes earlier, and no amount of snow was going to stop Mary Johnson from assuming the grandmotherly duty of watching her sleeping granddaughter while her second grandchild was being born.

"How are you feeling, Honey?" she asked as Ellen opened the front door. "Where's Jack?"

Before Ellen could answer, another contraction began, and Mary ran to get her son-in-law. Mary and Jack had a wonderful relationship—as long as nothing important was going on.

"Jack, get up! The baby's coming!" She screamed as she shook him roughly.

"Huh? What'sa matter? What are you doing here?" he sputtered, trying to gather his bearings.

"You're going to ruin the *second* delivery too, Jack! Except *this* one's going to be in your kitchen if you don't move your bum!"

The situation dawned on Jack, and he leapt into action and was dressed and ready to go within seconds. Despite the snow, the driving was not hazardous and Ellen and Jack arrived at the hospital in a matter of minutes. The admissions secretary started to ask for an insurance card, but changed her mind when Ellen started into her deep breathing. She instead whisked them both up to the maternity floor, where Sandy recognized Ellen from her previous pregnancy.

"Hi Ellen! How are you, Jack?" She saw that Ellen appeared to be in advanced labor and quickly helped her change, examined her and called Dr. Barron.

Joshua pulled into the doctor's parking lot at 3:15 AM, about thirty minutes after receiving Sandy's call. His transformation was now complete; the sleepy-eyed golf duffer had become an alert, take-charge professional. He ran to the emergency entrance and hurried to the elevator. This thing can't be tied up at three in the morning, he thought. Shaking his head, he opted for the stairs. At the mid-floor landing, he noticed an ache in his left shoulder and a tingling in the fingers of his left hand. The symptoms had been there before and he had dismissed it as a muscle strain. This time they lingered, and he found himself slowing his pace up the remaining steps. As the ache and tingling disappeared, his mind refocused on the clinical situation at hand.

"Hi, Dr. Barron," Sandy said. "Sorry to bother you again tonight. Mrs. Landry is pretty uncomfortable. She just broke her bag of water. The fluid is clear and the monitor strip is reactive."

"I guess I've just had a run of bad luck. Of course, if I keep doing my deliveries at night, I won't have to be disturbed during my office hours," he said sarcastically.

The sarcasm of Dr. Barron's logic was not lost on Sandy. It was well known that Joshua Barron had spread himself too thin and desperately needed a partner. Sandy knew that there were plenty of hospital personnel urging him to review applications, but she also knew that his practice was his life. His standards were simply too high, and he worked too hard, which worried her. What also worried her was Dr. Barron's current appearance—he looked quite pale, and a bit out of breath.

After listening to Sandy's report on Ellen's status, Joshua continued on to the obstetricians' lounge and changed into a green scrub suit. With Ellen's chart in hand, he made his way to her labor room.

"Hi Ellen," Joshua greeted her. "How're you handling them?"

Ellen answered with short *hooo haaahs* as her latest contraction reached its peak. Beads of sweat had broken out on her forehead as she sat Indian style on the labor bed, eyes fixated on the picture of her little girl, placed across the room strategically at eye level. As the contraction faded, she left her semi-trance.

"Hi, Dr. Barron," Ellen breathed. "I think I'm doing fine. Jack's in the waiting room this time—I told him it was okay with me. Besides, Sandy's been great."

Sandy smiled and blushed. She knew she was a good labor coach, but she never could handle a compliment well.

"I think you've really got it together, Ellen," Sandy said.

"You look like a great team to me," Joshua said, knowing that reassurance was the most important therapy at this time. He donned a latex glove and quickly examined Ellen before the next contraction started.

"Eight centimeters with the vertex at zero station," he reported to Sandy, who recorded it in Ellen's chart. "Have the lab draw a hematocrit and a second sample for blood typing. If the monitor isn't too uncomfortable, let's leave it in place. I'll go say hello to Jack." He left Ellen starting to breathe through another contraction while Sandy processed his orders.

Joshua found Jack in the father's waiting room. It was more like a large alcove than a room. The name had come from much earlier days, before societal changes had ushered (or perhaps unwillingly dragged) fathers into the labor room.

In more recent years, the room had become a hangout for other family members and friends. After his unfortunate experience with baby number one, Jack was opting for the old-fashioned way. Joshua found him in classic "pace mode" with a cup of coffee in his hand, his lips tight. If Joshua had asked for clean rags and boiled water, he would have responded immediately and fetched the requested items.

"How's she doin', Doc? Is she okay?" Jack queried.

"Ellen's fine, Jack. She's in great control and it shouldn't be terribly much longer. Try to relax."

Jack continued to pace. Joshua poured himself a cup of coffee and was just sitting down in a comfortable chair in the corner of the alcove when the ominous siren of the emergency alarm went off.

"What's that, Doc?" Jack asked frantically. He noticed a bright blinking light down the hall in front of Ellen's labor room.

"The baby's probably ready and they want me back there," said Joshua, aware of the control in his voice. He knew that the alarm was the nurse's signal for help, not delivery, but there was no point in rattling an already nervous husband. "I'll have to go, Jack. Try not to worry." He hurried to Ellen's room and disappeared inside. The blinking lights and siren subsided.

As the door of the labor room closed behind Joshua, the scene inside was worse than he had expected. Where before there was an uncomfortable yet calm laboring patient, pandemonium had broken loose. Ellen Landry was in a knee chest position with her buttocks up in the air and an oxygen mask covering her nose and mouth. The fetal monitor was showing a low heart rate of only sixty beats per minute. Sandy had acted appropriately, trying to position Ellen so that her baby would get the most oxygen and respond with a more normal heartbeat. To this point, this method had been unsuccessful. Joshua donned a glove. In examining Ellen, he found her cervix to be fully dilated and the baby's head just inside the vagina.

Sandy's voice was tense. "Dr. Barron, the heart rate doesn't appear to be responding to our usual maneuvers."

"I think I can ease the baby out with the vacuum extractor. Let's set her up for delivery and get me a pudendal set."

Sandy moved the appropriate instruments into place as Joshua helped Ellen turn onto her back with her feet resting on support plates, keeping her knees separated.

"My baby, my baby!" Ellen cried.

"Ellen, the baby is going to be just fine," Joshua reassured. "I'm going to help you deliver. Just listen to what I say and we'll get through this together." His voice was calm and reassuring.

Joshua injected the anesthetic. In seconds, both nerves that provided sensation to Ellen's birthing canal were numb, allowing Joshua to perform the necessary maneuvers to deliver her child. He attached a plastic cup to the baby's head while it was still in the vagina and Sandy attached the other end to a vacuum pump. After cutting an episiotomy to allow more room for the baby's head, he pulled on the plastic cup and gradually the head of the child appeared at the opening of the vagina. Ellen pushed hard, and in what took seconds but felt like hours, Joshua delivered Ellen of a large male child. He suctioned out the baby's nose and mouth and removed two loops of tight umbilical cord from around the baby's neck—the apparent cause of the sudden drop in fetal heartrate.

"I'm getting a heart beat of less than a hundred," Sandy said, listening to the newborn with a stethoscope. Joshua promptly rubbed the baby's back vigorously to stimulate respirations. He continued to suction the baby and stimulate him while Sandy covered the infant's nose and mouth with oxygen. The timer went off, signifying the infant was one minute old. Sandy and Joshua reviewed the baby's status.

"One for heart rate, one for tone, one for grimace. That's a total of three." Sandy was referring to the Apgar score, a list of five criteria which are graded and used to determine how well a baby is doing after birth. Suddenly, as if the infant had sensed that the poor adults in the room had suffered enough, he began to scream uncontrollably. A look of relief appeared on everyone's face. The baby responded quickly and by five minutes of age his Apgar score had reached nine out of a possible ten. The baby was fine and Sandy could continue with the more mundane activities of tagging and wrapping him in a warm blanket. Tears rolled down Ellen's face as joy and relief replaced anxiety and pain. Joshua easily delivered the placenta. The episiotomy was sewn up in short order and he began to fill out the chart.

"You okay?" Sandy asked Dr. Barron. Through the anxious moments of the birth, he had seemed his usual, controlled self. But now he appeared paler than before and was sweating profusely.

"I'm fine, Sandy," Joshua reassured her. He wished however that he could reassure himself as well. Something was wrong—very wrong. The shoulder pain was bothering him again and the fingers on his left hand were tingling. Feeling the room was closing in on him, he took the chart, and without congratulations to the new mother, headed for the doctors' lounge and a cold glass of water. In the lounge his breathing became easier and the shoulder ache settled down. He finished the chart and returned to the labor room to check on Ellen.

"Her uterus is firm and the flow is minimal," Sandy reported. Reassured, he congratulated Ellen and then went down to the father's waiting room to tell Jack the good news. He was now feeling considerably better and accompanied Jack to the labor room to visit with his new son.

As Joshua changed back into his street clothes in the lounge, his concern for the unusual symptoms resurfaced and he promised to speak to his friend and personal physician, Phil Lambert, in the morning. For now he wanted to get home and catch a few more hours of sleep.

Leaving the maternity floor he headed towards the stairs, then stopped at the top of the landing and opted for the elevator. This time there was no wait.

"Hi, Dr. Barron. Did you let another baby get you out of bed again tonight?" teased Joe O'Mally, the night guard.

"Yeah, I guess so," Joshua admitted.

"Well, you have a good rest of the night, Doc," the guard said as he headed down the hall towards the emergency room to complete his night rounds.

Joshua left the hospital moving a little slower than usual in the snow and frigid air. He opened the door of his Cherokee and got inside. As he started the engine, he clutched his shoulder, feeling the tingling again in his fingers. A warm feeling began to spread over his chest and neck and sweat beaded on his forehead. The inside of the car appeared to be getting smaller and smaller and his breathing became labored. But it was too late to act. The excruciating pain of dying cardiac muscles overwhelmed his being and as he lost consciousness, his body fell over the car's horn, sending out an urgent call for help.

CHAPTER TWO

JOSHUA BARRON HAD TO grow up fast in the summer of 1950. On a hot day in late July, the oldest son of Catherine Breed and Josiah Barron was out doing what most twelve year old boys did in the summertime—playing baseball in the schoolyard. It was Sarah Stewart, their neighbor and his mother's best friend, who came to fetch him. He never forgot that moment. He'd just finished singling home his teammate from third base and was proudly relishing the achievement.

"Joshua!" Sarah called urgently as she approached him at first base, "Your mother needs you. I've come to take you home." She spoke in a way that he knew not to protest.

"Mrs. Stewart?" Joshua asked, wrenched out of his glory. "What's wrong?"

"Your father has taken ill. Your mother needs you home right now." There was no further discussion. The momentary baseball hero sat in the front seat of the Stewarts' Chevy, lost in thought. As was true of most twelve year olds, Joshua saw his father as invincible. He was a doctor—doctors didn't get sick. How bad could it be? Still, he was worried. He shivered briefly, staring out the window as Mrs. Stewart drove in silence.

Along their drive, the Chevy sped past the mall with the statue of George Washington proudly mounted on his horse. This was a favorite place for Joshua. He still remembered the day when he and his father, out flying kites, managed to catch the string on the head of the steed. As they untangled the mess, his father had taken the opportunity to share the story of the statue, which commemorated an event that had occurred nearly two hundred years ago. Garrison Breed, an ancestor from his mother's side, was honored by General Washington for saving his life during The Revolutionary War.

"Was he really related to Mom?" young Joshua asked.

"Well, your mom's family has lived here a long, long time, and her last name is Breed. That story's been passed down through her family for years. I'm pretty sure she's done some solid research on it at the library, too."

"Did he really save Washington's life?"

"That's how the story goes," Josiah answered. "The circumstances are questionable. No one knows why he was so far away from his regiment when he came upon the sniper." At this point in the narration, his father picked Joshua up high and held him so he could reach the string around the horse's head. He felt so tall in his father's grasp.

"Can you reach it, Josh?"

"Got it!"

"Well done," he said, putting Joshua down and continuing on. "Breed was apparently wounded during the scuffle and never had to serve in the army again. They erected this statue here to commemorate his actions—the award ceremony took place right on this spot. They even changed the name of the town; it used to be called Salem's Crossing, after the engineer who built the first bridge across the Merrimack. Since he wasn't a local, they felt no obligation to keeping the original name."

"Wow." was all Joshua could say. His family was famous.

The front door of the house was open when they arrived. There were adults milling around, all speaking very quietly. The shades were drawn. He found his mother on the living room couch, her eyes red, with his sister and brother by her side.

"Oh Joshua!" she cried as she reached out to embrace him. A shiver again came over Joshua's body, but he did not cry. He held her as her tears ran to his neck and shoulder.

"Your daddy loved you so," she continued to sob. "You were his big boy, his helper. He was so proud of you."

The next few days were a blur. Memories of sitting next to his mother on the couch, being consoled by people he barely knew. Dressing up in his good suit and making sure his younger siblings behaved. There was the funeral, and the open casket—his father looking so calm and rested, the stethoscope in his hands. The cemetery, the big hole in the ground, the dirt scattered on the coffin as it was lowered down.

And then it was over. The endless flow of visitors stopped. They were left with countless vases of roses and a refrigerator full of casseroles and lasagnas—just twenty minutes to a home-cooked meal. His aunt and uncle lingered for a few days to help his mother get the details of Josiah's estate in order, but the house had never felt emptier.

It had been a heart attack that took his father from him on that sunny summer day. That's the story the autopsy told. Josiah had been at the hospital attending to a delivery when he slumped down in his chair at the nurse's station. Mother and baby were fine; the doctor was dead. A code was called. Another physician making rounds tried to revive him. No response.

After his father's death, Joshua quickly realized that his mother was not prepared to fill her husband's shoes. Catherine Barron was extremely loving and undoubtedly devoted to her family, but she was not able to pick up the pieces and be the strong pillar that her family needed. Josiah had been the protector, the planner, the disciplinarian. Joshua promptly took on the challenge of becoming the man of the house. It was he who made sure his younger siblings did their homework and made their beds. It was Joshua who took on the role of fixing things around the house—replacing light bulbs and mowing the lawn, installing insulation in the winter and cleaning out the gutters in the fall. He developed an inner strength and confidence in knowing that he had taken over for his father when the family needed him the most.

It only made sense that Joshua felt the drive to follow in his father's professional footsteps, as well. He matriculated at Dartmouth College, only two hours from home, allowing frequent weekends in Breedville to continue his family obligations. Boston University School of Medicine was next, followed by postgraduate training in obstetrics and gynecology at Boston Lying In Hospital. Many who knew Joshua's history felt he selected this specialty due to the circumstances of his father's death. They could have just as easily rationalized his becoming a cardiologist for similar reasons. But Joshua knew that he was his own man. He recognized the opportunity to be a primary care giver and a surgeon at the same time. He could be an expert in his field with little reason to refer for outside help. He would become the consummate physician—able to take charge and assume responsibility, instilling the utmost confidence. The qualities that made a superior ObGyn were a direct extension of the responsibilities that Joshua had readily accepted as a teenager, and he felt at home in his new profession.

There was never any question that Joshua would return to Breedville to practice. He was the first board certified obstetrician on staff at Breed General, and his presence had been the impetus for change at the hospital. Before Joshua Barron's entrance, most deliveries were attended by family practitioners (like Josiah Barron); gynecologic procedures and cesareans were done by the surgeons. Due to Joshua's standing in the medical community,the medical staff grudgingly assented to the addition of a specialist.

Breed General continued to grow over the years as the surrounding population expanded and the community needs increased. The labor floor was modernized in 1970 and a coronary intensive care unit was introduced less than a decade later. This unit was the pride of the hospital, having won several architectural awards for its unique design. Its cutting-edge technology had even inspired several prominent cardiologists to leave their big city posts and settle in the countryside on the banks of the Merrimack River. It was in Room 1 of this coronary unit that Joshua Barron was now residing, having been discovered unconscious, leaning on the horn of his four-wheel drive in the middle of a cold, snowy night.

CHAPTER THREE

ELIZABETH BARRON WAS SLEEPING soundly when the call came in from the nurse on duty in the intensive care unit at Breed General. As an obstetrician's wife, Elizabeth had developed a necessary defense mechanism—sleeping through a ringing phone. It never ceased to amaze Joshua that he could be woken up in the middle of the night, drive to the hospital, return home, and over his morning coffee be asked by his wife how he'd slept. He would tease her that a perfect stranger could take his place in their bed while he was at the hospital and she would never know the difference. So, with this habit deeply engrained in Elizabeth's sleeping patterns, the phone rang ten times before it was finally answered.

"Hello, Mrs. Barron? This is Betsy Cameron, the ICU charge nurse at Breed. Your husband was admitted here just a few minutes ago with chest pain."

Still half-asleep, Elizabeth could barely tell if this phone call was a dream or reality. "Wha—I mean, how—how is he?" she stammered.

"Dr. Lambert is on his way to the hospital to evaluate him. He seems to be stable for the moment, but you might want to come right in. I'm so sorry to have to relay this kind of news to you."

"Thank you for calling." Elizabeth was now awake. "Tell my husband I'll get in there as soon as I can."

She hung up, the gears in her head beginning to churn. After living with Joshua and his obstetrical practice for over twenty years, Elizabeth had come to rely on herself for the day-to-day handling of family business. Joshua was rarely home long enough to eat dinner or watch a movie with her on the couch uninterrupted, let alone attend to details like paying the bills, balancing the checkbook or managing the hectic schedules of their three children. All of these responsibilities fell squarely in Liz's lap. She was nothing if she wasn't self-reliant—a trait that she knew would help her through this family crisis.

The clock on her night stand hit 6:15 AM. Her daughter Julie, a freshman in high school, would be waking any moment to get ready for school. James, her older brother, was a senior and rarely got up more than five minutes before flying out the door to catch their 7:15 bus. Jeff, the youngest, still benefited from a junior high school schedule that ran an hour later than the high school. This gave Elizabeth the time she needed for that ever important cup of coffee and a chance to process this unsettling news. She would not allow her emotions or fears to get the best of her. There would be plenty of time for that later. Joshua was alive and apparently stable; now she needed to make sure everything else was under control.

As the caffeine made its way into her system, Elizabeth reviewed the planned activities of the morning—unfortunately, Wednesdays were usually quite busy. The library committee would just have to function without its chairperson, and the gas meter man would leave an estimated bill. The only other thing to do would be to call her friends later and cancel their plans for tennis and lunch at the club. Elizabeth breathed a heavy sigh. She had already decided not to tell the children.

She needed them in school this morning; there was no time to handle their concerns in addition to her own. She'd tell them this afternoon, once she had a chance to digest and evaluate it all.

Elizabeth toasted two slices of whole wheat bread and covered them with peanut butter before laying them out with napkins on the kitchen counter. The clock hit 7:10. On queue, Julie entered the kitchen, looking put-together and ready for school. She picked up a slice of toast as she slung her book bag over her shoulder.

"Thanks, Mom! I have cheer practice after school today. Love you!"

"OK, hun. Come home right after practice today, OK?" Liz kissed her daughter on the head as she left.

"Hey Mom. Who called this morning?" It was Jim, rushing into the kitchen with his books flying and his coat half on.

"Oh, just the hospital calling for your father. I told them he was already there and they should page him. Aren't you going to have breakfast?"

"I'm almost late for the bus already. Anyway, I'm really not hungry."

Despite his voracious appetite, her elder son spent more time picking out the perfect outfit and primping in front of the mirror than he did worrying about his stomach.

"You mean Dad spent another night in the hospital this week? I don't know, Mom" Jim grinned, "I think you oughta be more suspicious!" Before his mother could reply to this innuendo, Jim was out the door.

She made breakfast and put lunch together for Jeff before dispatching him to the bus. They were used to their father being away in the morning, so his absence didn't raise any suspicions. With her diversions gone, Elizabeth was now able to focus on her concern for her husband. As she dressed, she recalled several instances of Joshua complaining of being tired. It wasn't like him to complain of physical ailments, but at the time she hadn't ascribed any more significance to his complaints than he had. It was true he was overworked. His office schedule was always double booked and he was attending more than thirty deliveries a month. They had talked about him looking for a partner on several occasions or at least consider joining with the other obstetrical group in town. But her husband never seemed to have time for the former and refused to consider the latter. Although he was friendly with the other two obstetricians, he didn't consider them to be as compulsive nor as up to date as he thought necessary. They had covered his practice infrequently when Joshua was out of town, but invariably there would be a problem he would have to straighten out whenever he returned.

All things in order, Elizabeth finally prepared to leave for the hospital. As she put on her coat and grabbed her purse from the table in the foyer, she caught her reflection in the mirror. She was an attractive woman. Her long brown hair hung straight to the shoulders of her five foot five inch frame. The outline of her breasts beneath the white turtleneck sweater was proportioned to the rest of her slim body. The births of her three children had not taken their toll on her figure as it had on so many other women she knew, and her efforts to keep herself in shape helped maintain that figure. She looked far younger than forty-five. She dressed impeccably, even when appearing casual. No one ever would have guessed that this well-coordinated, neatly pressed woman had received such disconcerting news just a few hours prior.

The Barron's neighbor's son had fortunately plowed the driveway early that morning, and the driving was reasonably safe. Elizabeth was native to northern New England, as was her husband, therefore snow was never more than an inconvenience. She turned left on to Main Street and headed towards the hospital.

Elizabeth allowed her mind to wander to her husband as her station wagon moved down the street. Joshua had always been in excellent health. Although his practice gave him little time for himself, he ate sensibly, didn't smoke and he rarely drank. He was just over six feet, 180 pounds; aside from the gray hair, Elizabeth thought Joshua to be the healthiest, best looking fifty year old she knew.

Of course, she was aware of his father's early death from a heart attack. But the rest of the Barron clan had all lived well into their eighties. Still, Elizabeth couldn't help but find blame in Joshua's past—not physical, but emotional. She knew the stressors that had been put on her husband at such an early age, factors that ultimately fed into his adult and professional life. She vowed to take a more active role in helping her husband find an associate so he could slow down for the first time in his life. She would talk to Ann, Joshua's office manager, and see what the status was on the search.

As she passed the statue of George Washington, her memory flashed back to a very early memory with Joshua. He, a studious and slightly awkward senior at Dartmouth College, had tried to impress her with the fact that it was at this spot that the first president had presented a medal to his ancestor, Garrison Breed. At that time, she'd been much more impressed by his big shoulders and his dry wit and couldn't care less about his famous lineage. They had met at a college football weekend, each with another date. She was a "high school honey" of his roommate at school. Fortunately, Joshua's date had been more attracted to his roommate than to him, and the feeling rapidly became mutual. As a favor to his roommate, Joshua offered to take Elizabeth off his hands, and the rest was easy and natural. They spent the rest of the weekend in continuous conversation, both eager to know as much as possible about the other. Their dating throughout the rest of the year was sporadic at best, considering that she was only a junior in high school. He moved to Boston for medical school and she followed a year later, entering a liberal arts college just outside the city limits. Within three years of that football weekend, they were married.

As she reminisced, Elizabeth's eyes began to tear. The control that had been so evident at home that morning was now breaking down. She needed to release the tension before seeing Joshua, and she sobbed the rest of the way. By the time the station wagon entered the hospital grounds, she was back in control. She parked in the doctor's parking lot and entered the new wing of Breed General Hospital. Although she had been to the hospital many times before, it was always in the physicians' lounge on the labor floor. She was unfamiliar with the intensive care unit and needed directions from the front desk. Having no patience for the elevator, she took the stairs to the second floor and soon was on her way to Room 1 of the coronary unit.

CHAPTER FOUR

A PHYSICIAN IN THE INTENSIVE care unit represents irony at its highest point. For any doctor, this is a role reversal that would prove extremely difficult to transcend. In the ICU, independence is usurped, modesty is compromised and adults revert to babies requiring constant care and attention. Not only is the physician forced into the unfamiliar role of patient, but he must suffer the dependence of illness without the reassurance of ignorance.

Unable to muster his usual defense mechanisms, Joshua Barron had submitted to total dependence. He lay in his hospital bed, staring at the ceiling in a room where day and night did not exist, and the transition of TV programs from one to the next was the only reminder that time was, indeed, still ticking. The only persistent stimuli were the intermittent beep of the cardiac monitor and the steady click of the IVAC machine that was regulating his intake of intravenous fluids.

Fortunately for Joshua, his myocardial infarction was uncomplicated. He did not develop an irregular heartbeat nor the advent of pulmonary edema, a condition in which the lungs fill up with fluid. Ten milligrams of morphine sulfate had eased the pain and he was actually resting quite comfortably when Phil Lambert arrived.

"What's a nice guy like you doing in a place like this?" Phil said slyly upon entering. Phil checked the monitor by Joshua's bed, then quickly perused the pulse and blood pressure stats in his medical chart. He placed his stethoscope at a number of locations on Joshua's chest and listened.

"Lungs clear, heart steady. How's the pain?" he asked with concern.

"Actually, Phil, I'm feeling fine now. I thought it was all over in my car earlier. You know, buddy, you really do get that 'feeling of impending doom' thing." Joshua was referring to one of the classic symptoms of a heart attack that is taught in medical school—the "feeling of impending doom," along with pain running down the left arm along with diaphoresis, or sweating.

Phil picked up Joshua's chart and began to review the early test results that had already come in.

"No question about the diagnosis, I'm afraid. You've flipped your T waves, raised your S-T segments and have a brand new Q wave on the EKG." All of these changes on the cardiogram were indicative of recent injury and death to a portion of the cardiac musculature. "You're fortunate that you don't seem to have any complications. I think you're being given a warning and you're going to have to heed it."

"Well, Phil, I'm in no rush to get to the office this morning. Maybe we can do a round of golf once they clear the snow," Joshua quipped.

Phil smiled broadly. The two had known each other for over ten years and enjoyed each other's utmost respect and friendship. They had met at a medical meeting in Boston where Joshua was learning about heart disease in pregnancy. Phil was the cardiology fellow giving the lecture. Joshua approached him with a few questions after, and Phil had been impressed with Joshua's grasp of cardiac principles and pathology. "Not bad for an obstetrician!" he would taunt Joshua, years later. The two men continued their conversation over dinner that night. Phil was finishing his training and was looking to set up a practice. By the end of the course, Joshua convinced him to look at Breedville. Hailing from New York City, Phil had been skeptical of any town where it was safe to walk the streets at night. By the time he finished spending a weekend at Elizabeth and Joshua's home, he decided that the country was for him. For several years, he was part of the Barron family, sharing dinner with them on many occasions. After Elizabeth fixed him up with a close friend of hers, those dinners became a bit less frequent. Phil and Cindy married a year later and Joshua delivered their two children. The two couples remained close to this day.

"Seriously, Joshua," Phil continued, "You're going to have to cut back on your practice. You know that."

"I know," said Joshua with a hint of frustration. There was no denying his family history. "I guess it's back to the application pile. I'm sure I can get Breedville ObGyn to cover me for awhile at least."

"You're going to have to. I know you don't want to, but you have to. Take care. I'll see you later." Phil picked up his chart and went to find the ICU nurse.

"I'd like to see his cardiac enzymes as soon as they are available. Also, repeat a twelve lead EKG within the next hour. If he develops any additional pain or any cardiac arrhythmias, I want to know about them immediately—I'll be making rounds. And please let me know when Mrs. Barron arrives." This last request became moot when Phil bumped into Elizabeth as he was leaving the coronary unit.

"Phil!" Elizabeth cried. Her face was tense, her eyes red. "How is he?"

"He looks pretty good, Elizabeth." Phil gave her a reassuring hug. "It was definitely a heart attack, and we're going to have to see how he does over the next few days. He's resting comfortably now—he'll be so happy to see you," Phil paused. "You know, you're going to have to encourage him to slow down some."

"Thank God he's okay," said Elizabeth, too distracted to listen to the details that Phil had offered her. "Thank you, Phil," she said distractedly, and continued on to Joshua's room.

"Oh, my dear!" Elizabeth exclaimed upon seeing her husband in his hospital bed. Her control was wavering as she quickly moved to his side and kissed his forehead. "Are you in pain?"

"Actually, I feel okay," he answered weakly. "It's probably the morphine, though. I felt awful getting into the car to go home, and the next thing I knew I was in here. It was frightening, but Phil seems to feel that things could have been much worse. So, I guess I'm kind of lucky!" Joshua tried to smile.

The charge nurse was watching their conversation and could see that Joshua was getting a little winded.

"Mrs. Barron, I think your husband is getting pretty tired. Why don't you just sit here for a while beside him and give him a chance to rest."

Elizabeth nodded and sat by Joshua as he fell asleep. She asked the nurse for a pad of paper and pencil and began to compile a list of things to do. She always found this a good way to distract herself from emotional stress. On the top of her list was to notify Ann Stremp of Joshua's heart attack so she could arrange coverage and cancel out his appointments for the foreseeable future. Ann had been with Joshua for most of his twenty years. She was a fiercely loyal employee and a very take-charge kind of individual. With Ann on board, Joshua always had the luxury of focusing on his work, letting her handle the business side of things. To some extent, Elizabeth knew that Ann herself was one of the stumbling blocks in the way of Joshua obtaining a new partner. Her watchful guard over Joshua's practice and their professional relationship could be construed as jealous or controlling. But this was the breaking point. Elizabeth knew that she must convince Ann that a new partner was imperative.

Second on the list were the children. They would be anxious to see their father and she would bring them over to the hospital that evening as long as Joshua was well enough to see them. Third was the call to her friends to cancel their plan for lunch and tennis.

The longer the list became, the more confident Elizabeth felt. She glanced over to her sleeping husband. He looked so vulnerable in bed, hooked up to the myriad of medical instruments. Her eyes scanned the room, the blank television screen, the flimsy curtain by the bed for pseudo-privacy, the window providing a view of the nurse's station and the other ICU cubicles beyond. Her vision became fixed on the green blip of the cardiac monitor and its accompanying beep, counting out Joshua's heartbeat, reducing the measure of his life to its basic elements. Hypnotized by the monotonous noise and green lines of the monitor, Elizabeth felt herself begin to drift off. Almost instantly, the frightening blare of an alarm brought her back to the present with a start. A nurse hurried into the room. She turned off the alarm, took Joshua's blood pressure, then promptly went to the nurse's station and picked up the phone. Too jarred to speak, Elizabeth tried to listen in.

" . . . multiple PVCs . . . . 120 over 70 . . . respiratory rate . . . 20 . . . lidocaine drip . . ."

The nurse returned with a bag of IV solution and connected it to the line that was feeding Joshua's vein.

"What's wrong?" asked Elizabeth, fear rising in her chest.

"Dr. Barron's heart is producing extra beats and this medicine should straighten that out. Dr. Lambert is on his way back here, but I assure you, Mrs. Barron, this situation is not uncommon."

The nurse's reassurance was wasted on Elizabeth, who now sat helplessly in her chair. The pattern of green blips quickly returned to the more monotonous sequence. She was no doctor, but Elizabeth could derive at least some relief from this. Joshua slept right through this melodrama, though he began to stir as Phil entered the room.

"What's happening, Phil?" Elizabeth asked anxiously. "Is something wrong?"

"Cardiac irritability is fairly common following a myocardial infarction," Phil explained, studying the monitors. "The lidocaine drip should keep it under control." He saw no point in alarming her by further explaining that these irregular beats had the ability of throwing Joshua's heart into a potentially fatal arrhythmia.

"Hey, Phil. Any problems?" Joshua was now partly awake.

"You threw a few PVCs. The lidocaine drip seems to have put things back on course. The most important thing for you to do right now is rest." Phil tried to sound reassuring, but Joshua could detect concern. Nonetheless, he managed to drift back to sleep. Elizabeth reassumed her position on the chair in the corner and Phil returned to the nurse's station to check for lab results. The rest of the morning went uneventfully. Elizabeth left Joshua's room only briefly to make the calls on her list. Joshua continued to sleep peacefully while the monitor bleeped on.

Elsewhere in the hospital, the news of Dr. Barron's heart attack spread rapidly. A group of physicians sat in the medical records department downing coffee and doughnuts, philosophizing on the professional pressures that were capable of producing events like the one that had befallen Joshua Barron. Their fatalism was accentuated by the number of doughnuts consumed, the cigarette smoke that hung in the air and the obvious lack of physical activity of the bemoaners themselves. Joshua was a popular and well-respected member of the medical staff at Breed, and his fall from the ranks of the immortal was jarring. What shook them even more was the fact that Joshua was a non-smoker, exercised regularly and had never once partook of the endless supply of glazed confections in the break room. What chance did they have if coronary artery disease had dared attack such a specimen?

A similar group of physicians gathered in the surgeons' lounge, next to the operating room—no doughnuts here, just some nervous humor.

"I knew Joshua had a thing for the ICU nurses, but this time he took it too far!" joked Ted Dennis, a general surgeon. He was comparing theories on Joshua's illness with Frank DiMento, one of the staff urologists.

"Just goes to show what clean living will do for you. No smoking, no drinking, no fooling around. No wonder his heart broke," suggested Frank.

Though neither man was very close to Joshua, they both felt vulnerable in the wake of the news. It could just as easily have been them up in the unit and both felt, as did many, that they had dodged a bullet. By nature of their profession, physicians tended to build walls around themselves, allowing them to look at death, disfigurement and illnesses with a degree of cold aloofness. But the barrier of this defense mechanism would crack whenever disaster struck one of their own.

While this dark cloud hovered over the entire hospital, nowhere existed a more somber mood than the labor floor. For staff members who knew Dr. Barron, the event posed a personal hurt and worry. Morale was so low that a special meeting of the entire staff was held later that day. Many had tried to visit Dr. Barron, only to be turned away by the ICU nurses. Phil Lambert, anticipating visitors, had left strict orders that no one but immediate family was allowed to visit. He realized that these orders would be almost impossible to enforce, but he hoped to get at least 24 hours of relative isolation for Joshua to ensure his stability above all else.

The rest of the day was relatively uneventful for Joshua. Elizabeth brought the children over for a short visit after dinner and they found their father in good spirits. His heartbeat remained stable and he found himself sleeping less and less. Phil Lambert noted no further progression in the damage to Joshua's heart and within 24 hours the lidocaine drip was discontinued. Elizabeth stayed at home with the children that first night and returned early the following day to keep her husband company. She found him awake and watching the end of The Today Show.

"I missed you in bed last night." She kissed him.

"Mrs. Barron, don't you know you shouldn't be talking to a man in my condition like that?" He smiled up at her. "Besides, I haven't spent much time with you in bed this week anyway, so you have nothing to compare last night to."

This characteristic jocularity provided Elizabeth with hope that she might be able to discuss some future plans with Joshua today. She had spoken with Ann Stremp about the many decisions that needed to be made. Ann had been anxious to visit Joshua, but Elizabeth discouraged her for the time being, worried that Ann's intense energy would be too much for him at this stage. Despite acquiescing, Elizabeth sensed that Ann did not agree with her wishes. While there certainly was no love lost between the two, they had always respected the other's turf.

Elizabeth took a breath and began the conversation.

"I spoke with Ann. She is currently canceling all of your upcoming appointments, and has put in a call to Breedville ObGyn to arrange coverage. She will also set up new appointments for all of your patients who are close to term." She paused. "Ann is composing a letter that she will send to all cancelled patients, briefly explaining your situation, so that everyone knows what's going on. They will all be told that they'll be rescheduled as soon as you know when you will be back at work." No objection, not even the bat of an eye, from her husband.

"And lastly," Elizabeth continued, "I spoke to Ann about all of the applications you have sitting around. The ones for a partner." This time she waited for a response.

"And?" Joshua goaded.

"And I think it is time someone take a serious look at those. Ann promised that she would personally review them, select the most promising and check references for you. She will forward on her recommendations when you think you are well enough to interview."

That Ann herself planned to comb through the partner applications and separate the wheat from the chaff might have seemed presumptuous to some, but Ann knew Joshua's attitude regarding medical practice better than anyone else. She was more than capable of narrowing down a group of qualified applicants. Besides, Joshua wouldn't have the energy, and certainly not the interest, to be as compulsive as she knew Ann would be.

"I think this is the best way to move forward, given the circumstances," Elizabeth concluded. "It's time."

Joshua managed a smile after absorbing all the details. He could just picture the German tornado that was Ann Stremp, whirling around the office, straightening everything out and making all the preparations for this unexpected pause in his career.

"That all sounds fine," Joshua told his wife plainly, who was entirely pleased that the whole conversation had gone so well.

Later that afternoon, Phil came by to relay the good news that Joshua's condition was stable and that he would be transferred to the intermediate care unit the following morning. It was another four days until he was discharged, but at least he had a real window this time, looking out on the snowy landscape. By the time he went home, Joshua had entertained nearly every member of the hospital family. Even Ann Stremp was finally permitted to visit. She brought Joshua up to date and reassured him that the practice would be ready and waiting for him when Phil finally gave the word. Both obstetricians from Breedville ObGyn stopped by to touch base regarding his imminent deliveries. By carefully reviewing each patient with them, Joshua felt comfortable that the cases would be handled suitably. Both Sam Cronin and Bill Worth hoped that they might be able to talk Joshua into joining their practice, and so looked at this situation as an opportunity to pursue that course. They were extremely receptive to Joshua's concerns regarding patient management and promised to keep him informed on their outcomes. Although tentative, Joshua was willing to accept their help, and was grateful for it.

Ironically, that everything was going so smoothly during this transition period caused Elizabeth to worry. Joshua was being so reasonable regarding his practice and his own present limitations. She knew the perfectionist that she had married, and although pleased that he appeared so accepting of his situation, it simply was not like Joshua. Could it be a manifestation of depression, she feared?

Phil had told her that depression was a common occurrence following a heart attack and to inform him if she noticed any significant changes in his personality.

Despite his wife's worries, Joshua was well aware of a personal change in outlook, and it was not depression. He had seen the handwriting on the wall. He didn't want to end up like his father. The most intelligent solution was to focus on a full recovery and then pick up the pieces back at work. The key was finding a suitable partner to share the load, so there would be no compromise on quality. He knew it was just a matter of time, and now he felt he had all the time in the world.

CHAPTER FIVE

M ARIA SANCHEZ KNEW THAT something was very wrong. It had been nearly three months since her last period and she was quite confident that her fatigue, dry heaves and breast pain were due to a pregnancy. Maria was no stranger to pregnancy, having had four children in the last six years. But this time things were different. The pain in her left side had grown worse during the past two weeks and it now bordered on intolerable. She was incapable of taking care of her children in her present distress and had shipped them downstairs to her mother's apartment—thank God for her mother! She was always there when Maria needed her. God forbid Carlos ever be there to support her. Maria and Carlos had run off and eloped, to her father's dismay, at eighteen. She had been pregnant with their first child. Carlos dabbled at several jobs for a few years, but could never keep anything longer than six months, a year at most. The only thing steady about Carlos was his sexual appetite. Combined with his mistrust for contraception, ("The pill causes cancer, you know") Carlos rapidly became the father of four. He disappeared two months ago with Maria's girlfriend.

In addition to the intense pain, Maria had developed vaginal spotting. Never having availed herself of medical attention much before labor with her previous pregnancies, Maria had been hesitant to seek care. Now, she was desperate. The pain was tearing right through her. She frantically called an ambulance. As she hung up the phone, the pain suddenly ceased. The relief was overwhelming, but short-lived. The pregnancy that had been swelling up in her fallopian tube all these weeks had finally gnawed its way through the wall. The release of pressure provided the relief. The now unchecked flow of blood poured into Maria's abdomen. As her blood pressure dropped, her brain, deprived of its vital sustenance, was closing down her conscious state. She could see the flashing red light of the oncoming ambulance. After that, only darkness.

Alex Faber was having another busy night. She had to be available for two emergency cesarean sections performed by her residents. As luck would have it, both required her to bail the less experienced physicians-in-training out of a jam. In the first case, a tear had developed in the right uterine artery during delivery through the uterine incision. Blood began to squirt uncontrollably in to the operative field. Alex had quickly scrubbed and gowned, joining the operation to demonstrate to her residents how to handle this uncommon complication.

The second case was far worse. The baby had been delivered and the young physicians were having difficulty removing the placenta, or afterbirth, from the uterine cavity. Normally the placenta would shear off of its implantation site with little effort and minimal blood loss. This time however, the residents found themselves removing the placenta in fragments and the bleeding picked up. Alex diagnosed placenta accreta, a severe obstetrical complication, and scrubbed in once again. She quickly reviewed the principles of placentation, and how in rare cases, the afterbirth would not only implant into the uterine wall, but actually grow into the muscle layer and become an integral part of the uterus.

The patient rapidly lost several pints of blood before Alex was able to control the bleeding by performing an emergency hysterectomy in the delivery suite with the assistance of her resident staff. The patient would be incapable of future childbearing, but at least she would live to take care of her present newborn.

Now that the labor floor was under some semblance of order, Alex had a chance to finish her cup of coffee at the nurses' station.

This was not the way she envisioned her first year out of residency. After finishing her program in July at New York City Hospital, she had elected to stay on as a member of the attending staff. She enjoyed the academic setting and didn't feel ready for private practice. The few interviews she had turned her off to the outside world of medicine. One had been a small group of obstetricians on the Upper East Side. They had privileges to practice at several hospitals in the area and spent much of their time traveling from one to the other. The office itself had been professionally decorated and exuded a feeling of luxury and opulence. Though all four physicians had been well trained in their specialty, they had all seemed more preoccupied with the business of medicine and less with the practice of it. The other opportunity involved a position with an HMO, also in the City. In this setting, the physicians were totally divorced from the business aspects of the practice. Though all of their efforts were in the direction of patient care, there existed a nine-to-five mentality amongst the physicians she spoke to. Most were viewing their present position as a stepping-stone to eventual private practice, and she found the heavy physician turnover rate depressing.

Several other opportunities had developed, but she had not pursued them as of yet. Alex had elected to stay on in her current position, where she was responsible for resident training, both in the clinic setting and on the labor floor. She shared call with several other attending physicians and was required to stay in the hospital an average of every fourth night. She found her job both challenging and rewarding, but missed the opportunity of providing primary care to patients herself.

Alex's thoughts were interrupted by a call from one of the residents down in the emergency room. A twenty-five year old Hispanic woman had just been admitted in hypovolemic shock with a distended abdomen. The emergency room physician had smartly sent off a stat pregnancy test that had just come back positive. The gynecology resident had been called to evaluate her for a possible ectopic pregnancy. As the situation unfolded, it became clear to Alex that she would soon find herself in the operating room for the third time tonight. A female with a positive pregnancy test in severe abdominal pain with distension had a ruptured tubal pregnancy until proven otherwise. She advised a quick ultrasound in the emergency room to eliminate the possibility of a pregnancy in the uterus. As she expected, none was seen. The operating room was notified and within the half hour, Alex was once again trying to stop another woman from bleeding to death.

Instead of traveling down the fallopian tube and implanting in the uterus, Maria's fertilized egg had become trapped, and implanted there instead. While the initial implantation was successful, once the egg began to grow, the wall of the tube was not thick or strong enough to sustain its growth. The searing pain that Maria developed was a symptom of the breakdown of the wall of her fallopian tube, leading to uncontrollable bleeding in her abdomen.

Maria lay on a stretcher, a tube filled with blood running into her arm as she was rushed down the hallway by an army of green scrub suits. She heard voices trying to speak to her, but they sounded far off and garbled. She understood no English, and felt terribly afraid and alone. She wished she had her mother by her side.

As she was moved from the stretcher on to a metal table, Maria searched the room, afraid of what was going to happen next. The walls were covered in light green ceramic tiles, and there were stainless steel trays full of ominous instruments. Two bright lights were switched on, shining down on her abdomen. A figure in a paper mask and hat covered Maria's nose and mouth with a black rubber mask. She started to panic, and tried to turn her face.

"Relájese, Maria," a voice came. "Me llamo Doctor Faber. Tome una respiración profunda. Todo va a estar bien."

Hearing a soothing female voice speak recognizable words, Maria instantly relinquished her struggle. She felt the rubber mask close securely around her mouth and unconsciousness took over, like magic.

The anesthesiologist slipped a breathing tube into Maria's airway. After washing the abdomen with an iodide solution to prevent infection, the resident made a vertical incision from Maria's navel to her pubic bone. The several layers of tissue that comprised her abdominal wall were dissected open until they entered the abdominal cavity. It was obvious from the massive amount of blood in her belly that Maria had a major hemorrhage. Alex guided the residents through the case, trying to limit her instructions to verbal ones. The only way for them to learn, and for her to evaluate, was for the residents to handle the case without senior interference. To Alex's pleasure, they handled the procedure well.

Unfortunately for Maria, the aberrant pregnancy had cost her one of her fallopian tubes, which had been hopelessly destroyed. Another tube was still available for future pregnancies, although Alex was hoping Maria could be convinced to utilize one of the several effective forms of birth control available. Education was always the most neglected and ignored of the medical therapeutics.

When Maria woke, she was once again lying on a stretcher. She had left the room with the green tiled walls. Several men and women were standing over her, their faces no longer masked. Her belly hurt even more than it had before the surgery, but she was unable to cry out in pain. The tube running down her throat felt like it was gagging her. As she retched, the pain in her belly intensified. The doctors babbled on in English, not talking to her but at her. Finally, the woman with the soothing voice spoke to her in Spanish.

"Que está haciendo bien, Maria. Vamos a quitar el tubo de pronto."

Maria nodded, and felt a bit of her panic subside. One of the doctors pulled the uncomfortable breathing tube out of her throat. She eyed an IV pole with a bag of clear fluid by her stretcher, dripping medication into her arm. Drop by drop, her pain regressed. Dr. Faber, the kind woman who had comforted her in Spanish, sat down and explained what the doctors had done in the operating room.

Maria flinched when she heard that she would have to stay in the hospital for several more days—she worried about the cost, and about leaving her mom to deal with all four kids. Maria's previous hospital experiences had been horrific, leaving her extremely leery of doctors and the whole institution. But Dr. Faber seemed different. She was comforting. Dr. Faber was the first doctor who spoke to Maria as though everything was going to be OK.

"Where'd you learn to speak Spanish so well?" David Arnold, the chief resident who had operated on Maria asked Alex later in the surgeons' lounge. "Except for 'dolor,' 'sangre' and 'puje,' it's all as foreign to me as Russian." He was referring to the key words of obstetrics: "pain,", "blood,", and "push."

"Four years in high school and two years in college," Alex replied. "I also took Spanish for Medical Personnel during medical school, which was probably more helpful than those six years combined."

"That's really great," David replied. "Me, I'm just hopin' to get by till the end of residency. Once I finish at City Hospital, it's 'adios amigos' and 'hello suburbia.'" David never kept his materialistic goals a secret, and Alex had always found that a big turn-off. It was unfortunate, she thought, that a physician as capable as David Arnold would limit his goals to membership at a prestigious country club and a Mercedes 560SL.

"What about you?" David asked. "Are you going to stay here all your professional life or are you going to break out and experience the rest of the world?"

"I really wish I knew," Alex sighed. "I must admit I feel very safe here."

"Safe—hah! That's a relative term." David was referring to an incident in the ER several weeks ago where a twenty-year-old denizen of the streets took a few gunshots at a physician for failing to provide him with narcotics. Fortunately, the assailant was high as a kite and his shots were well off their mark. Nonetheless, the incident had shaken the entire staff and prompted demands for tighter armed security at the hospital.

"You know what I mean!" she said. "I'm just not sure what I want to do, and there is some security in the status quo, even at City Hospital."

"Come on, Alex. Don't you ever get the urge to buy a gorgeous condo, complete with a jacuzzi and a wide-screen, take out your Corvette and play tennis on the weekends with colleagues? You really want to be bogged down with this stuff your whole career?"

She had to admit that the vision was tempting. Still, the satisfaction of taking care of her patients throughout their entire pregnancies, and being there to welcome their new baby into the world was a far greater turn-on than the prospect of a tennis club membership and a sports car. Her own office, complete with support staff, a comfortable waiting room and patients whose lives she could become a part of, was her goal. Not a Jacuzzi.

"How about continuing this conversation over dinner tonight?" David asked, interrupting these thoughts.

Alex was caught off guard.

"Sure," she heard herself say. David wasn't exactly her cup of tea, but it had been so long since she had gone on a date. "Perhaps I can inspire you to more noble goals, David."

"Perhaps I can tempt you to taste the good life, Alex!"

She wasn't exactly sure what he had in mind, but she was too tired to pursue it further at this point. It had been a long night and fortunately she had the following day off. Alex bid so long to David, who as a resident didn't have the luxury of a weekday off. She headed back to her apartment for a shower and sleep.

Alex woke around 1 PM that afternoon. Five hours was all she ever needed to recharge her batteries. She had learned as a resident to survive on even less. Lazily, she sat up in bed, blinking at the sunlight that was peeking in behind the blinds. Her one bedroom apartment was furnished in the style of a college student. The wall unit housing her TV, stereo and medical books wasn't much more than unfinished pine and cinder blocks. The only semblance of artwork was her poster collection, mostly of the Grateful Dead and Woodstock variety (the concert, not the bird). An empty bottle of Mateus and a few half-melted candles sat atop the fireplace. She knew she was due for some more mature furnishings—she was, after all, an attending physician now. But she never managed to find the time.

Alex hopped off the bed and headed for the bathroom. She took a good look at herself in the mirror. Despite coming off only five hours of sleep, she was pleased with her reflection. Her straight blond hair cascaded off of her shoulders and partway down her back. She'd been blessed with good hair and good skin—lucky for a doctor, who never had the time or inclination for the time-consuming endeavors of make-up or curling irons. She rarely wore anything more than a quick swipe of mascara over the lashes that shaded her clear blue eyes. The pink pajamas that she'd been wearing since medical school were pilled and worn, clinging close to her body. Her breasts were small, barely a contour under the thin flannel. Feeling a sudden urge for exhibitionism, she pushed out her chest like a proud soldier, trying as she had as a teenager to maximize her bust. She turned from side to side, searching for the most seductive pose. When she could find none that pleased her, she returned to the more mundane duties of washing her face and brushing her teeth. Alex wasn't usually one to fawn in front of a mirror or dwell on her physical appearance, but her date tonight with David had stirred up feelings that had been too long suppressed. Although she did not consider David a potential mate, her libido had been unleashed.

As she sat at the kitchen table, sipping her first cup of freshly ground coffee, Alex's gaze fell upon a framed photo at her medical school graduation with her parents. Seeing their faces sent her mind adrift, back to her childhood in Queens.

She had grown up in an unpretentious, working class home. Her father had been a foreman at a plant that manufactured clothing in New York City. Though he never went to college, Peter Faber had a great deal of respect for higher education. He had a strong sense of responsibility and work ethic—both of which he passed on to his children. Although she had loved her father, it was always a love based on respect (and a little bit of fear). This was the compelling force behind Alex's drive to please her father by overachieving. Unlike her sweet and loving mother, who insisted that everything her daughters did was wonderful, it was making Dad proud that was the real challenge. Alex was the oldest of the four daughters, and was, for all intents and purposes, the ambitious son her father never had.

As a kid, weekends would always find her helping with lawn mowing, washing the car or helping paint the house. During the week, she delivered newspapers before school. All of this while maintaining an excellent academic record through high school.

"Ah, Alex my dear," he would say. "No father could ask more from a daughter." She knew that was the highest compliment she would be able to get from him. But her gender would always keep her a second-class citizen in his eyes.

Though an attractive girl, Alex spurned the advances of the boys in her school. She was always more interested in besting the opposite sex, in the classroom or on the athletic field, than she was in dating. "Give the ball to Alex," the boys would cry on the baseball diamond, "She's good! She doesn't know she's a girl!" With this drive to achieve came feelings of inadequacy, and Alex was never truly able to enjoy her successes. She was something of an outcast in her community—never dating much and avoiding close relationships with her sisters, and women in general. Her father's harsh judgments about women always made femininity seem like a weakness to Alex.

When she moved on to Columbia University, her contact with her family became tenuous at best. As an undergrad, she became very interested in animal and human reproduction and was active in the research lab. At the time, she envisioned herself as a research scientist and professor. In typical form, Alex's social life continued to stagnate as she struggled with her internal demons. This all changed in an instant when, as a graduate student in biology, she met Ron Dorcik,

Ron was the only child of a wealthy family from Connecticut. His father was a successful lawyer and hoped that his son would follow in his footsteps. Ron's path, however, took him through a business program as an undergraduate and then on to a masters in hospital administration. The formalized business of medicine was in its infancy, with managed care and health maintenance organizations struggling to find their place in health care. Ron saw this environment was a prime opportunity to escape from the inevitability of practicing in his father's firm. He remained close to his parents and reluctantly received his father's blessings as he began to forge his own career.

They met at a lecture on health care. Spotting this attractive coed, he promptly found a seat next to her. Ron's attempts at conversation were discouraged, as Alex proved to be a compulsive, focused note taker. After a while, he simply scribbled a note at the top of her paper: *How about coffee after the lecture?*

She looked up, distracted. His dark brown eyes met hers.

"Do you mind?" she asked in a hushed tone, obviously annoyed.

"I'm sorry." he whispered back. "Did I do something wrong?" His warm smile and bristly beard caught her off guard.

"I need to concentrate!"

"I haven't been able to concentrate since I've been sitting next to you."

"Then why don't you move?"

"I don't want to. I like being distracted by you."

Whether it was his persistence or good looks, Alex accepted a cup of coffee after the lecture. Minutes turned into hours as the students discussed the lecture, their backgrounds and anything else as an excuse to keep the date going.

He walked her back to her dorm room late that night and invited her to dinner the following evening.

As days became weeks, the two became a fixture on campus. For the first time in her life, academics were taking a back seat to a social life. Ron's apparent interest in her, his solicitous behavior, his sense of humor—all were disarming to Alex. She found herself in the lab, a beaker of organic solvents boiling in front of her, scribbling his name repeatedly on a sheet of graph paper, adding hers in there every so often, just to see how they looked together. The overachieving wallflower from Queens had fallen in love.

Ron was no less preoccupied. His wealth and good looks had afforded him ample opportunity for dating. But there was something very different about Alex. Underneath her drive was a tender vulnerability just below the surface. He felt challenged by her and protective of her at the same time, which was a beautiful, invigorating feeling. After only a few weeks of dating, Ron could see a future as the president of a prestigious hospital, living in a luxurious home in southern Connecticut with his wife Alex, and three children at their feet. He hoped Alex felt the same, and asked her to move in with him after just three, mind-blowing months. She must have, because she accepted. And, not long after that she said "yes" as Ron proposed; they were married soon thereafter.

Ron's first job was as an assistant administrator at a small hospital in southern Connecticut. Alex became a biology teacher at the local high school. They were still very much in love, though Ron's vision of their future slowly began to look less appealing to Alex. At first, the idea of being the model Connecticut housewife sounded adorably quaint. She didn't realize that she would feel unfulfilled in her high school teaching job, and that she didn't exactly like cooking dinner every night. As their first year of marriage became the second, a schism began to appear.

"You know, I was thinking," Ron mentioned over pancakes one morning. "I'm earning a good living, and with the interest on my trust funds from my family, you really don't have to work." This was not the first time this conversation had come up.

"But I want to work." Alex said. "As a matter of fact, I was thinking of applying to the state university for a teaching position at the end of this term."

Ron paused. "Don't you want to start a family soon? I was hoping we could ditch the diaphragm. Besides, there are some opportunities in Boston I was thinking of checking out." He got up from the table without waiting for a response or clearing his dishes, kissing Alex on the top of the head and heading out the door.

As she cleaned the breakfast dishes, a familiar voice from her past returned.

"Alex, no father could ask more from a daughter."

Tears began to well up in her eyes as she envisioned the future that Ron was planning out for them. She truly loved him. But she could not stifle the feeling of intellectual and individual suffocation that was coming over her. This was not what she had worked and strived for all of her life.

That conversation continued at dinner, not only that night but for many days and weeks thereafter. Ron was interviewing for other jobs and was pressuring Alex to start trying for a baby.

"What's the matter with you? Every woman wants to have children. Money's not a concern. Besides, you can always go back to work once they're older."

Alex felt something inside her boil over. "What about my life, Ron? My needs? When we met, we were equals; I was on a path that was going somewhere. Why is it that you got to stay on your path, and I had to get off the road?"

The smirk on Ron's face was the painful final straw in Alex's realization that her husband just didn't get it. "I don't know, babe. I've heard raising children is very challenging!" He laughed as he walked away from the table, and she knew that the marriage was over.

The coffee in her second cup was getting cold. Alex sat in her pink pajamas, pondering her upcoming date. She'd known David for several years, always in a supervisory position. He was a fine physician with excellent technique in the operating room and good diagnostic skills. He was also extremely handsome and confident. He developed a reputation among the house staff as a Romeo-type, but managed to remain well liked by most. It was only Alex who seemed to intimidate him, and David had never made a pass at her before. She found the prospect of a date with him entirely intriguing, and she was actually looking forward to it.

Alex dressed and returned to the hospital to make rounds. Because the residents managed the post operative care of all her patients, she actually wasn't required to go in. But as the attending physician responsible, she felt compelled to check in on everyone to see how they were doing. It was a brisk February afternoon and she bundled up for the ten-block walk. The first patient she was anxious to see was Maria Sanchez, the ectopic pregnancy from the night before.

"Buenos dias, Señora Sanchez. Como esta hoy?"

Maria complained about the pain in her abdomen and appeared unsure of what had happened the night before. Alex described to her again in detail the operation and how important it was for her to rest in the hospital for several days. Alex listened to her lungs and heart and examined her abdomen and incision. Upon reviewing the chart, she noted that David had already made rounds on Maria, performing many of the same maneuvers several hours earlier. He had also noted that her blood count had dropped considerably after surgery and had already ordered additional units of blood for transfusion. It gave Alex personal satisfaction to see her residents so on top of the clinical situation.

After leaving Maria, Alex visited with the two other women who had undergone surgery the night before. They too had already been seen, and were in good shape. Realizing that her presence on the floor was superfluous at this point, Alex went to her office to catch up on her mail. It was there amongst the rubble of unsolicited journals, articles and miscellaneous debris that she noticed a letter marked "Personal and Confidential." These envelopes were not that uncommon—she received at least one a day from physician recruitment services. What was special about this one was its return address: it had come from a single physician, not an agency.

The letter began with the uncommonly personal touch of "Dear Dr. Faber." It went on to describe a solo practitioner in obstetrics and gynecology in a small New Hampshire town who was searching for an associate. The physician sounded up to date and quite patient-oriented, and the setting sounded utterly bucolic. If interested, a resume was requested. The letter was signed "Joshua Barron, MD."

At first, Alex was confused as to where this Dr. Barron would have found her name. Then she remembered that she had been listed as "available for practice" last year. This list, sponsored by a pharmaceutical company, acted as a service to the medical community to help match available physicians with practice openings. The letter sounded intriguing, so Alex sent along her resume and cover letter, not thinking much of it. This was not the first resume she had sent out and she was sure it would not be the last. She went on reviewing her mail and thinking about her quickly approaching date.

The evening with David began quite pleasantly. He met her at the entrance to her building, and they went to dinner at a small Italian restaurant on the Upper East Side. The food was excellent, and Alex was pleased to find David's company stimulating and thrilling. They continued their conversation regarding the material benefits of practicing medicine. David was quite comfortable with his previously stated goals, while Alex continued to emphasize the care of the patient and that the personal satisfaction it gave was reward enough. Both knew that neither would be successful in convincing the other of their point of view. Nonetheless, they continued in earnest to argue their points. It made for a stimulating evening and the dinner was over far too soon for either one's liking. Alex was turned on by the handsome resident physician and let her fence down low enough to consider intimacy. She was actually looking forward to having him return with her to her apartment.

David needed very little encouragement. He had an eye on Alex ever since they had met when he had joined the residency program. Her beauty and intelligence had intimidated him for a long time, and he had been fantasizing a torrid affair with her for months. He didn't need to be asked up to her apartment twice.

They enjoyed a glass of wine on Alex's second-hand sofa until it was clear that neither wanted to talk much more. David turned her face to his with a gentle movement of his hand, and their lips met, first hesitantly and then with a rising intensity. He moved his lips to her neck, his hands sliding beneath her sweater, exploring every detail of her yielding body. He was surprised by Alex's aggression, her left hand feeling the curly hair of his chest while her right was freeing his stiff member from the confines of his slacks.

Their mounting excitement left no time to move to the bedroom as they quenched their passion there on the couch. He could feel her body rock and quiver beneath him as he spent deep within her. Exhausted, they drifted off, only to awaken less than an hour later to continue their lovemaking with renewed strength and enthusiasm.

David, a creature of habit, was the first to arise at six. Alex, as befitting an attending physician, woke at eight to an empty apartment. She replayed the previous evening over coffee, relishing the deeply intimate moments. She had no regrets—it was exactly what she wanted. With her inner-self satisfied, she headed over to the hospital for rounds and a morning in the gynecology clinic.

Maria Sanchez was making good progress, as were the other patients in Alex's care. As the day before, David had already seen the patients and written the appropriate orders for the day. A repeat blood count was ordered on Maria Sanchez to see how her body had responded to the transfusion. Alex could see that Maria's spirits were up as she began to bounce back from the surgery. The timing seemed right for her to spend a few minutes reviewing Maria's various options for birth control. As expected, she met a tremendous amount of resistance, based mainly upon false assumptions and hearsay from her friends. She reassured Maria that the available forms of contraception were all quite safe. She left her bedside with Maria's resistance beginning to drop, reassuring her that she would stop by later that day to discuss the issue with her again.

Clinic duties at City Hospital never ceased to frustrate Alex. Her role was to be available to the residents as a consultant—opportunities like the one she'd just had to talk with Maria were rare. If there was a complex issue or a surgical procedure required, then she became actively involved. But most of the time, she and the patient were on either end of the equation; the residents acting as go-between. She missed spending time with patients—seeing a problem through from diagnosis to a successful conclusion. It was that one on one contact that she yearned for, without the additional member of the resident house staff in-between. These were the moments when private practice seemed so alluring.

Despite frustrations surrounding clinic duty, this day happened to be an active one for Alex. The first woman she was asked to see was forty-five years old. She had come to the clinic complaining of a few days of stomach pain. She had tried castor oil at home, trying to relieve her assumed constipation. She appeared unaware of the basketball-sized mass that was distending her abdomen. She knew that pregnancy was out of the question, due to a sterilization ten years earlier. She'd written off the abdominal distention as gas, hoping for relief from the castor oil. A pregnancy test had been run by the resident and came back negative. It was clear to Alex that this woman was carrying around a large ovarian tumor and would need surgical exploration as soon as possible. The only question left to answer was whether the mass was benign or malignant. The answer would have to wait until surgery. She left the resident to work the patient up and schedule her admission to the hospital.

Alex's second patient was certainly unique. This woman came to the clinic, complaining that something was sticking out of her vagina. The resident had examined her, and agreed that there was indeed something lodged in her vagina, but couldn't determine what it was. Alex was called in and sat down on the stool facing the woman's exposed groin. She saw a long, pointed, pink object protruding from the lips of the vagina. Further exploration revealed the object to be made of plastic forming the tongue of an evil looking face. Alex gently extricated the foreign object and placed it in a small basin on the instrument tray. Noting that there were no injuries to the soft tissues of the vagina, she reassured the patient that everything was fine.

"What was it?" the woman asked urgently. Alex showed her the plastic devil's head that she had removed from her vagina. The dumbfounded resident who had witnessed the extraction left the cubicle, trying to suppress the grin that was quickly forming on his face.

"How'd that get up there?" The woman was now rather angry, realizing quite well how it got up there and just who was responsible for its placement. Alex had no plausible explanation that would not embarrass the patient, so expressed ignorance.

"I want that thing back. It's mine, isn't it?" The woman was getting more agitated by the second. Alex returned the plastic head to the woman and left her to dress. After dressing, she left the clinic in a huff, mortified by the findings and intent upon wreaking revenge. Alex knew that the patient's next stop was surely her boyfriend's house, where someone was about to undergo payback.

The devil's head story was the main topic of conversation in the cafeteria amongst the residents that day. Even Alex, who had tried to sympathize with the patient's plight, found herself joining in the humor. The next day, the clinic staff presented her with a small jewelry box, inside which rested a plastic devil's head complete with plastic necklace. Clinic duty did, after all, have its bright points.

The remainder of Alex's week was fairly uneventful. She found herself spending more and more time in her office, reviewing career options and sending out resumes. She was not spending every night with David, an arrangement that suited her. Both were able to put their relationship into perspective. They saw each other a few nights a week, here and there. Alex gave up trying to convince David of the virtues of helping people as its own reward, preferring to utilize their time together for her more basic needs. David completely agreed, saving his intellectualization for the hospital. As far as that job query from the practice in New Hampshire, Alex had totally forgotten about the response she'd sent back until she was reminded of it a few weeks later, when a letter arrived from Breedville.

CHAPTER SIX

I T WAS NEARLY SIX weeks after his heart attack in the parking lot at Breed General that Joshua Barron finally returned to his practice. He spent the weeks at home catching up on journal reading and taking an audio video course on selected topics in obstetrics and gynecology. The enforced vacation also gave Joshua time to spend with his wife and family and reacquaint himself with these people who mattered so much in his life. Though he received daily reports from Ann and patient updates from the physicians in Breedville ObGyn, he cherished the time he had at home. Perhaps for the first time, Joshua realized just how much he wanted to be a part of his family's life.

He was also finally able to get around to reviewing those applications. Ann Stremp had it all organized for him—each applicant's file contained a CV and the letters of recommendation that she had requested. They were presented to Joshua in order of preference, just to make it that much easier. After reviewing it all intensively, Joshua selected four applicants and asked Ann to set up interviews for when he returned. The practice would offer paid transportation to those willing to make the trip to New Hampshire.

His first day back at work was purposely booked lightly, mostly obstetrical patients who were due over the next two months. Routine visits usually consisted of checking blood pressure and urine, measuring the abdomen and listening for the baby's heartbeat. Though somewhat monotonous, Joshua was quickly aware of how much he'd missed his work while he was recovering. These visits were also his opportunity to interact with his patients on a more personal level—to hear their questions and give them answers, to address concerns and try to allay their fears. He was convinced that few people knew how to speak to a pregnant woman properly. Much of the art of obstetrics was about reassurance, which could come from just a few extra minutes of his time at the end of a check-up. It was these few minutes that Joshua cherished, and had greatly missed.

The morning flowed by quickly as Joshua found himself savoring every aspect of patient contact. He only hoped that he would be able to find an associate who would feel the same way. He knew he would find out soon enough, as his first interview was scheduled for that afternoon. As lunch time approached, Joshua broke tradition and invited Ann Stremp and Lois Wilner, his office nurse, to join him at the local deli in town. Both women jumped at the opportunity to have lunch with the boss. Lois had been working in Joshua's office for four years, having spent the previous thirteen on the labor floor at the hospital. She took the office position due to her fondness for Dr. Barron, and her relief at eliminating night and weekend duty. Her husband Peter had been likewise thrilled to have his wife home on a regular schedule.

The three sat at the new delicatessen across from the library in the commercial section of town. Ann ordered a ham and cheese sandwich and Lois a bowl of chicken soup. Joshua nursed a salad.

"You guys sure are a sight for sore eyes. It's been great getting back to the office." Joshua was glad to give his team members a chance to get out of the office and relax for a bit. He knew that both women had been very busy these past few weeks, despite his absence and the lack of patients. Lois answered patients' questions over the phone, and was constantly reviewing charts with the ObGyn group that was covering for him. She was the active link between practitioners, therefore played a crucial role in making sure all of Joshua's patients were being properly cared for. Ann, of course, was busy managing accounts, paying bills, sending out financial notices and insurance forms. The business of medicine did not stop when the practitioner did. Joshua was lucky to have such a strong core team in place when he needed their support.

Over their lunch, Joshua had a chance to discuss the applications a bit more in-depth with Ann. Amidst the selection process, Ann had formed her own opinion regarding the four applicants who'd be coming to Breed to interview over the coming weeks. Although all of Joshua's selections were at the top of Ann's preference list, only one had really caught her attention. She wasn't sure what it was about Alex Faber that she found unique. Nonetheless, she was looking forward to meeting this man in particular, though his interview was scheduled last. She would have the opportunity to meet with each of the candidates to review the benefits package offered, and was more than ready to size them up.

The three returned to the office for a light schedule of gynecologic patients prior to the first interview at 3 PM. Joshua's first patient of the afternoon was a twenty-one year old college student who had received abnormal pap smear results at her school health clinic. She was very worried, as her mother underwent a hysterectomy for cancer several years before. Joshua reviewed the pap smear report from the college clinic and had recommended a colposcopic exam. He explained that it was necessary to look carefully at her cervix in order to find the abnormal tissue. He reassured her that most of these pap smears could be handled with office procedures and rarely progressed to a hysterectomy. With Lois assisting, he methodically scanned the area in question, biopsying what he considered suspicious. The procedure lasted five minutes, though from the frightened look on the girl's face, he could tell she felt it was an eternity. The biopsy samples were sent off to the lab, along with a repeat pap smear. She was scheduled for a follow-up appointment in several weeks to treat the abnormal area once the biopsy reports were back.

His second patient complained of a foul odor and persistent bloody discharge from her vagina for several days following the end of her period. Joshua was able to make the diagnosis of a retained tampon as soon as he entered the examination room. The patient's history combined with the rancid smell that met him at the door, made the diagnosis obvious. The hardest part was explaining to this very poised, thirty-five year old elementary school teacher what the cause had been without making her wish to cover her head with a brown paper shopping bag. After removing the tampon, Joshua emphasized the positive by describing the successful treatment of her "condition" and praised her for such vigilance in seeking medical attention before a serious infection had set in. The school teacher was so pleased with the expeditious solution to her problem that it wasn't until she arrived home that the embarrassment set in. Her husband's insensitive remarks about the doctor finding a "needle in a haystack" did not help the situation either, except to provide her with a full night's sleep after she banished him to the couch for the night.

Joshua had several more patients to see before his interview. One needed her IUD removed and another inserted, the next suffered from a vaginal yeast infection. A birth control prescription, a sterilization procedure, and the final patient of the day had taken her leave. By three, Joshua found himself a little tired, but invigorated still.

"When Dr. Ransom arrives, just send him in to my office," Joshua called to Ann. He sat down at his desk, reviewing charts while he waited for his first applicant.

Joshua's mind wandered back to his own start in private practice. He'd met a great deal of reluctance from the medical community, who saw a specialist like him as infringing on their territory of family practice. To that point, they were the ones delivering the babies and the general surgeons performing the cesarean sections. It was only through his persistent efforts and diplomacy that he was able to find a niche in the medical staff at Breed. Of course the fact that he was a local boy from a prominent family didn't hurt. Over time, the family practitioners began to refer their more complicated obstetrical patients to him, and he reciprocated by returning the patients back to them after the baby was delivered. The general surgeons were far more reluctant to accept this new kid on the block. But the writing was on the wall for them, too, as other specialists like orthopedists, urologists and gastroenterologists began taking over their turf, bit by bit. Joshua had forged new ground, and his presence as a member of the medical establishment made it easier for other specialists to set up practice, including two other gynecologists. Despite the growth of the medical staff, Joshua prided himself on the practice he had established, and jealously guarded it from the incorporation of additional obstetricians. He liked working alone, and was, for the most part, unimpressed by his obstetrical colleagues. Ironically, it was his excellence in practice that was making his solo-status increasingly unmanageable. All of these thoughts churned in Joshua's head as he waited. By the time he looked up at the clock, it was nearly quarter to four. Just before he buzzed Ann to ask about Dr. Ransom's whereabouts, she announced the arrival of his first applicant.

Dr. Gerald Ransom's stature was befitting of his name. All six feet four inches and two hundred pounds of him was wrapped in a three-piece gray flannel suit. His vest was studded with a Phi Beta Kappa key. His tortoise shell glasses and long, well-coiffed hair gave him an aristocratic appearance that was not far from accurate. Born into an old Boston family, Gerald had been schooled at Phillips Academy in Andover, Massachusetts, matriculated at both Harvard College and Harvard Medical School, and received his ObGyn training at Brigham and Women's Hospital in Boston. After residency, he continued on for two additional years as a perinatology fellow. Looking to escape the suffocation of high society life in Boston, Gerald was preparing to build his own dynasty in this modest New Hampshire town.

"Dr. Barron. It's a pleasure to meet you," Dr. Ransom said as he extended his hand to Joshua. "I'm so sorry I'm late. I took the liberty of driving around town while it was still daylight, and must have lost track of the time. You have a lovely city—any man could be very content practicing here."

"Thank you, Dr. Ransom. Please, sit down." Joshua sensed his mildly pompous nature, but this man's credentials were so impeccable that he felt obligated keep an open mind. "I hope you had no trouble finding us. We are a bit off the beaten track compared to Boston." Joshua couldn't believe he was making excuses for Breedville.

"Not at all," Gerald retorted. His eyes scanned the room noticing Joshua's diplomas on the wall. "I see you're a Boston man, yourself."

"Not really. I'm a native here, but I did train in Boston. Let me show you around." Joshua walked through the office with Gerald, stopping in the examination rooms to point out his instrumentation. They next passed through the medical chart area, the waiting room and finally the laboratory, where they ran into Ann and Lois.

"Lois Wilner; Ann Stremp, I'd like you to meet Dr. Ransom." Joshua kept things on a formal note.

"Ladies." Gerald acknowledged them with a nod, without extending his hand. "Please to meet you both." His highfalutin air wafted over Ann.

"My pleasure, I'm sure," she said stiffly, making a point of extending her own hand to Dr. Ransom. "Welcome to Breedville."

Lois, on the other hand, was bowled over by Dr. Ransom's looks and "charm." She stood by Ann's side, speechlessly smiling and clutching onto a patient file.

The men returned to Joshua's office.

"Did I miss the ultrasound machine?" Gerald queried.

"No, you did not. Because we are attached to the hospital, I usually send patients over to radiology if I need one. They're very accommodating."

"Oh, I see." Gerald was obviously not impressed. "I'm used to performing my own scans in the office, rather than relying on the radiologist. But I'm sure it wouldn't be too much trouble to get a machine in here."

Joshua bristled. This guy sounded like his name was already on the door. He paused and collected himself.

"Medicine is handled a little differently here, outside of the tertiary center. The politics of medicine respect the turf of the various specialties. As long as we receive the high quality service that we demand, we try not to encroach on another physician's territory."

"I see," Gerald replied. "At The Brigham we consider ultrasound the province of the high risk obstetrician."

"Would you like to see the hospital?" Joshua queried.

"I would be delighted."

The two men walked the short distance to the hospital. The labor floor was in the old wing, and Joshua found himself taking the same stairs which had been such a chore on that fateful night six weeks earlier.

Michelle Singer, the charge nurse on maternity, greeted them at the nurses' station. "Hi, Dr. Barron. How're you feeling? It's great to have you back."

"Michelle Singer, I would like to introduce Dr. Gerald Ransom." Joshua made the introductions. "Dr. Ransom is visiting with us today. He is interested in joining our staff."

"Welcome, Dr. Ransom," Michelle said, smiling at the visitor.

"Thank you, Michelle. It is a pleasure to be here."

Joshua took Gerald down the hall toward the birthing rooms. He showed him the fetal monitoring system, the cesarean section room and several postpartum rooms. The two finished up in the lounge. Joshua was impressed with the quality of his interviewee's questions. The man was obviously well-trained, and it became clear that he would be a tremendous asset to the obstetrical staff at Breed. Unfortunately, he just could not warm up to the man. Gerald Ransom appeared to be Gerald Ransom's own biggest fan, and this was a trait that Joshua found off-putting. Nonetheless, he would reserve final judgment until after Gerald met Elizabeth.

"I hope you can stay for dinner. My wife is looking forward to meeting you."

"That won't be a problem for me—thank you for the kind invitation. I already made a reservation at the local inn, and plan to look at some real estate in the morning."

The same bristling came at the back of Joshua's neck. Clearly, Gerald looked at this position as a fait accompli. Didn't Dr. Ransom realize that Joshua had some input into who joined his own practice?

The physicians continued their tour of the hospital, stopping by the operating room suites, the intensive care unit and one of the medical-surgical floors. They finished up back at Joshua's office where Ann, just finishing her work for the day, spent a few minutes with Dr. Ransom reviewing the salary and benefits package that she and Joshua had put together for the prospective applicants. Meanwhile, Joshua called Elizabeth to confirm the timing of their dinner reservation.

When Ann was finished going over the benefits package, she left for the evening. Joshua was pleased to find that Gerald had no questions for him regarding these financial details, albeit a bit surprised. Obviously, Ann had been very thorough, which pleased him. Joshua preferred not to discuss these details, and those matters were best left to Ann.

Before leaving, Joshua checked in with his answering service. This was his first night on call since his illness, and luckily, things were temporarily quiet.

He and Gerald walked out together to the parking lot. Eyeing Gerald's Mercedes 450SL, he shook his head and laughed quietly to himself, expecting nothing less from this Boston Brahmin. Gerald followed him back to their house.

Elizabeth greeted the two men at the door. Joshua hadn't briefed her on his own impressions of Gerald, wishing her to come to her own opinion. "It's a pleasure to meet you, Dr. Ransom," she said warmly. "Welcome to Breedville."

"You have a lovely community, Mrs. Barron. I feel my wife and I could be very happy here."

"I'm sorry she wasn't able to join us today. I would have enjoyed meeting her." Elizabeth said.

"I felt it would be better to travel here alone the first time. I didn't want her to fall in love with the area before I had a chance to personally evaluate the professional opportunity. Her presence would have been a distraction from the task at hand." He flashed a smile. "You know how women are. But now that I've seen what I have today, I'm sorry that she didn't join me. You two would have gotten along quite famously."

Elizabeth did not know how to respond to such a remark. She simply nodded and smiled, figuring Dr. Ransom would be comfortable with such a response.

With all three kids busy in the kitchen with homework and other activities, the adults adjourned to the living room for a sherry.

"I must say, I was very impressed with the quality of your girls that I met today. They run a tight ship!" Gerald said breezily as he sat down.

Elizabeth raised an eyebrow, thinking that the only girl for Dr. Ransom to potentially meet would be their daughter.

"You mean Ms. Stremp and Mrs. Wilner," said Joshua purposely. "Thank you. They're a very loyal twosome; I'm privileged to have them work with me."

"If you think Joshua's girls are nice, let me introduce you to my girl and two boys," Elizabeth chimed in, calling the kids. Each shook his hand, said the obligatory "Hi" or "Nice to meet you" and promptly returned to the kitchen. Joshua was sure that the freshly baked chocolate cake in there was much more entertaining than meeting Dr. Ransom.

The Barrons took Gerald to a charming restaurant in town, where they dined on fresh fish and Caesar salad. The conversation remained light, bouncing around from standard topics such as Gerald's family, how he met his wife, and the Red Sox. From his manner, it was clear that Gerald was already looking forward to moving north. He had plans to see several homes with a local real estate agent before returning to Boston. After a short nightcap back at the house, Gerald took off, promising to stop by the office the following day before he left. Joshua checked in with his answering service again before retiring for the night. Still quiet, though it was barely nine and the night was still young.

"Well, what do you think?"

"That chauvinistic, pompous ass!" Elizabeth was never one to mince words. "You aren't serious about him, are you?"

"It's unfortunate that his personality leaves so much to be desired. He's extremely well trained and his expertise would be good for the department. We all could benefit from his presence on the medical staff," Joshua admitted. "I just don't think he would fit in with my practice," he went on. "Gerald might fit in with the other two guys, who frankly could use someone with his training and academic orientation. My concern is that he appears ready to move in and take control. It may be difficult, if not impossible, to turn him down. I think I'll tell him that I have several others to interview and that I'll get back to him in a few weeks. That will give me a chance to talk to Sam and Bill about it. I know they're interested in adding another physician to their group. Maybe by taking Gerald, they'll stop pressuring me to join them."

"Can the area really support five obstetricians?" Elizabeth said, bringing up a good point.

"I think so. Besides it wouldn't hurt to talk it over with them."

Duty called, and later that night Joshua ran into Sam Cronin in the doctors' on call room on the maternity floor. Sam was following a patient with a prolonged labor pattern and had begun pitocin, a contraction-stimulating medication. Joshua's patient was moving much more quickly towards delivery. Sam was propped up in bed half-heartedly watching the 1 AM news.

Joshua started the conversation. "I met a fine prospect today, Sam."

"I meant to ask you how your search was coming." Sam's glazed eyes were still glued to the television set.

"His name is Gerald Ransom. He's well-trained and is presently working as a perinatologist in Boston. Appears to come from an old Boston family."

"Why's he interested in leaving the big city?" Sam finally moved his eyes off the screen.

"I don't understand that one myself yet. He definitely appears interested in Breedville. Maybe he's had enough of his ancestors."

"That never stopped you, Joshua. Sounds like you two should have a pretty common bond, considering how far you trace your family roots."

"I think he could be quite an asset to our medical staff, what with his training and experience."

"Sounds like you've found yourself a new partner, my friend. When is he going to start?"

"Christ! You're sounding as presumptuous about this as he does! Truth be told, I find him a little overwhelming. But he's such a strong candidate, I thought you and Bill might want to consider him."

Sam groaned as he changed positions in bed. "You got us all wrong, Joshua. It was you Bill and I were considering. We really weren't looking for an additional partner."

"Well, you've mentioned to me on more than one occasion how you and Bill were hoping to expand your practice to take some of the pressure off. Not that I'm such a good example of that, you understand. I just thought that if you two were interested in meeting this guy while he's still up here, I could introduce you in the morning. We don't even have to discuss possibilities with your group. It could be just an opportunity for him to meet some of the members of the medical staff. I could give you a copy of his resume after he leaves."

"How're you planning on leaving things with him regarding your practice?" Sam asked, sounding a bit more interested.

"I've just started the interviewing process. I was planning on telling him that I'll get back to him in a few weeks. Besides—" Joshua's words were interrupted by a knock on the door.

"Dr. Barron." It was Sandy. "Mrs. Foley is crowning up."

"Duty calls, my friend. We can talk later." With that, Joshua was on his way to the birthing room where Susan Foley was about to become a mother for the second time. Unlike his last delivery over six weeks ago, things went very smoothly. When he returned to the on call room, he found Sam fast asleep with a local TV station showing a rerun of "Mash." He changed quickly and left for home.

When Joshua arrived at his office at 9 AM, there was a message waiting for him from Gerald Ransom. He would be by around 11:30 before leaving for Boston. Ann had already adjusted Joshua's morning schedule to accommodate the visit. Between patients, Joshua called Ann into his office.

"Well Ann, what did you think?"

"About what?" Ann asked, playing dumb.

"You know exactly what I'm talking about, Ann. Out with it! What did you think of Ransom?"

"Frankly, I found him somewhat overbearing. However, I'm sure he is very well qualified for the job."

"Don't worry Ann. He's not what I'm looking for. I think we'll both know the right one when we see him."

Ann's smile was weak.

"Ann, don't give it a second thought," Joshua said, reading her reaction. "I would never hire another doctor without your approval. We're a team, remember?"

Her smile grew more robust. Joshua relied on Ann's insight to help him in many a circumstance, and although her knowledge of medicine was limited, her judgment of people was almost frighteningly accurate. Yes, he wouldn't consider an applicant without her input.

His next patient was Ellen Landry, whose middle of the night delivery had ended with his admission to the ICU.

"Hi, Ellen. How are things going?"

"Oh Dr. Barron, it's so good to see you back to work! I felt so horrible when you got sick. I was convinced that it was my delivery that sent you to the hospital!"

"Not at all, Ellen", he reassured her. "I'm afraid that this doctor wasn't following his own advice! How's your baby?"

"Oh, he's wonderful!" Just the thought of her new son was enough to light up Ellen's face. "Jack has already filled his room with enough sporting equipment to satisfy the local athletic club." She laughed.

Joshua proceeded to examine Ellen, first checking her breasts for any sign of infection, obtaining a pap smear, and examining her uterus to determine that it was back to normal size. He left her to dress and met her in his consulting room. "Everything looks good, Ellen. I should see you again in about a year. Have you considered what you want to use for birth control?"

"Actually . . . Jack and I haven't, you know, done anything since the delivery. He doesn't seem to be interested," Ellen looked at the floor with embarrassment, tears welling up in her eyes. "It doesn't look like we're going to need to worry about birth control."

"Ellen," Joshua said gently, "A lot of men are afraid that they'll hurt their wives by becoming sexually active soon after delivery. Didn't Jack behave similarly after your first delivery?"

"Well, yes, as a matter of fact, he did. I practically had to seduce him after Emily was born!" Ellen's face cast a red glow as she recalled the scenario. Jack came home to Ellen in her honeymoon nightgown and the baby spending the night at her mother's. Dinner got cold waiting for the two of them to finish in the bedroom.

"I'm sure it's just a matter of time. Maybe I should write you out a prescription for birth control pills so you can be prepared." Joshua handed Ellen the prescription and she left his office with a little more self-esteem. He remained at his desk when Ann called to mark Gerald's arrival. Joshua met him at the door and ushered him in.

"Good to see you again, Joshua." Dr. Ransom said, extending his hand.

"I hope your accommodations were adequate."

"Oh, they were fine enough. In a more exciting vein, I think I found the perfect house for us this morning. I told the real estate agent to keep a hold on it for a day or two until I had a chance to talk to my wife." Gerald paused and cleared his throat. "Well, Joshua, I've decided that this is where I want to be. What do you think, do we have a deal?"

"Frankly, Gerald, I'm sorry to delay the decision, but I have several more interviews scheduled. It would only be fair to the remaining applicants who are planning to come up. I just can't give you the thumbs up right now."

"Well I certainly understand the position you are in, Joshua. But it seems purposeless to have the others come all the way up here when there is no potential for them."

"Well, Gerald," Joshua said brightly, "I would feel better carrying out my plans as already scheduled. Why don't we go over to the hospital cafeteria for a bite of lunch before you leave."

"Sounds good to me."

The two men left the office and headed towards the hospital cafeteria. As they were getting on line, they bumped into Sam Cronin and Bill Worth. After making the appropriate introductions, as if on cue, Joshua's beeper went off and he excused himself to answer the call.

"Thanks, Ann. This worked out just right. Gerald is with them now. I'll see you later," he said into the phone.

"Gerald," Joshua said, approaching the group of three men standing on line, "I'm afraid I have a patient bleeding in the emergency room and I'm going to be tied up for some time."

"We'll keep him company, Joshua," Sam told him. "We'll try not to snake him from you!"

"Thanks, Sam. Gerald, it was a real pleasure meeting you. I'll be in touch as we discussed in the office."

Joshua hurried off in the direction of the emergency room as Sam, Bill and Gerald perused the available selections for lunch.

Joshua's afternoon was filled with the ironies of life that are quite routine for a gynecologist.

His first patient in the afternoon was a thirty-two year old woman who had a miscarriage several weeks ago. She was a longtime infertility patient of Joshua's who had been pregnant three times before, all ending in miscarriages in the first trimester. Her most recent loss had occurred while Joshua was on leave. She was now returning to discuss her chances of carrying a pregnancy to term. Joshua discussed several tests that he felt might help bring to light the cause of her recurrent losses. He scheduled her for these tests over the next few weeks. She was extremely frustrated, as was expected in women with infertility issues. She spent nearly twenty minutes in the consulting room, her mood swinging from anger to tears and back again. Joshua attempted to reassure her and do his best to comfort her, but he knew the test results would help more than his words ever could.

His next patient was a scared seventeen-year-old who had missed her period and received a positive result from an at-home pregnancy test. She was a freshman at the local college and her parents were out of state. She had never met Joshua before and had never had a gynecologic exam. After examining her and confirming her early pregnancy, he had her come back to his office to talk. She managed to maintain her composure until he closed the door.

"I don't know what I'm going to do!" the girl said, sobbing into a tissue offered by Joshua. "My boyfriend and I were so careful. We were using a condom and it broke. I can't believe I'm pregnant." And then with a sudden internal resolve, she blurted out, "Dr. Barron, I want an abortion."

In his mind, Joshua could see his infertility patient who had been sitting in the very same chair not ten minutes earlier. Life had a way of being cruelly ironic.

Joshua was dedicated to his obstetric patients, and his practice was centered on assuring healthy outcomes. Generally, this meant a healthy baby. And sometimes, fortunately not often, it meant terminating a pregnancy. Joshua approached all of his services with the same goal—to put the health, needs and desires of his patients above all else. Though pregnancy termination was not something that Joshua actively sought out or was personally comfortable with, he took it on as his professional duty. He felt a moral obligation to be there for the women who needed the expertise of trained professionals to ensure their own safety. He made it a priority to spend time with any patient considering abortion, counseling them prior to their making their decision. His only concern was that the patient was making the right decision for herself.

"Are you sure that is what you want to do?" he asked the sobbing girl. "Would you want to talk the decision over with your parents?"

"I don't have to, do I?" she asked him desperately. "They'd never understand. They'd kill me!"

"How does your boyfriend feel?" Joshua asked.

"He wants me to have the baby. But we've only known for a few days! How does he know?" The tears began to flow again. "I'm so confused."

"You don't have to tell your parents if you don't want to—that is your right. But I would encourage you to think about this some more. You're still early enough in the pregnancy to put off a final decision for a few weeks if necessary. I would consider calling your parents and giving them a chance," Joshua said, his mind briefly flashing to his own teenage daughter. "If you decide to have the abortion, I will take care of you whether you speak to your parents or not. We will set up an appointment for you to see me again in one week. This should give you time to arrive at a decision that you are comfortable with."

"Thank you, Dr. Barron. Maybe I should speak to my mother. I can't really imagine her not knowing about this." With that, she left his office and stopped at Ann's desk to make a follow up appointment.

As the days went by, life began to return to relative normalcy for Joshua Barron. His office hours were busy, but not unreasonably so, thanks to Ann fiercely guarding his schedule from the double and triple appointments that had become common prior to his heart attack. Joshua was still sharing night call with Sam and Bill, thus giving him two out of three nights without disturbance. Meanwhile, Sam expressed interest in Gerald Ransom, and requested a copy of his CV. Joshua was pleased, and encouraged Sam and Bill to keep in touch with Gerald. They agreed to delay contacting him until after Joshua had finished his interviews.

The next two applicants were unfortunately disappointments. The first arrived just two days after Dr. Ransom left. He appeared at Joshua's office with his mother, who sat in during Ann's benefits overview, constantly asking questions on behalf of her son, The Doctor. Joshua gave him a perfunctory tour of the hospital and sent both home by the end of the day. That evening, Joshua and Ann sat in the office re-reading his application, trying to see where they had gone wrong.

The next applicant arrived in a sweater and jeans. Though his resume revealed a specialization in infertility and reproductive endocrinology, his area of interest was definitely finance. The man just couldn't suppress his enthusiasm for the financial potential of Joshua's practice, expressing dismay at the current lack of fiscal initiative. Through a combination of target marketing to a wealthy segment of the population and streamlining patient flow, he mapped out how Joshua could triple his receipts in less than a year. Once again, Ann and Joshua pored over his resume after he left, trying to figure out how to better screen applicants in the future. Gerald Ransom was looking better day by day.

Ann still held out hope for the final applicant, Alex Faber, who was expected on Monday. Joshua, on the other hand, was getting very discouraged. It might come down to hiring Ransom or merging with Breedvile ObGyn.

Monday morning went by quickly, but the day began to drag after lunch. Dreading the thought that Dr. Faber might be his last decent chance for a partner, Joshua found himself going through the motions with his afternoon patients. He was anxious. By 2:30, Joshua was at his desk, making a mental list of the possible shortcomings of this last candidate. Perhaps he'll be a sex maniac, or maybe a child molester. As he was rounding out the list with "social misfit" and "awful body odor," Ann called to signal Dr. Faber's arrival. Before he had a chance to leave his desk, the door opened. An attractive blond with fine features, dressed in a well-tailored suit, entered the room.

"Dr. Barron, it is a pleasure to meet you," she said, extending her hand to his. "My name is Alex Faber."

CHAPTER SEVEN

JOSHUA NEVER CONSIDERED HIMSELF a male chauvinist. He was aware of the many contributions to the field of medicine that were credited to female physicians. Furthermore, he had established his practice during the advent of the feminist movement in America, and was comfortable, even welcoming, of their ever-growing role in society as well as his specialty.

Despite this enlightened attitude, Joshua had never considered a female partner. The appearance of Alex Faber at his door took him completely by surprise, and it was written all over his face. As he shook Alex's hand, embarrassment replaced shock on his visage. There was no way Alex wouldn't notice.

"Perhaps you were expecting someone with a deeper voice, Dr. Barron?" This was not Alex's first exposure to a physician who had assumed the male connotation to her unisex name. Of course, she could have used her full name on her resume to clarify, but she hadn't been called Alexandra since grade school. Besides, Alex was rather enjoying seeing Dr. Barron squirm.

"I'm terribly sorry to appear so shallow, Dr. Faber, but I must admit that you caught me quite by surprise!" Joshua laughed. "Regardless, it is certainly a pleasure to meet and welcome you to Breedville." He was slowly regaining his usual composure.

He offered Alex a seat, and decided to take the chair next to her. He picked up her resume from his desk and thumbed through it. Of course he had already reviewed it several times—this move was just a way to break the ice and distance himself from his opening embarrassment.

"So, Dr. Faber, why would someone from New York City want to look at a practice in rural New Hampshire?"

"Please feel free to call me Alex, Dr. Barron."

"Only if you'll call me Joshua."

"Certainly." She went on, crossing her legs comfortably. "It's true that my whole life has revolved around the New York metropolitan area. Frankly, I never considered working this far away from the center of my universe. But medicine has changed a lot, especially in New York, and there was something very special about the way that you described your practice in your letter." Joshua leaned in, listening intently.

"You emphasized patient care and pride—not the typical benefits package, easy hours and vacation allotment. It was really refreshing to hear some old fashioned values. Plus, the idea of living in the country sounds amazing after so many years in Manhattan."

Joshua felt instantly drawn to Alex. He quickly forgot that this was an interview, and instead dove into an in-depth discussion on recent trends in the field of medicine. This was a passionate topic for him, and the two spent the better part of an hour discussing the growing nature of medicine as business. They lamented how much of their art was being lost under the deluge of prepaid health plans, malpractice litigation and peer review committees. These days, there were more and more obstacles put between the physician and the patient, turning that relationship into an adversarial one. Alex expressed her dismay at how doctors saw patients as potential litigants, while the patients were ready to sue for anything less than perfection. Even the technology was interfering with this relationship, Joshua added, as fetal monitors were turning contractions into blips on a screen and ultrasound and CAT scans were replacing clinical judgment. Not that the technology was unimportant, they agreed—the quality of medical care had improved dramatically because of the advent of these instruments. But both Joshua and Alex felt that all of these factors were increasing the distance between them and their patients, ultimately diminishing the quality of care. Joshua was utterly impressed at Alex's stance, especially for a young doctor like herself.

"Well!" Joshua exclaimed, checking his watch. "We really should move along here. Why don't we grab you a cup of coffee and begin our tour?"

Their first stop was an exam room, where Alex noticed the homemade quilted covers shielding the steel stirrups, and the heating pads in the speculum drawers—subtle touches of a practitioner who cared about his patients. A colorful but tasteful mobile hung over the examination table, another example of his attempts to put the patient at ease. There was literature on subjects ranging from breast self examination and sexually transmitted diseases to prevention of osteoporosis, all organized in clear plastic containers attached to the wall.

As they moved through the office, Alex saw other signs of a progressive, education-oriented environment within the confines of a comfortable atmosphere. The chairs in the waiting room looked plush and fairly new, with end tables containing current issues of *Women's Health*, *Newsweek*, *Redbook* and *Mademoiselle*. As she perused several patient charts in the records area, she was fascinated by Joshua's fastidious organization, and the clarity and completeness of his notes.

There was even a separate section of the chart for personal and social notes about each patient.

Back at the front desk, Joshua introduced Alex to Lois and Ann. Lois extended her hand immediately, while Ann maintained a cordial though cool propriety.

"It's a pleasure to meet you, Dr. Faber." Lois said with a vigorous handshake.

"Thank you Lois. Please, call me Alex." Alex was never one for titles between medical personnel. "And it's a pleasure to meet you again, Ms. Stremp." Formality, she assumed, was best met with formality.

"Dr. Faber," Ann said, extending her hand.

"I'm going to show Dr. Faber around the hospital, Ann. I'm sure you can review the details of the benefits package with her in the morning if you have an opportunity to leave early," Joshua said casually, trying to warm up the chilly atmosphere.

"Whatever you say." Ann returned to her work, while Lois offered Alex a second cup of coffee. The two physicians then left for the hospital.

"I don't think Ann approves of female physicians," Alex mentioned as they climbed the stairs to the second floor.

"Well, we've all got our hang-ups, Alex. Ann has been with me a long time and she's fiercely protective. I'm sure it's simply a matter of adjustment—which is one thing Ann is not used to. But once you win her over, she can be a valuable ally." Without realizing it, Joshua found himself making similar assumptions about Alex's hiring as Gerald Ransom had about his own. This time, however, it all seemed very natural.

Joshua continued the tour, eventually bumping into Michelle Singer at the nurses' station. He introduced Alex to Michelle, as well as several of the other labor floor nurses who were congregated around coffee and doughnuts in the nurses' lounge. For a change, the labor floor was quiet. Alex couldn't help but notice the look of surprise on several of the nurses' faces when she was introduced as a doctor. It was becoming clear that the female physician market had yet to break into Breedville, New Hampshire.

They took their leave of the maternity floor, stopping briefly in the operating room. There they met urologist Frank Dimento who was just finishing dictating an operative note. His eyes roamed over Alex's body as he signed off his dictation.

"Frank, this is Alex Faber from New York City. She is visiting here today, looking at a position in my practice. Alex is currently on the obstetrical staff at New York City Hospital."

"What a pleasure to meet you." He extended his hand to Alex, who felt obliged to provide a firm, masculine handshake. Frank's smile made it clear that he was mentally undressing her on the spot. "I always knew that old Josh had good taste in colleagues, but you really outdid yourself this time," Frank leered.

"Well," Alex stammered, "Good to meet you." She turned, excusing herself with Joshua before the situation became any more awkward. They headed through a medical-surgical floor on their way back to the office.

"I'm really sorry for Frank's behavior, Alex. He can be a bit obnoxious."

"No need to apologize. You get used to those types when you're a woman in a man's world, especially in the city. Where I come from, we'd just call Frank a degenerate sleeze!"

Joshua laughed, thinking how ridiculous Frank had come off, worrying about the impression he'd made on Alex.

"Somehow I think you're probably quite capable of handling yourself in those circumstances. I would just hate you to think that Frank is typical of most of our staff here."

"Nothing to worry about. Every hospital has its characters," Alex replied with a smile.

Lois was just getting off of the phone as Joshua and Alex returned to the office,

"Dr. Barron. I was just talking with Mrs. Sanders. She was hysterical. Her six-year-old daughter fell off her sled and complained of stomach pains. She saw some blood around her vaginal area when she took off her clothes. I told her she could come right over and you would see her. I hope that is okay?"

"Of course. Just set her up in exam room one and see that we have the pediatric specula available."

"Well, I guess you're going to get to see some action here today," Joshua said, ushering Alex into his office.

The upcoming emergency served as a springboard for the two to discuss a variety of clinical situations and the various means of handling them. Joshua found the discussion stimulating. Alex asked many questions regarding his management of several clinical situations that she had faced recently. By the quality of her questions, he had no doubt in the excellence of her training. Yes, she could be an excellent addition to the team, he thought.

"Breedville is a really small town, Alex. Could you see yourself—a single professional woman—finding a satisfying life here?"

"Would you be asking the same question of me if my name were Alexander?" Alex asked, trying not to sound defensive. She really liked Joshua's practice and did not want to appear too feministic.

"Probably not, I must admit. But I would still have some concerns about any unmarried individual moving up here with regard to their chances of staying." He took a breath. "Frankly Alex, I think you would be a tremendous asset to my practice, but I am concerned about the long haul. Would you still be happy here after five, ten years?"

Before she could answer, Lois stuck her head in the office to tell Joshua that Mrs. Sanders and her daughter were ready for him in the examining room.

"Mind if I join you, Joshua?"

"Not at all. You can be the famous consultant from New York City."

Joshua smiled at her as they left the office. He gave Alex one of Lois' white coats and the two entered the examining room.

Carolyn Sanders was covered in a white sheet from the waist down. She looked scared and her cheeks were wet with fresh tears. Her mother Beth, a long time patient of Joshua's, was holding her daughter and rocking her back and forth. This was the first time Joshua had seen Carolyn since he delivered her six years ago. He introduced Alex as a visiting gynecologist from New York, then approached Carolyn with a slow and friendly manner.

"Hi Carolyn, I'm Dr. Barron. I'm going to help figure out why you're hurting. Can you tell me what happened?"

Over choked back tears and hugs, Carolyn's story slowly unfolded. She had been sitting on her sled, riding down a hill behind her house. She had hit a rock, throwing her off the sled and right on top of a broken branch sticking up from the snow. The branch had pierced her snowsuit.

"It went into me and hurt a lot," Carolyn finished, bursting into tears and burying her face in her mother's shoulder.

"Does anything hurt you now?" Joshua asked, trying to gently lift Carolyn's face to look at him.

"It hurts me right here." The girl pointed to the lower portion of her abdomen, just above the pubic bone and to the front of her vagina.

"I'd like to try to help you, Carolyn," Joshua said softly. "Will you let me help you to feel better?" The girl nodded, continuing to sob.

Lois helped Carolyn lie down on the examining table, asking Beth to move up by her daughter's head.

"This may hurt a little, Carolyn. But I am going to be very gentle. Okay?" Joshua gently palpated the girl's lower abdomen, eliciting tenderness just above the pubic bone. He then pushed down on her belly, holding his hands there for a few seconds. Carolyn wailed softly, but soon calmed.

"You're doing great, Carolyn! Keep up the good work."

He quickly released the tension on the abdominal wall. Carolyn responded with a jump and a scream. Definite rebound tenderness, Joshua thought. There was probably some peritoneal irritation, and most likely some internal bleeding.

"Carolyn, I'm going to need to have you spread your legs out like you're pretending to be a frog. Will you do that for me?"

Lois helped Carolyn move her knees out to the side so that Joshua could examine her. The area around the vagina was badly bruised with several small cuts. Of concern was the small trickle of blood coming from up inside the vagina. Joshua attempted to insert a small metal speculum into the young girl's vagina to find the source of the bleeding. As gentle as he was, this was the final straw for Carolyn, who screamed, locked her knees together and tried to squirm off the table.

"Okay, honey, we'll give you a little break for right now."

Alex managed to catch Joshua's eye and motioned for him to leave the room with her. The door closed behind them, leaving the hysterical girl with her mother and Lois.

"I know that this is an interview, but would you allow me to examine Carolyn?" Alex asked, looking quite serious. "I don't want to appear presumptuous, Joshua, but I've had a lot of experience with young girls with genital trauma. New York City Hospital is one of the designated rape centers in the city, so I've had more than my share of experience."

Normally, Joshua would be reticent to allow an interviewee to examine one of his own patients in his own office, or anyone other than himself for that matter. But as she said, Alex had seen many child trauma cases like this before, and she was more than suited to care for Carolyn. The camaraderie that had already grown between the two over the past few hours only solidified his decision.

"Yes, please take a look and see what you can find." The two re-entered the examination room. Carolyn's crying was down to an occasional sob.

Alex made her way over to Carolyn and began to stroke her hair. "Hi honey, my name is Alex. I'll bet that was pretty scary, falling off the sled. Did you hurt any other part of your body?"

The girl shook her head.

"Did anyone else get hurt or was it just you?"

The girl remained silent, though noticeably calmer during Alex's conversation. The mother explained to Alex that Carolyn was the only one on the sled at the time.

"Carolyn, can I please take a look at you so that I can see how bad the hurt is?" Reluctantly, Carolyn reassumed the frog leg position. "That's a big girl, Carolyn." As she continued to speak softly to the girl, her gloved fingers touched the sensitive area, allowing Carolyn the time to get used to the exam.

"You're being very helpful, Carolyn, and I really appreciate it. I'll be finished real soon, okay?" Although she didn't respond, the tenseness left Carolyn's thighs as she relaxed for Alex's probing speculum. Using several long cotton swabs, she wiped away the blood and peered up into the girl's vagina while Lois guided her with a flashlight. After a minute, she removed the speculum.

"You were a very brave girl, Carolyn. Why don't you get dressed now, okay?" Alex and Joshua left the room. When they were alone again, Alex reported her findings.

"The bleeding is coming from deep in the posterior fornix. I'm afraid she's got a nasty laceration. Combined with your examination of her abdomen, we're going to have to assume that the laceration goes clear into the peritoneal cavity. She's going to need an exam under anesthesia with repair of the vaginal tear and probably a laporoscopy to evaluate for internal injury and bleeding."

"I agree with you completely—nice job. Betcha didn't expect this on the interview schedule!"

They returned to the examination room where Carolyn was now dressed. Joshua and Alex invited Beth to join them in the office while Lois watched Carolyn. Once inside with the door closed, Joshua explained to Beth the potential gravity of the accident, including the possibility of continued bleeding, internal infection and injury to the child's other organs. He suggested that Carolyn be taken to the operating room tonight and with luck could be home in the morning.

"Are you sure she really needs an operation?" Beth asked, visibly distraught.

"Yes," Joshua stated unequivocally. "And the sooner the better. Chances are the injury is small, but without a thorough exam, a simple injury could turn far worse and she could develop a serious infection. Carolyn can't tolerate this type of procedure while awake."

At this point, Beth submitted a look of worried resignation and asked to use the phone to call her husband. Joshua and Alex left her to make the call in private.

"Lois, call the hospital and set Carolyn Saunders up for emergency surgery tonight." Then he turned to Alex. "My wife and I have a lovely dinner scheduled for you for tonight, which I'm afraid will be a bit delayed. Would you like to join me in the operating room?"

"I'd love to." Alex said. "Do you think you could get me emergency privileges for tonight?"

"I'll see what I can do!" This was going to be a tricky case—having Alex's extra set of hands meant Joshua wouldn't have to call in another surgeon to assist. Plus, he'd be able to size up her OR skills in person.

Beth left Joshua's office and Lois began to help her with the details of an emergency admission. Fortunately, Carolyn had not had anything to eat or drink since lunch, so her surgery would be able to be performed within the hour. Joshua returned to his office to call Liz and tell her they would be late.

"What's he like?" Liz didn't want to wait until dinner to judge for herself.

"She's wonderful, Liz. I know you'll like her," Joshua answered.

"She? What do you mean? I thought it was Alex Faber today," Liz asked, even more taken aback than Joshua had been.

"It's obvious what I mean, Liz! I'll call you as soon as I get out of the operating room. Love you!"

The phone went dead before Liz had a chance to ask any more questions.

Joshua called the president of the hospital, and with Lois's help with the paperwork, arranged for emergency privileges for Alex Faber. By 6:00 PM, the operating team had assembled. Joshua spoke briefly to Carolyn's father Russell, then he and Alex accompanied Carolyn to the operating room. Alex walked alongisde her, speaking to her in sweet, comforting tones. The little girl was unusually calm, and anesthesiologist John Stands had her asleep in no time.

With the six-year-old fully anesthetized and with the proper instruments in place, Alex and Joshua were able to visualize the tear high up in the little girl's vagina. They also noticed several small pieces of broken bark within the vaginal canal. This debris was removed and the entire vulva and vagina were washed with an iodine antiseptic solution. As a precaution, Joshua started Carolyn on intravenous antibiotics and planned to give a tetanus shot later in the recovery room.

While Alex continued to inspect the vagina and vulva for additional tears, Joshua began the laporoscopy, a procedure in which an instrument is inserted into the abdomen through the umbilicus in order to visualize the peritoneal cavity. In his usual methodical fashion, Joshua inserted the insufflation needle first, distending the little girl's abdomen with carbon dioxide so that the bowel and other vital organs would not be in the way of the laporoscope. Next he inserted the scope itself through the same umbilical incision, careful to angle it away from Carolyn's aorta. In short order, he was able to visualize the young girl's internal organs and find to his satisfaction that there were no internal injuries. However, he did find another sliver of bark behind the uterus, at the point of insertion of the branch.

Alex was able to remove the foreign object through the vaginal tear with Joshua's verbal guidance. The two worked beautifully as a team. Joshua washed out the internal cavity with saline solution through a second incision in the girl's abdomen while Alex sewed up the laceration in the vagina. The two finished, and less than an hour after she was taken into the operating room, Carolyn awoke with her parents by her side.

Joshua explained to them what he and Alex had done, reasssuring them that their daughter should recover uneventfully and could be back on a sled (if they permitted!) in less than a week. He decided to keep Carolyn in the hospital an extra day so that she could get additional intravenous antibiotics before being discharged.

Later on in the surgeons' lounge, Dr. Stands couldn't keep his thoughts to himself.

"Man! You two are a real team. I wouldn't let this girl go!" John said jovially as he sipped his coffee with his feet up. Coming from a sixty year old, gray haired yankee who rarely had a good thing to say about anybody, this was the highest compliment Alex could get.

It was Joshua who broke the ice at that point, turning to Alex with a big smile on his face.

"John, I have no intention of letting her go!"

Chapter Eight

THE SCENE SHOULD HAVE been perfect. Joshua and Elizabeth Barron were sitting down with Alex Faber for dinner at The Tavern, one of the finest restaurants in Breedville. His obstetric colleagues were covering his practice that night, leaving Joshua free to enjoy the moment. The food was excellent. The swordfish was fresh as could be, the stuffed cod was bursting with flavor, and the roast duck was moist and succulent. After an incredible interview, both parties couldn't have been happier. Alex had found the private practice that she'd been looking for, and Joshua had finally found his elusive ideal partner. His workload would be cut in half, as would his night call. Elizabeth was finally going to have all of her wishes met—she would be able to enjoy much more of her husband's company, he would be more available to his family, and his health would benefit from the decreased stress.

But all was not, as it seemed, right.

Elizabeth's worries had been piqued when Joshua referred to Dr. Faber as "she" on the phone just a few hours earlier. The idea of a female partner had never even crossed Elizabeth's mind. She wasn't typically the jealous type, but her sensitivity ran much deeper. After hanging up the phone with Joshua, Elizabeth caught herself thinking about her own father and her childhood. She had been just twelve when her parents divorced, spurred on by his infidelity. The vision of her father in the arms of another woman had been traumatizing to Elizabeth as a young girl, and similar, sickening thoughts had begun to creep into her head even before they all sat down to dinner at The Tavern.

Although no contract had yet been carved in stone, Joshua and Alex were talking of the future as though it had already arrived. Elizabeth felt awkward and ignored at the table, fiddling with her white linen napkin and rustling about in her purse for things she didn't need. She felt entirely excluded from the process, and Alex Faber's good looks and youthfulness were not helping matters.

"So," Elizabeth interjected, deciding to make herself a part of the conversation, "Why would an unattached woman who has spent all of her life in New York City want to permanently move to rural New Hampshire?"

Alex looked up from her conversation with Joshua, slightly startled by the tone in Elizabeth's voice.

"Frankly Mrs. Barron, I found your husband's letter intriguing and his philosophy regarding medical practice quite similar to my own," she answered warmly. "I spent many, many months considering other practices. None were nearly as compatible with my thinking as this one. The fact that it was in rural New Hampshire only made it that much more romantic." Alex decided too late that the use of the word "romantic" may have been a poor choice.

"Perhaps I shouldn't tell you this," Elizabeth replied, "but since you're practically in the family—Ann Stremp wrote the letter for Joshua."

At this retort, Joshua shot Liz a glance that could have sunk a battleship. Luckily, Alex handled his embarrassment with poise.

"Ms. Stremp seems to be a very dedicated employee, and I'm sure she knows Joshua's practice and outlook well enough to represent it accurately." Alex looked briefly at Joshua, then returned her attention to Liz. "And she did. The attitude in the letter was adequately confirmed during my interview today."

"I'm glad to hear that, Alex," Liz said flatly.

Throughout dinner, Joshua noticed that Liz was very quiet and listless. She refused to make eye contact with either him or Alex, and ate little of her swordfish. Joshua knew something was wrong—Liz was generally so effervescent and welcoming at these kinds of dinners.

After dinner, the Barrons dropped Alex off at the Town Inn and headed home. Storm clouds were gathering in the sky. As they approached the statue of George Washington, Joshua steered the car to the side of the road and stopped. He turned to his wife.

"Liz, can we talk about this?"

"What's to talk about?" She folded her arms and turned her head to look out the window. "You've made up your mind. It's your business and you don't have to include me in your decision making." The clouds thickened overhead.

"But Liz, she's perfect for me." He stopped. "For the practice."

"You can say that again!" Liz scoffed. "Tall, thin, long blond hair. I'd probably pick her too if I were a guy."

"What are you talking about Liz? She's a physician!"

"She's one hell of an attractive woman!" The tears were starting to fall.

"Liz, honey, you're the one I love, the only one I love." And, as if reading her mind, he went on, "I'm not your father! Alex is going to give me the chance to spend more time with you and the kids. My family comes first. You come first. You know how hard it is for me to find someone who is a fit. Alex is a fit—and it has nothing to do with the fact that she's a woman." Joshua paused, wishing Liz would turn to look him in the eye. "I really would like to hire her, but if it's going to cause a rift in our marriage, I'll turn her down and look further."

Liz turned finally, and her tears were coming fast and furious. Joshua's eyes began to moisten as well. He reached to give his wife a reassuring hug, but was stopped short by the swift tug of his seatbelt. They both started to laugh, thinking of a moment almost thirty years ago in his Mustang convertible where two seat belts had kept two young lovers at bay. Their tears and laughter mingled as he kissed her deeply, their lips fused together in an attempt to erase any doubt. They were deep into the kiss when a tapping on the window startled them. They had obviously not seen the blue flashing light in the rearview mirror. Joshua opened his window and the patrolman's flashlight invaded their private darkness.

"Oh, I'm terribly sorry Dr. Barron! Mrs. Barron," he nodded. "I didn't recognize the car. My deepest apologies."

"That's okay, officer. You just made my wife and I feel about thirty years younger. We're grateful to you." The red-faced patrolman slunk back into the night and turned off his flashing lights.

"My place or yours, Mrs. Barron?" Joshua turned to his wife who was ready with another kiss.

"Do you want to get us into some more trouble, young lady?"

"Yes, lots of trouble, Dr. Barron."

The thirty-year newlyweds returned home. They didn't even check their sleeping children as they hurried like teenagers to the bedroom, where a line of discarded clothes led to the bed.

The following morning the two lovers awoke, still in each other's arms. Joshua kissed Elizabeth again, telling her how much he loved her.

"Liz, I meant what I said last night about continuing my search for a new partner."

Liz put a finger tenderly to his lips. "No, my dear. I was being a fool. I can't believe that jealous woman last night was me. Alex is a perfect candidate and will be a tremendous asset to your practice. I don't want you to look any further. I just needed some reassurance, and I was hurt that you seemed to have made your decision completely without me."

"You're right, Liz. I'm sorry. But she seemed so right that it felt like there was no real decision to make. It was just so natural. Hey, she hasn't heard the salary offer yet. She may turn me down."

"You make sure you offer her whatever it takes for me to have my husband home, not worrying whether his practice is going down the tubes," Liz said, rubbing his back. "When can she start?"

"Liz, have I told you recently that I love you?"

"Not nearly enough, my dear," she said, smiling.

Joshua met Alex at the office at 9:00 AM. Ann went over the details of the salary offer and benefits package, and Alex seemed quite satisfied. She then sat down with Joshua for a few minutes before his first patient of the day arrived.

"I don't think your wife likes me, Joshua." Alex began. Joshua wasn't surprised that Alex had felt Liz's chilly attitude last night.

"Liz not only likes you," he reassured. "She told me this morning to make sure I offered you the most enticing package I could so you'd be sure to sign."

"Wow," Alex said, slightly surprised. "Gee, maybe I ought to have given Ann a harder time!" she joked.

"I better get you to sign a contract before the price goes up!"

"Are you sure there won't be any problems with Liz? I'm not the home wrecker type."

"I'm sure. As a matter of fact, Liz would like you to stop by the house on your way out of town for a little brunch."

"I'd like that. It is important that we get along."

"So, when do you think you could start?" Joshua asked.

"Well, my contract runs until July first, but I could give them sixty days notice. As much as I would like to start immediately, I feel an obligation to finish out the medical year with them. I'm sure that they'll let me have the last two weeks of June off for moving, so why don't you count on me for July first."

Joshua walked Alex to the door. He gave her directions to his home and then to the highway. "It certainly has been a pleasure meeting you, Alex, and I'm looking forward to July."

"So am I, Joshua. Take care of yourself. I'll probably be back in May sometime to look for housing. Thanks again."

Alex found the Barron home without much difficulty. Liz greeted her at the door with a handshake and a hug. The Barron's home was warm, tidy and bright. Liz led the way to the kitchen, where she had prepared a light brunch of waffles and fresh fruit. She motioned for Alex to take a seat at the kitchen counter, where two place settings were waiting. She poured two cups of coffee, and took a seat next to Alex.

"I'd like to start by saying that I'm very sorry about last night. The last thing I want to do is put myself between my husband and his new partner—someone who is going to make his life *easier*," Liz emphasized. "I was jealous, and unjustifiably so. It is just that I never thought Joshua would consider a female associate, and such an attractive one at that." She blushed. "It sounds so juvenile, but it is the truth."

"It's OK, Liz. I accept your apology, and thank you. Your husband is a wonderful physician, and I think we are going to work very well together." Alex took a sip of coffee. "Your concerns about an unattached professional woman in Breedville are reasonable," she went on. "But I have been on my own for many years, and I know I'll find my niche here."

"I hope you'll let me help you get started in town. I know a lot of people, including some excellent real estate brokers. I'd just like to help make your transition as easy as possible. We're just so excited to have you."

"I appreciate the offer. I plan to be back sometime in May to look for housing. Maybe we can touch base, and set some showings up then?"

The rest of the conversation was light and friendly—Liz had effectively removed the tension that she'd created the night before. They talked about the area, where the skiing was good, and what kind of cars drove best in the New Hampshire snow. By the time their plates were clean, it was as though nothing had ever happened.

"Thanks for the brunch, Liz!" Alex said at the door. "I appreciate it. Take care and I'll be in touch." They hugged, and Alex hopped into her rental car and drove off.

"I hope I'm not making a big mistake here," Liz thought to herself as she waved goodbye. Alex may seem well intentioned, but come July first, she wasn't going to turn her back for a minute. Nothing was going to come between her and Joshua.

CHAPTER NINE

ALEX RETURNED TO THE city on Saturday. In addition to her highly successful trip to Breedville, she'd spent three days learning how to ski at Waterville Valley in the White Mountains of New Hampshire. After dropping off her luggage at her apartment, she headed to the hospital. David Arnold found Alex in her office, rummaging through the pile of mail that had stacked up in her absence.

"Welcome back! How'd it go?"

"Well, I learned how to ski," Alex said coyly, "and . . . I got myself a job!"

"Congratulations!" David exclaimed. "So you're finally going to earn the big bucks," he added, giving Alex a playful nudge. "How about celebrating by taking me out to dinner?"

"You're on!" Alex giggled. "I just want to catch up on some paperwork. Why don't you stop back here around four. What are you still doing hanging around if you're not on call tonight, anyway?"

"You know how hard it is for me to leave this place. I'm one of those real dedicated docs!" David said, veiling a smirk. "Actually, I'm just covering for Len Schantz this afternoon in exchange for a seat to the Rangers game tomorrow night."

"Ah, David. Always the opportunist. Well, check back with me at four. If you're a good boy, this soon-to-be private attending will take you out for a dinner that'll knock your socks off."

"That's okay, Alex. You can take me out for a decent pizza and knock my socks off later," David winked as he leapt out the door. "See ya!"

The pizza that night was good, but the sex was even better. The two devoured a large pizza with everything on it, washing it down with a bottle of Chianti. Alex described her trip to Breedville, the practice, and her impressions of Joshua Barron. She left out the awkward dinner and follow-up brunch with Elizabeth Barron.

David was more interested in the financial package. She told him she was starting at $70,000 and would be a full partner in three years, at which time she'd probably be earning about twice that amount. David wanted all the details: the buy-in, the fringe benefits, the expense accounts, vacation time, insurance coverage. Alex was amazed at how much more aware David was of this side of medical practice than she—but on second thought, she wasn't all that surprised. She started to tell him more about Joshua's office, the quality of his patient charts, his practice philosophy, but could tell from his wandering gaze that David couldn't care less. David's professional outlook was clearly the antithesis of hers; nonetheless, she was so physically attracted to him that she eagerly asked for the check, and enjoyed David's quiet discomfort as she paid the bill.

The walk to her apartment was quiet, each lost in their own thoughts. Both Alex and David knew that things could not go on as they were after June. David hadn't yet made plans for after residency, thinking he might take some time off to travel and find that perfect place to practice. He definitely would not be at City Hospital next year. Nonetheless, Alex's new position made the finality of their affair much more real.

Back at her place, they could both appreciate this sense of finality in the passion of their lovemaking. They undressed each other with building excitement; their first kisses were longer, hungrier. He explored very inch of her body with his hands and mouth, resisting a hurried climax. This slow exploration produced multiple orgasms in her, giving her the desire to explore him as well. By the time he entered her, David was ready to explode. With each spasm came mounting pleasure for both. Despite the shattering climax, she was able to hold him in her, reluctant to let go. Exhausted, they fell asleep, fitting comfortably into each other's warm curves. An hour later, renewed, they continued their sexual endeavors, sinking and surfacing several times throughout the night, till they finally passed out together in each other's arms.

As was his habit, David was the first awake. Since it was Sunday and he had the day off, he lay in bed watching Alex sleep, thinking how beautiful she was. A few minutes later, she stirred.

"Good morning," she said through her sleepy eyes.

"Good morning to you, too," he said, kissing her. "You know, you even taste good in the morning."

"Oh David," she said with an exaggerated sigh. "You say the most romantic things. Well, did I knock your socks off last night?"

"I think it speaks for itself!" he said, pointing to his bare feet at the other end of the covers.

On Monday, Alex notified her department chief of her plans to leave at the end of June. He wished her well and saw no reason why she couldn't take off the last two weeks of June to move up to New Hampshire. He was sorry to see her go, but was used to junior attending staff leaving City Hospital soon after residency. Many had outstanding loans to pay off, which they were not able to afford on the hospital salary. Others were anxious to get their careers going and many just wanted to leave the city for the suburbs.

As soon as Alex gave notice, she had trouble keeping her mind off her impending move. She began making plans for her new life in Breedville, and started the process of wrapping up her current one in New York. She informed her landlord that she'd be moving out in mid-June, and booked a moving company. She researched banks in New Hampshire, and made plans to transfer her accounts. Most importantly, she contacted Liz Barron and made plans for a quick trip to Breedville in May. When the time came, Liz followed through on her promise and helped Alex find a small condominium in the center of town. Things were falling into place smoothly, and Alex began packing up her apartment in full force.

As for David, she saw him less and less. He wanted to keep their relationship going, but Alex felt it best to let things cool off. Very reluctantly, David acquiesced. They shared a few more nights together, but none with the passion of that night when Alex had just accepted her new job. David made plans to join an HMO on the west coast in September, giving himself the summer to travel. It was a first job that did not bring with it the obligations of private practice, just the money necessary for him to finally begin enjoying the good life he always knew he'd have.

Meanwhile, spring slowly came to Breedville. George Washington lost his white cap and the village green regained its emerald hue. Sleds were replaced with bicycles, and cars lined up at the local garages to have their snow tires removed. The trees continued to look bare, though a closer look at the branches would reveal the tiny leaf buds just waiting for the middle of May to blossom.

Joshua was back at work full time, though he still shared coverage with Breedville ObGyn. The hospital was abuzz with the advent of two new obstetricians joining the staff in July. Alex Faber was to be the first female physician in town. Many women who had put off their annual gynecologic exams for years were looking forward to the opportunity to see a woman doctor, and Alex's schedule for July was already filling up fast.

The second obstetrician was Gerald Ransom. After having lunch in the hospital cafeteria with Sam Cronin and Bill Worth that day, he'd left with certain simpatico that he didn't feel for Joshua Barron. Sam and Bill told him that they might be interested, in the case that things didn't work out with Joshua. Less than two weeks after he left Breedville, Gerald received the phone call. Joshua told him that, though he had had impeccable credentials, he'd picked an associate who he felt would fit in better with his manner of practice. Just as Joshua predicted, Gerald was unfamiliar with rejection.

"Would you mind my asking whom you picked for your associate?" Gerald had asked.

"Her name is Alex Faber. She is a member of the attending staff at New York City Hospital."

"You picked a skirt from that city dump over me? Joshua, you must have taken leave of your senses. Don't you see the benefit of my training? I can have my pick of any practice I want!" Gerald was exasperated.

"I am perfectly aware of your credentials, Dr. Ransom, and I will try to ignore your derogatory slur about my new associate. Dr. Faber is a highly skilled and well-trained physician. The determining factor in my decision was that I felt her attitude and compassion were a better match for my practice."

"You may be interested to know that I am seriously considering joining your competition in town," Gerald said.

"Well, Dr. Ransom, if that is the case, then it would probably be in everybody's best interest if we forget that this conversation ever took place." Joshua began to regret his decision to hook Gerald up with Sam and Bill.

"Very well then, Dr. Barron. Good luck with your new associate. I must say, I didn't feel that you were a good fit for my talents, either." And with that, Gerald exited the conversation having resumed his sense of control.

CHAPTER TEN

"GRANITE GREATNESS" WAS THE name given to the week-long celebration in Breedville that culminated with a fireworks display on Independence Day. Each year the town would bedeck itself in American flags and everyone was running out to pick up extra charcoal for their backyard grill. The town population nearly doubled during this particular week of summer, and between the sidewalk sales and the flea markets, the merchants in town counted on it for a fair amount of their yearly revenue. Each day was packed with events where citizens were invited to intermingle in the name of community spirit. The firemen had the opportunity to continue their winning streak over the policemen in the annual tug of war. The high school faculty would try to break their perennial losing streak to the graduating senior class in the softball tournament. The river was alive with boat races, canoe tipping competitions and fishing contests. Every church and civic organization held a clambake, a bean supper or potluck. On July fourth, a parade passed through town, complete with fire engines, marching bands, local scouting troops and sponsored floats. The mayor and town councilmen road through in a procession of antique cars. Following the parade, families went on to stake their claim to a picnic site on the town green, awaiting the fireworks display at dusk. It was Breedville at its finest.

Alex Faber was on duty at the hospital the night of the fireworks. For the first time in years, Joshua Barron had had the opportunity to spend the holiday with his family. Mary Brown, a relative newcomer to Joshua's practice, was in the middle stages of an active labor pattern. It was her first pregnancy and she had been handling the pain very well. Her husband Tom, a graduate of Breed General's natural birthing classes, was breathing right along with her—stopwatch in hand, providing words of encouragement. Mary was the third obstetrical patient who Alex was attending on this long holiday weekend—none of whom she'd met before. This situation was common when a new physician starts in an established practice. Alex entered the birthing room to check on Mary's progress.

"How's it going, Mary?"

"I think I'm starting to lose it, Dr. Faber. The contractions are tough and my back is killing me!" Mary said just as her next spasm began.

While Mary began her rhythmic breathing, Alex reviewed the monitor strip that had been run just a few minutes prior. Although the fetal heart was steady at 135 beats per minute, there was an uneasy consistency to the rate, without any variation. "Beat to beat variability" was the medical term used to describe the changing heart rate pattern of a healthy fetus, never remaining at the exact same number for more than a few seconds at a time. A sleeping baby or medication given to the mother for pain relief could both account for this unvarying pattern that Alex saw. Still, she would be constantly on the lookout for subtle signs of fetal compromise.

"Mary," said Alex as the patient regained her composure following this latest contraction, "I'd like to examine you and break your bag of water."

"Is something wrong?" Mary asked with a mild degree of anxiety.

"No. I'd just like to see what kind of progress you're making and to check on the baby's fluid. It might help to move you along a little quicker as well."

Alex donned a latex glove and examined her patient. She was seven centimeters dilated—well into the active phase of her labor—and the fetal head was descending into the birth canal. Michelle Singer, who was taking care of Mary, handed Alex a long sterile stick to help her break the amniotic sac. A moderate amount of brownish-green fluid escaped from Mary's vagina as Alex withdrew her hand.

"Michelle, let me have an internal clip."

In less than a minute Alex had fastened a small wire to the baby's head and had hooked it up to the electronic fetal monitor.

"What's wrong, Dr. Faber?" Mary requested a second time.

"Probably nothing, Mary, but I'm just taking precautions. I noticed a pattern on the monitor before that can be associated with fetal distress. The amniotic fluid was discolored with meconium, which means the baby had a bowel movement while inside you. This can also be a sign of distress. Right now, the baby is doing fine. I just want to make sure he's not trying to send out subtle signals that he is not happy in there. The internal clip is attached to the baby, and provides me with a more accurate measure of fetal well-being." Knowing how frightening this news sounded to a mother in labor, Alex did her best to explain her actions calmly.

Another contraction distracted Mary before she could respond, though she looked scared. Alex's eyes remained on the monitor. She knew that Mary was two and a half weeks overdue; that fact together with the meconium-stained fluid were worrisome signs. Five years at New York City Hospital had taught her that things could go downhill quickly when a woman was in labor, but subtle warning signs were generally available if she would be vigilant enough to look for them.

What Alex saw on the monitor began to confirm her suspicions. In addition to a flat heart rate baseline with no variability in the pattern, there occurred a small deceleration just following Mary's latest contraction.

"How does it look?" Tom asked.

"It's too early to say, Tom," Alex said. "We'll just have to watch it for awhile."

Meanwhile, Alex wrote an order for the lab to draw up two units of blood for Mary, just in case an emergency cesarean section became necessary. Over the course of the next fifteen minutes, the deceleration pattern after each contraction became more obvious. Alex had Mary turn over on her left side to provide a better return of blood flow to her heart and thus to the baby. This was usually the first maneuver performed in response to such a monitor tracing. In addition, Mary was given oxygen by mask to help increase the oxygen load to her child. Though each maneuver appeared to improve the tracing temporarily, the ominous flat pattern with the late decelerations returned. Alex examined Mary again.

"We're still seven centimeters, Mary." Alex said with some discouragement in her voice. "I don't think we can wait much longer. We're going to have to take the baby by cesarean section."

Mary and Tom took the decision in stride, with deep breaths and squeezed hands. The happenings over the past half hour had prepared them for a more complicated birth than they'd hoped for. Michelle began to prep Mary for her operation by shaving her abdomen, placing a catheter in her bladder and starting an intravenous line. Alex called the switchboard and requested that the operating room crew, anesthesiologist and pediatrician be ready to go for an emergency C-section. The monitor continued to show an ominous pattern—with each contraction, the heart rate dropped lower and recovered more slowly to its original baseline. Occasionally, there was a tachycardia, with a rapid rate of over 180 beats per minute before returning to the steady 135. The baby was having progressive difficulty dealing with what had turned into a hostile intrauterine environment.

A second nurse from the maternity floor set up the room for the cesarean section while Michelle prepared the patient. To Alex's dismay, both the anesthesiologist and the pediatrician called in during the surgery prep to let Alex know that they were both stuck in the traffic caused by the festivities in town. It was backed up for over a mile. Beginning to worry, Alex beeped Joshua, as well, who was caught up in the same mess as the other two. They would be in as soon as they could; Alex wasn't so sure it would be soon enough.

With the patient ready for surgery, Alex glanced back to the monitor that now showed a failure to return to the 135 baseline and was instead hovering around 100. When the fetal heart rate began running between sixty and seventy beats per minute, Alex felt that she couldn't wait any longer. She had never performed a cesarean section under local anesthesia before, although she knew the technique required. She turned to her anxious patient and her husband.

"Mary, I can't wait any longer for the anesthesiologist. I'm sure he will be here very soon. I'm going to numb you up as well as possible so that you don't feel what I am doing, but I must deliver your baby now. If

I don't act, the baby will be at increased risk with every minute he stays inside you. Just try to bear with me."

"Tom, just keep your hands by her head and talk to her. The drapes will be up and you won't be able to see me. Your job is to talk her through this. Lamaze classes don't train for this kind of situation, but you two are a great team and together we're going to get through this."

Tom was nearly as pale with fright as his wife, though Alex's message came through and he rose to the occasion. He continuously talked to Mary, caressing her forehead and telling her how proud he was of her. Meanwhile, with Michelle scrubbed in, Alex prepped Mary's abdomen briefly with an antiseptic solution and covered her with the surgical drapes. Using multiple injections of novacaine, she anesthetized the skin and deeper tissue layers as she methodically cut through Mary's abdominal wall to reach the baby. After making an incision in the uterus, Alex delivered the Brown's baby boy. There was no muscle tone and the baby was not breathing. She quickly cut the umbilical cord and took the baby to the warmer. There she suctioned the baby with the help of the second obstetrical nurse, removing the meconium-stained fluid from his windpipe.

"Michelle," Alex called to her nursing assistant. "Keep steady pressure on the uterine incision to cut down on blood loss while I work on the baby."

A heart rate of sixty was the only sign of life as she continued to suction out and then stimulate the baby to respond. The nurse provided oxygen with a bag and mask while Alex listened for any increase in the heart rate. After two minutes, the baby began to respond, first clenching his fists and then grimacing. A loud cry was next, followed immediately by a consensual sigh of relief by everyone in the room.

After five minutes, the baby was pinking up, crying, and thrashing in the warmer.

"I get an apgar of nine, Dr. Faber," nurse Susan Hall reported.

Seeing that there was nothing left for her to do with the baby, Alex returned to Mary where she found both parents crying with relief. Tears began to well up in her own eyes as the tension began to fade. John Stands was the first of the medical colleagues called to arrive, and promptly put Mary to sleep for the rest of the case. Tom was ushered out of the room with the baby.

Over the next thirty minutes, Alex finished putting Mary's anatomy back in order. Joshua arrived, full of apologies, as she was just finishing sewing up the skin. They left the operating room and headed over to the nursery, where they found a proud father holding his newborn son. Art Hill, the pediatrician, was finishing up some paperwork at the desk.

"Joshua," said Art, looking up from his desk at the two obstetricians, "You didn't tell me you hired such a gutsy associate!" Then he turned to Alex. "I'd like to shake the hand of the physician who pulled that one out of the fire. My name is Art Hill."

"I'm Alex Faber. Sorry to have to meet you under such trying circumstances."

Art extended his hand to the new associate. "It's a pleasure to meet you, Alex. I wasn't kidding before. It sounds like this baby was going down the tubes rapidly. I understand that the cord pH was 7.12." Art was referring to a sample of blood taken from a segment of umbilical cord that Alex had analyzed in the lab. The degree of acidosis was considerable and indicative of a high degree of distress to the infant.

"Well, Art," said Alex in response. "I appreciate the vote of confidence. I'll try to deliver most of our mutual clients with less fanfare." She smiled.

Alex and Joshua took their leave from the nursery, heading into the obstetricians' lounge where Alex began the paperwork.

"Sorry to have to bother you on your first July fourth off," Alex offered.

"No problem, partner." He was quickly growing to like the sound of that word. "Let me echo Art's admiration for your efforts. It was a gutsy call. But remember for the future: you're not at New York City Hospital anymore. Residents aren't available 'round the clock for emergencies here. You should probably lower your threshold for calling a cesarean section or any emergency where you will need back up. There would have been more time for anesthesia and pediatrics to get here if you hadn't waited as long into the distress pattern." Joshua paused. "Don't get me wrong," he added. "What you did was exemplary. My only question is whether it was necessary."

"I understand what you are saying, Joshua," Alex said, a little subdued from her glory. "I probably should have pulled the trigger sooner."

Joshua got up to leave. "I hope the rest of your night is less hectic than this. I should be home if you need me." He left to pick up his abandoned family who, with their attention skyward, had hardly missed him as Granite Greatness came to a close over Breedville's skies.

As the fireworks display dazzled down on the town green, the action at Breed General Hospital was not limited to the labor floor that night. Mark Uber, a fifty-year-old barrel-chested auto mechanic, was admitted to the ICU with chest pain. He had been on his second six-pack of Moosehead beer, stuffing down franks and chips at the green with his coworkers, when he began to experience the onset of moderate chest pain. He first wrote it off as too much greasy food, but when a series of vulgar belches failed to lessen the intensity of the pain, he began to worry. One of Mark's friends drove him to the emergency room, where he was evaluated by a moonlighting physician from Dartmouth Medical Center who was covering for the holiday. Though the EKG was not typical for coronary artery disease, he was admitted with a diagnosis of angina. Phil Lambert, on call for the medicine department, was notified of his new admission by the moonlighter. By the time Phil arrived, Mark Uber's pain had increased tremendously and the nurses were having trouble maintaining his blood pressure. As Phil initiated a dopamine drip, Mark convulsed and went into shock. A code blue was announced, and half a dozen hospital personnel converged on the intensive care unit. Despite the persistent efforts of this group under Phil's leadership, Mark Uber was pronounced dead thirty minutes later.

Julie Barron, fifteen-year-old daughter of Joshua and Elizabeth Barron, was not with her family on the green when her father was called into the hospital. She had gotten permission to hang out with her friends instead. Julie promised Liz that she would return to the family blanket by the end of the fireworks so they could all go home together.

Julie had grown up a lot over the past year, stretching several inches beyond her mother's five foot five stature. She benefited from her parents' good looks and had filled out into a woman's body. She wore her dark brown hair loose and curly, and needed a minimum amount of make up to look a lot older than a soon to be sophomore in high school.

Julie met her friends at the statue of George Washington. There were two other girls and three guys, all from her class at school. The six teenagers took off for the local Burger King, the main spot to hang in town. After polishing off a few hamburgers and bags of fries, they returned to the green to find a place to watch the fireworks. The spot they found had a poor view, but it was fairly secluded, which suited everyone's taste. The blankets were laid out and they all coupled off.

Julie's date was Brad Hancock. Brad was taller than most of the boys in Julie's class, and playing junior varsity football last year had filled him out with a muscular form. He and Julie had several classes together, and it was no coincidence that she had shown so much interest in cheerleading this past year. Liz and Joshua hadn't paid much mind to their daughter's activities, assuming that her evenings out after practice or the football games were filled with innocent teenage fun. But as the sun went down, the hormone levels went up. The two starry-eyed teenagers gazed at each other, and Brad couldn't help but let his hands roam all over Julie's body, who did not discourage his advances. As their explorations reached new levels, they rolled over onto the grass, covering themselves in the blanket. Brad pulled down on Julie's shorts and panties. As the first set of fireworks exploded into the sky and the reaction of the crowd rebounded into the trees, he entered her for the first time.

CHAPTER ELEVEN

THE CAFETERIA AT BREED General Hospital was abuzz with the excitement of the previous evening. Most of the staff had yet to meet Alex Faber, yet they were already circulating her reputation as an obstetrician par-excellence. This fanfare did not sit well with Gerald Ransom, who had just come on as a partner at Breedville ObGyn. Gerald was having coffee with Sam and Bill when Art Hill stopped over to join them.

"Hi Sam, Bill," Art greeted them. "Did you hear about Faber? Joshua seems to have found himself a real cracker jack! Sure hope it works out for him."

"So do I, Art," said Sam. "Art, I'd like you to meet our new partner, Gerald Ransom."

"Pleasure to meet you, Gerald," Art said, extending a hand as he sat down with his coffee and doughnut. Despite Gerald's presence, Art continued extolling the virtues of Joshua's new partner, assuming everyone would be pleased to hear of Dr. Barron's successes. His assumption, it soon proved, was wrong.

"Performing a cesarean section under local anesthesia is no tremendous feat," Gerald remarked snidely. "In my program, we all were encouraged to perform several this way to gain proficiency. If anything, it sounds like she might have let things go on too long before acting."

Caught somewhat off-guard, the smile quickly faded from Art's face. He saw no point in continuing the discussion, and quickly changed the subject to the other excitement of the previous night.

"Have either of you heard whether they've performed the post on 'the heart' from last night in the unit?" he asked, shifting his attention to Bill.

"Haven't heard a thing, Art," Bill said. "I hear Lambert is taking it pretty hard."

"I can imagine. Phil always takes his patients' medical problems personally. Great for the patient, but it must do a number on Phil." Art trailed off, lacking further fuel for the conversation. "Well, I've got to go. The nursery calls! Nice meeting you Gerald. Have a good day, guys."

Sam turned to Gerald as Art ambled out of the cafeteria, a perturbed look on his face.

"Look. I know that you and Joshua didn't mesh well in terms of his practice. But we all have to get along. This is a small hospital and a close-knit medical community. We can't afford any infighting."

"I guess I shouldn't have opened my mouth," Gerald said as he crossed his arms. "It just bothers me to hear reality being stretched into legend."

"Look, Gerald," Sam said, "With your credentials, you've got nothing to be defensive about. Bill and I have maintained an excellent relationship with Joshua over the years and we'd hate to spoil it over an inadvertent comment."

Bill nodded in silent agreement, signaling the end of the coffee break. All three excused themselves from the cafeteria, Sam and Gerald heading to the office for morning hours.

Sam showed Gerald a shortcut back to the physicians' office building that took them through the basement of the hospital. The heating ducts and water pipes running along the ceiling made the going slow for Gerald, who was nearly half a foot taller than Sam. As they made a turn heading towards their office, they passed a simple gray windowless door. The word "Morgue" was stamped on the door in black ink letters. Sam and Gerald continued on, far too accustomed to the general ebb and flow of a hospital to let the morbid implications of such a room enter their thoughts. Just inside that door was the body of Mark Uber, lying on a stainless steel table with running water. On the left side of the table stood Randall Adams, chief of Pathology. On the right stood an anxious Phil Lambert.

For Dr. Adams, this was just another autopsy. He had performed hundreds during his thirty-five year tenure at Breed General. His thin gray hair barely covered his balding top. Thick wire rimmed glasses and a stooped posture bespoke of years bent over a microscope. To Dr. Adams, this autopsy was a mere early morning roadblock to a large pathology load that had built up over the long holiday weekend. There were at least thirty cases waiting for him up in his office that needed to be reviewed and reported on. Furthermore, the surgeons, already eagerly back in action, had posted at least four frozen sections for him to analyze before morning's end. Despite these impending burdens, Dr. Adams methodically performed the autopsy on Mark Uber, dictating his observations into an overhead microphone and analyzing the decedent's remains in an attempt to pin down the diagnosis.

Not unlike many of his colleagues, Phil Lambert never felt comfortable in the morgue. Whether it was the irreverent way their patients were gutted or perhaps the frustration of having failed in their healing art, most physicians would only pass the morgue in order to get from the cafeteria to their office as Gerald and Sam had done moments before.

Randall opened up the abdomen and cut through the rib cage, freeing the viscera from the encumbrance of its shell. He laid out the organs en masse on a wooden board adjacent to the stainless steel table. Knowing Mr. Uber's working diagnosis upon entering the unit on July fourth, Randall had removed the heart from its adjacent organs and was looking for signs of recent disease. Not only did the walls of the heart look healthy, multiple transections of the coronary arteries that fed oxygen to the cardiac muscle failed to reveal any significant plaque formation. Right away, Dr. Adams could see that this was not the heart of a cardiac victim.

"Perhaps the slides will give us more information, Phil," Randall told his younger colleague. "I'll have more information in a few days."

Frustrated, Phil prepared to leave. Randall called him back just as he had reached the door.

"Take a look at this, my friend." Randall was referring to a gaping hole with purulent drainage on the posterior surface of the stomach, near where it entered the esophagus.

"I think we've found the culprit," Randall stated, lightly prodding the area with a steel tool. "Mr. Uber seems to have perforated his stomach with an untreated gastric ulcer. I would venture to say that we're going to find overwhelming acute infection in the blood samples with seeding of many of the organs. It's an unusual presentation, but I think this case will ultimately be signed out as septic shock secondary to a perforated gastric ulcer.

Phil was aghast as he peered at the culprit organ. He had not even considered the gastrointestinal tract. Of course he had little time to consider anything since Mark Uber had arrested shortly after his arrival at the hospital that night. Nonetheless, losing a patient due to an errant diagnosis was anathema to Phil's very being. Knowing that Randall's findings were more than likely accurate, he promptly assumed the lion's share of the blame.

"Sorry to ruin your day, Phil," said Randall as lightly as he could. He knew how hard Phil would take this type of news, and he didn't want to make his load any heavier. "You can't blame yourself, son," he added in his signature fatherly fashion. "You didn't have time to make a diagnosis, let alone call in a surgeon and treat him."

"Thanks, Randall," Phil said glumly. "I did discuss the case with the moonlighter in the ER before he was admitted. Seemed like an atypical case. I should have pushed for a more complete work up before admitting him to the unit."

"Well, it sounds like everything just happened too quickly with this one," Randall said with soft smile as he returned his focus to his work. Phil turned to the exit once more.

"Well, call me when you have a final report. I'll wait until then to discuss it with the family."

Phil headed towards the hospital end of the long basement corridor to begin morning rounds. While waiting at the elevator, he saw Joshua Barron leaving the cafeteria and heading his way. Joshua seemed upbeat.

"Hi, Phil. I heard you lost a tough one last night. Sounds like he wasn't as fortunate as I was."

"Hey there, Josh," Phil said, not in the mood to discuss the Uber case again. "Yeah, it was a tough one. As it turns out, this guy appears not to have been a cardiac victim. Adams spotted a perforated ulcer with evidence of sepsis in the lesser sac of the peritoneum during the post. I blew the diagnosis."

Joshua's wide smile instantly left his face, replaced with thoughtful empathy.

"You shouldn't be too hard on yourself, Phil. It sounds like you didn't have a whole lot of time to do anything but react to his arrest."

"Maybe you're right." Phil took a deep breath. "But I still can't help feeling like I failed the guy. I should've been more demanding of the moonlighter's work-up over the phone." The elevator announced its arrival with a soft ding, signaling Phil's opportunity to change the subject. "By the way, I hear your new partner is becoming a legend in her own time. Art Hill can't seem to say enough about her."

Joshua gave a short laugh.

"It's probably just as well that she has the day off today. Give the place a chance to settle down." He smiled. "I wouldn't want all this publicity to go to her head!" The elevator doors opened and the two men headed off into Monday morning.

That same Monday morning found Julie Barron having second thoughts about her interlude under the blanket with Brad Hancock the night before. Although her mother was letting her sleep in, Julie was awake before six-thirty with horrible cramps in her lower abdomen. She went to the bathroom, hoping that urinating would relieve the pressure. Julie was frightened and confused when she saw bright red blood passing in her urine. Her period had been over for at least two weeks. She returned to her room, her mind pacing with all types of fears. The pain and feelings of urgent urination persisted as she lay in bed.

I must be pregnant, Julie thought as a wave of panic washed over her.

Tears began to fall as she thought of the events of the previous night. Everything with Brad had been so much fun till now. She had a crush on Brad Hancock for nearly the entire school year and it was only in the last few months that he'd begun to notice her. They'd gone to the final ninth grade dance together, and no one could separate them that evening. She couldn't believe it when he leaned in to kiss her—it felt like she was living in a dream. They saw each other several times since school had ended, walking hand-in-hand in the park, riding their bikes by the river; he'd taken her to the movies just the week before. Spending time with a guy felt so much more sophisticated than hanging out with her girlfriends in their pink bedrooms, where they only dreamed about what it would be like to have a boyfriend. She had been a little nervous last night, but it wasn't nearly as scary as she always thought her first time would be. Brad had made her feel warm and safe. Having him caress her breasts for the first time was amazing, and from that point she'd just stopped thinking and only felt. Even when he had entered her, it did not hurt like she had heard it would. But now there was something wrong. They hadn't used a condom and Julie was sure she was pregnant. How was she going to tell her parents?

The cramps and pressure in her abdomen intensified, sending her back to the bathroom. Once more she passed a small amount of bloody urine, still feeling like she had to go but couldn't. She sat there on the toilet wondering what she should do next. She didn't have to wait long. Her sojourns to the bathroom had raised the maternal antennae of Elizabeth Barron, who knocked softly on the door.

"Julie, are you in there?" she asked. "Are you okay, honey?"

When she received no answer, she opened the door to find her daughter sitting on the toilet, her head in her hands.

"What's the matter, baby?"

"Oh mommy, my stomach really hurts and I'm bleeding. I really don't feel good." She made no mention of last night's activities. After Dr. Mom gleaned a few more symptoms from her daughter, she recognized the pattern of a bladder infection. She had experienced similar problems earlier in life, usually after an exceptionally passionate weekend with Joshua in Boston. Unwilling to concede that the cause was similar, Elizabeth wrote off the infection as a result of poor hygiene. She was only fifteen, after all.

"It's okay, honey. It sounds like you have a bladder infection. I'll call your father and he'll prescribe you something that'll take care of it in no time."

Julie was tremendously relieved that she didn't have to confess to her mother what had happened with Brad, and hoped that she was right about the bladder infection. Elizabeth called Joshua—as she suspected, he asked her to take Julie to the hospital lab to leave a urine sample. Julie did, in fact, have a bladder infection, and Joshua started her on ampicillin for the infection and pyridium for the pain. Joshua was a little more concerned about the true cause of his daughter's infection than his wife. He would speak to Elizabeth about it tonight.

Chapter Twelve

AS THE MEDICAL STAFF at Breed General was singing her praises, Alex Faber was enjoying a relaxing Monday off. She took a leisurely walk from her new townhouse to the local bicycle shop. She had spotted a ten-speed Schwinn in the store window several days before, and her interest was piqued. She hadn't ridden a bike in nearly fifteen years. She had traded in her old two-wheeler for the family Chevrolet the minute she hit seventeen and had never looked back. Besides, the thought of riding a bike in New York City seemed ludicrous. But now, things were different. The topography of Breedville and the surrounding area was absolutely gorgeous, and compared to Manhattan, traffic was non-existent. There were so many beautiful streets and trails to explore.

Alex walked into the cycling shop. It didn't take her long to settle on the Schwinn from the window display. She looked at the purchase as a gift to herself—between landing a great new position and starting off with a bang, she felt she deserved it. She added a sturdy bike lock to her tab, and less than thirty minutes after entering the store, Alex was off to explore her new world. She was grateful to feel her body adjust quickly to the new equilibrium, and in no time it felt like it used to when she was a kid. She'd pay for it later with some unfamiliar muscle aches, but for now, an irrepressible smile spread across her face as she peddled her way first towards the river, then back past the green, all the way to the hospital at the east end of town. It was a glorious day and she was feeling good about her move to New Hampshire.

After spending the afternoon exploring Breedville by bike, Alex returned home for a quiet dinner and a good book. She was enjoying her relaxing evening when the shrill ring of the telephone broke her peaceful solitude. It was Frank Dimento, the urologist she'd met at the hospital while on tour with Joshua several months before.

"Hello, Alex—this is Frank Dimento. Joshua Barron introduced us a while back while you were touring Breed General."

"Hello, Frank," Alex said, a grimace growing as she remembered their first encounter. "How are you?"

"Fine, thanks," Frank said. "You seem to have made quite a first impression with your heroics of last night."

"I wasn't aware there was that much to talk about," Alex said. "I'm just glad things worked out as well as they did."

"No, really," Frank continued. "Everyone was talking about it this morning in the cafeteria."

"I'm sure Joshua would have done the same thing in that circumstance, so it really isn't a big deal." Alex said very matter-of-factly. "Look Frank, I'm really tired and have a busy day tomorrow. What can I do for you? Surely you didn't call me up to extol my virtues." Her tone took on a professional demeanor.

"Actually, I wanted to ask you out for dinner this weekend. Being that you're new in town, I thought I could help make your welcome a warm one. I know a cozy restaurant just outside of town that has great food."

Alex clenched her eyes shut, wishing she could vanish into the deep cushions of her couch. After their meeting in the surgeon's lounge that day, she had seen more than enough of Frank Dimento.

"Well, Frank," she replied, "I appreciate the offer, but the Barrons have been doing a great job of acclimating me, and my schedule is pretty booked." There was short silence on the other end of the phone.

"Oh, well sorry to hear that," Frank said hopefully. "Maybe another time."

"Good night, Frank. I'm sure I'll see you around the hospital."

"Sure, Alex. See you around."

That had gone fairly smoothly, Alex considered. But she had the feeling she hadn't heard the last of Frank Dimento.

By Tuesday morning, the awkward phone conversation with Frank was a distant memory. Alex arrived at work, thrilled to finally have her new office space decorated and complete. Her reference books were lined up neatly on a tall bookcase by the window. Her diplomas hung with authority over a brand new mahogany desk, accented with a desk set, blotter and a few framed photographs. The piece de resistance was the door plaque engraved with her name, which had just arrived yesterday. Ann Stremp was just screwing it into the door when Alex arrived.

"Good morning!" Alex greeted her with a smile in her voice, determined to win over the ever-feisty Ann.

"Good morning, Dr. Faber."

"Please call me Alex, Ann."

"If that's what you wish, Dr. Faber. Alex, it is!"

Alex figured she better not press her luck. She sat down at her desk, taking a moment to soak in the sensation of being in her office for the first time—a warm feeling washing over her body, similar to the sensation of returning home after a long trip. Reviewing her schedule for the day, she noticed that she was being booked exceptionally light in comparison to Joshua. This was her partner's idea, so that she would have the opportunity to learn where everything was and also to get herself adjusted to the new practice.

Her first patient of the day was a thirty-two year old newly pregnant woman. Jody Pinkham had been seen by Lois Wilner for her initial visit. This was her first visit with the doctor and she was more than a little nervous. She had noticed a small amount of bloody discharge after intercourse several days ago, and was concerned. Much to her husband's chagrin, her panic over causing a miscarriage had stymied any further romantic endeavors. As a very concerned pregnant woman, Jody had already taken every precaution she could for her baby—she stopped smoking as soon as she missed her period; she suffered through several headaches for fear that Tylenol could cause a birth defect. She even exchanged her occasional beer for three full glasses of milk a day.

Alex greeted Jody in the examination room. She sat with a hospital gown covering most of her body, a sheet over her lap. Alex briefly reviewed her history. She reassured her that a small amount of bleeding after sex was not all that uncommon in early pregnancy, although she deferred to her physical exam before completely ruling out pathology. Since she was already twelve weeks pregnant, Alex listened for a baby's heartbeat with the doptone. The reassuring beat of life sent a smile through the patient's face, at once providing excitement and security. Alex never grew tired of seeing the glow on a woman's face the first time she heard the fetal heart beat. There was a love that would pervade the examination room, and even the doctor herself was not immune.

Alex's warm and friendly manner had had the desired affect, at once providing a relaxing atmosphere where before there was only fear and trepidation. However, the relaxing ambiance in the examination room did not prepare the practitioner for what came next. Sitting on the stool in front of the patient's exposed lower body, Alex gently inserted the speculum. She opened the beak of the instrument to visualize the cervix and perform a pap smear. What confronted her instead was an angry mass of red tissue which had replaced nearly half of the woman's cervix. A twelve-week-old fetus was not the only entity growing within her body. Her cervix had spawned a malignant neoplasm, destined to terminate the new fetus and potentially its mother, as well.

Alex was devastated with what she saw. She realized that a definitive diagnosis could only be made by biopsy, but she was confident of her clinical impression. She reached for the instrument drawer, removing a long metal object with a scissors-like handle on one end and a metal cup with sharp teeth and a steel jaw on the other.

"You might feel a bit of pinching, Ms. Pinkham, just hold tight," Alex said calmly. She attacked the mass, taking several samples with the cervical biopsy punch, dropping them into a small container of formaldehyde.

"Is anything wrong, Dr. Faber?" the woman asked anxiously.

"I'm not sure," Alex said. "You have a small sore on the cervix and I needed to get a sample of it to see what it is." Alex's answer lacked conviction.

"Is the baby going to be all right?" Jody asked, sensing the worry in Alex's voice.

"The baby appears to be fine. I'll be finished in a moment." Alex's mind was racing as she wondered how she would deliver this news to her patient. She finished the exam, painting the biopsy sites with a resin solution to stop any bleeding. Moving on, the last steps of the exam went smoothly—the size of Jody's uterus was consistent with a twelve-week gestation. Fortunately, there were no physical signs of spread of what Alex was sure was a malignant tumor.

"Why don't you get dressed and join me in my office," Alex suggested, leaving the examination room. She gave the bottled sample to Lois, requesting that the report be sent directly to her attention as soon as the pathologist could have it ready. She took a deep breath and returned to her office.

Alex concentrated on the pregnancy during her discussion with Jody, making light of the biopsy for the time being. They discussed Jody's due date, the anticipated prenatal care and reviewed the routine blood test results that had already come back. She suggested that Jody return near the end of the week so that Alex could examine the biopsy sites. To Jody's questions regarding the significance of the "sore," Alex said that she could not be sure what it was without a pathology report. She reassured her that she would definitely have more information when she saw her later in the week. Jody appeared to accept this answer, and seemed hesitant to ask any more questions. She left with the contentment of having heard her baby's heartbeat.

The rest of Alex's morning was uneventful. Birth control pills, diaphragm fittings and a woman who wanted a sterilization made up the rest of the appointment slots. Alex was relieved by the mediocrity of the appointments that followed Jody Pinkham. She was sitting at her desk dictating a note when Joshua knocked at her door.

"Doing anything for lunch, Dr. Faber?" Joshua had just returned from the operating room, where he had finished a full case load and was now taking a break before afternoon office hours.

"Hi, Joshua," Alex said, trying to sound upbeat.

"Why so glum, Alex?" Joshua asked. "Private practice getting you down already?" Alex shared her concerns over Jody Pinkham with her new partner. Joshua looked equally concerned upon hearing her findings.

"Any question in your mind about the diagnosis, Alex?"

"I wish there was. I'm afraid Ms. Pinkham is going to have a very short pregnancy and an abbreviated reproductive potential. I just hope we can save her life."

Thankfully, the afternoon session did not hold the same dark atmosphere that the morning had. Most of Alex's patients were pregnant and in for routine exams. She had purposely been booked for patients late in their pregnancies, in order to minimize the number of women whom she'd meet for the first time on the labor floor. Office obstetrics was almost always an emotionally up-beat session. Complications were uncommon and reassurance was usually the only therapy needed. As long as one was a stickler for details, methodically reviewing the lab work and serial measurements of fetal growth and blood pressure, there was rarely trouble. The two greatest concerns would be spotting a subtle abnormality on the prenatal record, or being unable to pick up the fetal heartbeat. Fortunately, Alex did not encounter either problem that afternoon, which sped by rather quickly. She was actually looking forward to being on call that night.

Before heading home for the day, Joshua signed out his fresh post-ops and introduced Alex to a patient he had admitted in early labor a few hours earlier. She would likely be delivering sometime that evening.

"Before I go," added Joshua, "I just wanted to remind you about the reception tomorrow evening for the new hospital president. It'll be pretty informal, but important that you show up."

"No problem! I'll be there," Alex assured, waving him home. After finishing up some paperwork, Alex headed to the cafeteria for a bite to eat, then adjourned to the labor floor with a book to await the progress of the latest mother-to-be.

Gerald Ransom was on call for Breedville ObGyn that night and also had a patient in early labor. This was the first opportunity for the two newest members of the obstetrical staff to meet. With the logistics of one large on-call room for the two attending physicians, they were destined to spend a lot of time together that night. Though preparations had never been made in anticipation of a female attending on the labor floor, the sleeping arrangements were of no concern to Alex. As the only female member in her residency class, she was used to having to find her place in a male-dominated specialty. It was Gerald who was having more issues with the call room logistics.

"Alex," Gerald said, "don't you find it awkward sharing your call room with a man?"

"Not really, Gerald," Alex answered, looking up from her book. She was seated in a chair in the corner, bare feet resting comfortably on her bed. "You're an obstetrician; I'm an obstetrician. We're just going to have to get used to it." Alex shrugged and returned to her book. She had not meant to be short with her new colleague, but she resented the smarmy expression on Gerald's face.

Despite her attitude, Gerald found himself utterly distracted by Alex. She looked great, he thought, even in the shapeless green scrub suit. He left the call room frequently, ostensibly to check on his patients but more to relieve himself of the frustration he felt in her presence. He wandered the halls of the labor floor, aggravated that he had to share his call room with a female, and even more burned that she wasn't giving him the time of day.

In addition to covering for his practice, Gerald was also on back-up gynecologic call for the emergency room. As he was pacing, his beeper went off, requesting he come down for a consult. The patient was a sixteen-year-old girl with heavy vaginal bleeding and a positive pregnancy test. She had no idea she was pregnant and had been brought to the hospital by her bewildered boyfriend. The moonlighter had diagnosed her with an incomplete abortion or partial miscarriage, and had consulted Gerald for a probable dilatation and evacuation. Gerald briefly examined the frightened girl, confirming the diagnosis. He set her up for a D and E in the emergency procedures room and dismissed the boyfriend to the lobby.

"Were you using anything for birth control, honey?" he asked.

"No," she said. "My boyfriend wouldn't let me take the pill. He said it isn't good for me and besides, he wants me to have a baby."

Gerald couldn't help but scoff. "You're a baby yourself!" he said strongly. "If you're going to fool around, you need to protect yourself, regardless of what your boyfriend thinks. He's not the one who has to have surgery now, and who knows if he would have even been around months from now to be a father if you carried this baby to term!"

The girl began to cry and turned away from Gerald. The emergency room nurse, appalled by Dr. Ransom's harsh insensitivity, tried to reassure her that everything would be okay.

Gerald administered twenty-five milligrams of Demerol and ten milligrams of Valium intravenously and then began to suction out the blood and pregnancy tissue. The bleeding quickly subsided and the procedure was over. Gerald wrote out directions and prescriptions for the nurse to review with her and her boyfriend and quickly took his leave.

Stupid girl, he thought angrily as he returned to the labor floor. Gerald went to check on his patient, who had progressed to four centimeters. It was definitely going to be a long night.

By the time he returned to the call room, it was dark except for a night light in the bathroom. Alex was fast asleep. He stared at his sleeping colleague for a moment, then slipped under his covers. Though he usually had no trouble falling asleep, he felt himself getting hard as his thoughts returned to Alex, asleep only a few feet away.

God damn it, he thought. I've got a patient in early labor and I can't convince my penis to go to sleep!

It turned out to be long night for both Alex and Gerald. Each of their patients progressed slowly through their respective labor patterns, necessitating frequent interruption in their sleep to perform vaginal examinations. Alex's patient finally delivered around five AM and Gerald's around six. After her delivery, Alex returned to her call bed until 7:30, at which time she showered and began rounds on her patients. Gerald had the rest of the day off, so took a cold shower at the hospital before heading home to take out his sexual frustrations on his un-expecting and half-asleep wife.

Morning rounds went quickly for Alex. There was Joshua's hysterectomy from yesterday, Alex's cesarean section from two days before and a few women recovering from their vaginal deliveries. Each woman appeared to be doing well. Alex performed brief examinations, discussed postpartum instructions with the new mothers and wrote the necessary orders on the post-operative patients. This was much more pleasant than when she rounded at City Hospital, where she usually ended up feeling like the fifth wheel amongst all the residents. Now she was in charge and directly responsible for their care, and Alex loved every minute of it. She spent her extra time introducing herself to Joshua's patients, answering their questions and instructing them on what to expect in the postoperative period. Despite her lack of sleep, she felt good about the care she was providing and the new responsibilities that she now had.

After completing rounds, Alex moved on to morning office hours, which began simply enough. She had several patients who were in excellent health, merely returning for their annual pilgrimage to the gynecologist. Her next patient requested a sterilization. In reviewing her chart, she noticed one of Joshua's notes from a previous visit—the woman's husband, a prominent member of the city council, had undergone a vasectomy. Because she saw no change of last name or marital status, Alex questioned her about the previous vasectomy and need for contraception. As tears began to fall, Alex realized that she had stumbled into a social quagmire. The patient admitted that she had been having an affair, which resulted in an unwanted pregnancy. Unbeknownst to either her husband or her lover, she had driven to Manchester where she had undergone an abortion several weeks before. Not wishing to lose her marriage or her lover, she decided to have a sterilization, hoping that Alex would help her cover her tracks by finding an alternate diagnosis for the procedure and perhaps leave out that her tubes were being tied.

Alex explained to the patient that it would be possible to perform the laporoscopy for other indications, such as pelvic pain, or a possible ovarian cyst, but that the operative note would clearly state that she was undergoing a sterilization as well. She reassured her that her chart and medical history were strictly confidential and it was unlikely that her husband would ever find out. Satisfied, the patient agreed and Alex scheduled the surgery.

After the patient left, Alex returned to her office to quickly sort through her mail. Just as she was leaving to see her next patient, the phone rang.

"Hello, this is Dr. Faber."

"Dr. Randall Adams from pathology is on the phone for you," came Ann Stremp's voice.

"Thanks, Ann. Put him through." Alex sat back down in her chair. "Hi Dr. Adams. What can I do for you?"

"I'm afraid you have a patient with a pretty nasty cervical lesion, Alex," Randall told her.

"I take it you're referring to Jody Pinkham. You know, Dr. Adams, she's three months pregnant."

"I'm sorry to hear that. My final report will read out as invasive squamous cell carcinoma of the cervix. At least it is well-differentiated." This comment referred to the more orderly array of abnormal cells found under the microscope, portending a less aggressive cancer if it was found early enough in its clinical course.

"Well, I appreciate your getting back to me so quickly. Thanks again."

Alex was beginning to feel the weight of the world on her shoulders. There was more pathology out here in suburbia than she thought. She would ask Joshua for a recommendation for a gynecologic oncologist for referral. She realized that Jody would need a radical pregnant hysterectomy as soon as her metastatic workup was back, and hopefully negative. There was no question in her mind about waiting out the pregnancy. There was just not enough time to allow the fetus to develop and be delivered safely. She had an appointment with Jody Pinkham in two days, which would give her enough time to make whatever arrangements were necessary.

A bit shaken by Randall's confirmation of her suspicions, Alex moved on to her final patient of the morning. Betty Travis worked as a natural childbirth instructor at Breed General Hospital, and her pregnancy was close to term.

"It's a pleasure to meet you, Dr. Faber." Betty extended her hand. "I was hoping to ask you a few questions about your feelings regarding the management of labor before the exam, just to get acquainted."

"Of course, go right ahead," Alex replied, happy to be distracted by the discourse. Betty asked many advanced, well-informed questions about pitocin, episiotomy, indications for pain medication during labor and the use of epidural anesthesia. Alex sensed that her answers were reassuring to Mrs. Travis, whose skeptical manner soon abated.

Following the discussion, Alex led her to an exam room where she palpated the fetal parts within her abdominal wall. She was not convinced that the baby's head was directed down. After hearing a healthy fetal heart, Alex performed a vaginal exam. As she thought, the baby's head had not descended into the pelvis. Since the patient was less than a week shy of her due date, Alex suggested an ultrasound to determine the fetal position. Lois Wilner scheduled her for an ultrasound in the hospital early in the afternoon and she would return to the office to discuss the results with Alex later that day.

"I know she's got a transverse lie," Alex said to Lois as the patient left for the hospital. "I'm going to offer her an external version, but if it doesn't work and she doesn't turn on her own, our Lamaze instructor will be on the receiving end of a cesarean section!"

As she had expected, the ultrasound revealed a transverse lie—a fetal position that was impossible to deliver vaginally. Alex scheduled her patient for an external version after office hours to attempt to physically turn the baby into the correct position. Since it was Joshua's day off, Alex would once again be taking call for the practice that night. As she left the office, beeper on her belt, she headed upstairs to the labor floor, confident that her luck had to change.

Alex arrived on the labor floor a few minutes after Betty. Susan Hall, one of the maternity nurses, was running the external fetal monitor on her when Alex entered the birthing room.

"Hi again," Alex greeted Betty. "So, I assume you understand what I'm going to try to do?"

"Yes. Susan has explained everything to me. I just hope the baby cooperates."

"Me too," Alex agreed. She wrote out the orders for the intravenous fluids and dose of terbutaline, a drug used to relax the uterine musculature.

"This medicine may make you feel a little shaky," Alex explained. "The effect will wear off soon after I stop the IV fluids." She turned to Susan. "Has ultrasound been notified of the version attempt?"

"Yes, Dr. Faber. They said to call when we are ready for them."

"Great. Call them now, since it'll take a few minutes for them to come upstairs. The monitor tracing looks fine. Why don't you start dripping in the terbutaline. I'll be back soon."

Alex went to check in on Joshua's post-op patient again. When she returned to Betty's room, the ultrasound technician was already identifying the transverse lie she had detected earlier.

"Well, the baby seems to like this position," Alex stated. "Let's see how easily he or she can be persuaded to move." Alex filled her hands with mineral oil, liberally dousing the patient's abdomen with the slick liquid. Then using ultrasound guidance, she placed one hand on the baby's head and the other on its bottom. Using as much strength as she could muster, she pushed down on the head, trying to direct it into the pelvis while at the same time pushing the baby's bottom towards its mother's chest. However, the baby would not budge much beyond its original position. Meanwhile, Betty Travis was experiencing a significant amount of pain from Alex's manipulations.

"We're not making much progress," Alex reported. "I'll try moving the baby in the opposite direction." Once again Alex pushed with as much effort as she could. Her hands began to cramp up on her from the exertion. The baby still showed no sign of moving. By this time it became clear that success would be elusive that night and the mother had had about all she could take. Alex stopped. She reattached the monitor to evaluate the fetus and left the room to clean off her hands and allow the circulation to return.

"What do we do now?" Betty cried, in a bit of a panic as Alex re-entered.

"We'll just have to let nature try it on her own," Alex said. "Your due date is not for several days and it could be more than a week before you go into labor. If the baby doesn't turn, you're facing a cesarean section. It's very important," she continued, "to let us know if you break your bag of water, since a baby in this position carries a greater risk of having the cord drop into the vagina when the membranes break."

The repeat monitor tracing showed no ill effect on the fetus from the version attempt, the intravenous line was removed and the patient given an office appointment in one week. Alex finished rounding on the maternity floor. She was also covering back-up for the emergency room, so she called down to see if there was anything for her.

"Not unless you want to examine a forty year old guy with chest pain, Dr. Faber," the emergency nurse offered.

"I'll pass," Alex responded, "Thanks anyway."

With her beeper remaining silent, Alex left the hospital, bumping into Joshua at the front entrance.

"Hi Alex," Joshua greeted her. "You didn't forget about the reception tonight, did you?"

"Oh, that's right," she remembered. "I'm not big on hospital politics, but I guess since I'm on call anyway, it's hard to complain." The two headed towards the hospital conference room.

"What do you know about him?" Alex asked her partner.

"All I know is that he came highly recommended. The search committee seemed to be pleased that he took the position."

Joshua and Alex entered the conference room, where a large group of physicians were milling around a buffet table.

"There he is, Alex. Let me introduce you."

Alex turned and as her gaze cast upon the tall man with dark brown eyes and a mustache. she felt an instant twinge of attraction that was entirely unexpected but not unfamiliar.

"Alex, I'd like you to meet Ron Dorcik, our new hospital president." Ron's eyes sparkled and a warm smile spread across his face.

"Hi, Alex," he greeted her, nearly having to support her with both of his hands. "It's so good to see you again."

CHAPTER THIRTEEN

SEEING RON DORCIK FOR the first time after all these years instantly flooded Alex's head with memories. She was amazed at how the mere sight of him could take her back so quickly—and the immediate recollections were some of the most painful ones.

In a flash, Alex was in an exam room, lying on her back, naked from the waist down. She still recalled the harsh bright light directed between her legs, so bright that it felt like the sunshine baking her from the inside out.

"You're going to feel me touching you," the doctor said. "Try to open your legs as wide as you can."

"What a lovely ring you have," the assistant commented as she held Alex's hand, trying to offer a distraction.

"Now you're going to feel some pressure on the inside. You're doing fine. I just need your legs a little bit further apart."

Alex lay on the table, eyes clenched shut. So stupid of me! she thought. There must have been a hole in the diaphragm. How could I go months without checking it? She couldn't believe she was actually pregnant.

"You're now going to feel a stick and a burn. This is the numbing medicine. It works very quickly," the doctor reassured.

"Try to take some slow, deep breaths, dear."

God, I hope I'm doing the right thing, Alex worried, her mind spinning with thoughts and fears and questions. He'd never understand if I told him. I have to make the decision that's right for me. I have to.

"Now you will feel some cramps as I dilate your cervix. The medicine should help keep them tolerable. You're now going to hear a bit of noise. There will be a pulling sensation and some cramps. We are down to only a few minutes more," the doctor explained.

The suction machine began to whine. Alex could feel a pulling sensation, but thankfully no pain. The pregnancy was suctioned from her womb as she took slow deep breaths.

"You're doing great, honey," the assistant said encouragingly. "Just a little more and then you'll be able to rest."

The noise was over as quickly as it had begun. Menstrual-like cramps were setting in. The speculum was removed and the physician stood up.

"You did very well, Alex," he said. "You'll be able to rest now."

She closed her legs as the nurse assisted her in lying down. A cold cloth was placed over her forehead.

"Make sure you start the methergine as soon as you get home," he instructed. "I've given you a prescription for Percocet and birth control pills. Start the pills on Sunday. If you have any questions or feel that you are bleeding or cramping too much, call the emergency number in the pamphlet. Everything went well. You were a great patient." He then left the room.

Alex would need to read the directions later, as she hadn't absorbed any of the doctor's instructions—his voice sounded faint and garbled in her head. She was assisted to the recovery area, where several other women were also resting and recovering. Thirty minutes later, Alex was out the door.

When Ron got home from work that night, Alex was already in bed. The hospital meeting had run way over and he was exhausted. Ron went upstairs, where he found Alex curled up far on her side of their king mattress, fast asleep. He kissed her on her forehead.

"Alex, honey, I'm home," he whispered. His wife's eyes remained closed, and her breathing was uninterrupted. Ron sighed, and went down to the kitchen to pour himself a bowl of Frosted Flakes and milk. Unfortunately, the mediocre sandwich and chips at the hospital didn't suffice, and he was too tired to prepare anything more elaborate. Alex didn't cook as often as he hoped she would, so cereal was rather common for dinner. After his second bowl, he returned to the bedroom. He changed, turned out the light and slid over towards his wife.

"Alex, you sleeping?" he asked.

There was no response. Alex's huddled position made it impossible for him to get close to her. He rolled over and went to sleep.

It was at the breakfast table the following morning that Alex told Ron that she wanted a divorce. She then turned around in her terry cloth robe, her eyes red and hair unkempt, and returned to bed. She didn't give an explanation and she wanted no alimony. She was moving back to the city. There was no changing her mind.

Alex was gone by the time Ron returned from work that night. She didn't leave a note. He had no idea why it had come to this, but was powerless to stop it. Ron eventually returned to his parents' home in Connecticut, emotionally drained. An uncontested divorce followed.

In the conference room, Alex could feel Ron's strong arms wrap around her in an embrace, while her knees struggled to regain their stability.

"It's great to see you again, Alex." Ron said as he gently lessened his grip. "It's been an awfully long time."

Alex felt a tug of emotion as she looked at Ron's face. Never before had she experienced such a feeling of happiness and dread all at the same time.

"Yes it has," said Alex, taking a deep breath. "A lifetime ago."

"You two know each other?" Joshua asked, surprised.

"Yes. We used to be married," Alex answered matter-of-factly.

"I must admit," Ron continued. "I knew you were here when I took this job. I probably should have gotten in touch to let you know—I just didn't know what to say," Ron said with a slight nervous laugh.

"You two were married?" Joshua said. He didn't know Alex had been married before, let alone to the new hospital president.

"Yes," she answered him again. "We married soon after graduate school and were divorced three years later. That's when I decided to go to medical school, and Ron moved on in his career—and has apparently gotten where he always wanted to be!" she said with a shaky smile.

"Well," said Ron, moving on, "since this is a welcome reception, I guess I better introduce myself to some other members of the medical staff. Perhaps we can catch up a bit later?" he asked Alex.

"Sure, Ron," she answered. "I'll see you later."

John Stands, president of the medical staff, came over and took Ron by the arm. "Come on, Ron. Let me introduce you to a few of the internists at the hospital." Ron moved off to the next group, looking back to offer Alex a smile as he went.

Ron finally caught up with Alex later that evening on the labor floor. Alex was free for the time being, so she led him to the more private doctor's lounge where they could talk. She certainly did not want to have a personal discussion with her ex-husband, the president of the hospital no less, in the middle of the labor floor.

"I've got to say, Alex, you look great!" Ron blurted out as the door closed, a broad smile forming under his mustache.

"Thanks, Ron. I'm feeling a lot better about myself than the last time you saw me." Alex still wasn't quite sure how to handle herself around Ron.

"Do I dare ask you what happened back then?" he asked with some hesitation in his voice. Alex paused, looking away.

"No. It was a long time ago. I don't want to go there." She offered him a cup of coffee.

"You know, Alex, you're just as distracting now as you were the day I met you in that lecture."

"Ron, don't," Alex pleaded. She shook her head. "There must be someone else in your life after all these years."

"I never remarried," he answered. "You?"

"No. Medicine has been my companion, for the most part. Between school and residency, there isn't much time for anything else."

"I see," he said, a tiny glint returning to his eye.

"No, you don't," Alex said softly but with assurance. "I'm not the same person anymore." Ron couldn't think of what to say next, and they both grew quiet as they stared at their coffee.

"Well, I should be off; it's getting late." Ron got up and headed for the door of the lounge, stopping as he put his hand on the knob and turning back to Alex. He had so many questions for her, so much he wanted to know.

"Dr. Faber—my name is Ron Dorcik. I'm the new hospital president. It was a pleasure to meet you." He nodded with a smile, and left.

CHAPTER FOURTEEN

WHILE ALEX WAS HAVING an impromptu run-in with her ex-husband at the hospital, several of Mark Uber's friends had gathered at his home across town to keep his widow company.

"You lost a hell of a guy, Sally," one of Mark's coworkers said, shaking his head.

"One of the best guys I knew," added another. They were gathered in the small kitchen, sipping fresh cups of coffee with a plate of homemade cookies that a neighbor had dropped off earlier.

"Yeah, Sal. We all feel real bad about what happened to Mark," George Baker offered. George had been one of Mark's closest friends. "It just don't seem right, him dying like that from an ulcer."

"Ulcer?" said Sally, turning quickly from her stance at the kitchen sink where she was vigorously washing dishes. Everyone had tried to convince her to sit down and relax, but to no avail. "How do you know what it was that killed him?" she asked, her voice agitated. "The doctor said it would be several more days before the autopsy results are back!"

George hoped he hadn't said something he shouldn't have. But Sally was Mark's wife—he thought she knew. "I overheard Mark's doctor talking to another one at the hospital on the morning after Mark died," he went on carefully, "I was just waiting in front of the elevator, having

picked up Mark's wallet and keys like you had asked me to. I heard him say something about an ulcer." George paused, then added, "I'm pretty sure it was Dr. Lambert. He sounded real down about it—like he was real sorry."

Sally stood for a moment, sponge in hand, feeling perplexed and angry. "He promised to call me as soon as he had more information. Last I heard, they still thought it was a heart attack." She felt herself getting more upset by the second.

"Well, you know these doctors, Sal," George said, trying to soften the situation. "They have one diagnosis one minute, and another the next. Maybe I misheard them."

"Well, I don't want to talk about it anymore tonight," Sally said firmly, looking distraught. "It's upsetting enough having to bury him tomorrow without thinking that some doctor made a mistake." She dropped the coffee cup that she had been scrubbing into the sink, and turned the faucet off with a thud.

Sally marched into the living room, where she starting opening and shutting cabinets, searching for something to organize or clean or purge. The television was on, showing some primetime drama. The volume went up as the show went to commercial, and Sally heard a booming voice permeate her living room, even with her head deep in the china cabinet.

Have you suffered a loss or disability at the hands of a doctor? Do you feel you have been a victim of medical malpractice? Know your rights! I can help you. Call the law offices of Jeffrey Stanislav. The number is 1-800-JUSTICE. The phone call is free and so is the consultation.

Sally peered around the corner of the cabinet door to catch a glimpse of the man on the screen. He was sitting behind a large desk, wearing a three-piece pin striped suit. The pinched features of his face were not inviting, but there was something about the sympathy in his voice that was credible and comforting.

The volume on the commercial was so loud that the others could hear it from the kitchen. George gave his friends a sidelong glance, quite sure of what had really happened to his dear friend, Mark.

Joshua Barron had been a little disturbed when he heard about Julie's urinary tract infection. There had been no question of the diagnosis; he had treated thousands of them in his career. Bladder infections were very common in women, much more so than in men. The short urethra provided easy access for bacteria to traverse the body's defenses from the external genitalia to the internal bladder wall. In females, a bladder infection was rarely the sign of a more serious medical condition. What bothered him was the cause. Although hygiene was always a possibility, sexual intercourse was usually the more common cause—in sexually active women. Joshua had trouble thinking of his fifteen-year-old daughter as sexually active. But with a certain pubescent football player on the top of Julie's priority list these past few months, Joshua knew that he couldn't chock this one up to parental overreaction.

He was anxious to leave Ron Dorcik's welcome party so he could get home and talk to Elizabeth. Unfortunately, she was still out at a library meeting, and it was Julie who met him as he opened the front door.

"Hi, honey. How're you feeling?" he asked with concern.

"Better, Dad," she answered with a smile. Was it him, or would Julie not look him in the eye? There were so many more questions he wanted to ask, but figured he'd better speak to his wife first. No point in creating a family crisis if one didn't exist.

Actually, Julie didn't give him much opportunity anyway, turning from him and heading into the kitchen to warm up his dinner which Elizabeth had prepared. By the time he had washed up and was sitting down to eat, Julie had excused herself and had returned to her room for an evening of telephone conversations with her friends.

The dinner table was empty except for the plate which Julie had warmed up for him. Jim was visiting at a friend's summer home on the Maine coast for the week, before coming back to start his summer job at a local warehouse. He had just graduated from Breedville High and was heading to Dartmouth in September. He was, to some extent, following in his father's footsteps, though Joshua knew that his squeamish son had no intention of studying medicine. He figured Jim would go into law or business, but not before he had his fair share of coeds and frat parties. Even Jeffrey had a full agenda that evening, and was out at the movies and then a sleepover. Joshua looked around at the empty table before him.

It sure is great to be home in the bosom of my family, he thought wryly.

It wasn't till the following evening that Joshua was able to talk with Elizabeth about Julie. He was not surprised that the same concerns had already crossed her mind.

"Do you think it's . . . possible?" his wife asked.

"I like to think it's not the case, Liz, but we have to be realistic. Those two have been seeing a whole lot of each other over the past few weeks. We have to consider it as a possibility." He paused, wondering at what point along the way had their children grown up. There was an uneasy silence.

"It might be less threatening if I talk to her," Liz offered. Joshua was relieved, as he agreed this was a mother's job.

"I was hoping you would say that, dear," Joshua said.

"You wimp!" Liz said, grinning at him. "You just waited me out long enough! I was hoping you would volunteer!"

That same Wednesday night, Jack and Ellen Landry were in bed watching television. Ellen had finally gotten their four and a half month old son to sleep. He had been irritable all day, suffering from belly cramps and diarrhea. She'd taken the baby to the pediatrician, Dr. Hill, who had diagnosed a viral gastroenteritis. He had given Ellen several suggestions for diet changes and a prescription for an anti-diarrhea medicine. With the baby fast asleep, this was Ellen's first chance of the day to unwind.

With his interest in the sitcom rerun waning, Jack turned to his wife and put his arm around her, planting a soft kiss on her cheek.

"You feeling frisky? I've got a little friend who wants to visit with your little friend."

Ten years of marriage hadn't changed his routine opening line. As silly as it sounded, Ellen was in fact in the mood for some romance. She giggled and rolled on top of her husband for a long, deep kiss. He reached up under her nightshirt, following the softness of her inner thigh and grasped the bottom of her panties. With a little help from his wife, he removed them in one stroke. As his penis became stiffer and their kisses wetter, something rubbery and wet dropped into his groping hand. With the light still on, Jack looked down past his wife's half-naked body to see a slimy red clot in his grasp.

"Yeecch!" was all he could say, pulling his hand away and frantically wiping it in disgust on the bed sheet. "Why didn't you tell me you had your period?" he demanded.

"I don't know . . ." Ellen said, feeling bewildered and a little embarrassed. "My period isn't due for another week." Jack was in the bathroom by this time, vigorously washing his hands with a grimace. "I don't understand it. I used to have such regular cycles. But ever since Jack Jr. was born, my periods are so erratic, and much heavier."

Jack returned from the bathroom, his face a bit pale.

"Your periods are screwing up our sex life! Every time we're both in the mood, you're having your period. We don't even have to worry about birth control; it's already built-in!"

"I'm sorry Jack," Ellen said tearfully. "You know I want to."

Jack finally softened at the sight of his whimpering wife. "That's okay, honey." He stroked her hair. "I know you want to. I should be more patient. Why don't you call your doctor in the morning and see if he can figure this out for you."

"Okay," Ellen sniffed. "Maybe Dr. Barron can help me."

"And . . . just one other thing . . ."

"What's that, dear?"

"Could you change the sheets before we go to sleep?"

CHAPTER FIFTEEN

Joshua ran into Alex on the maternity floor the following day as they were rounding on their patients. Joshua also took some extra time to check in on Alex's deliveries, since he'd taken care of the women early on in their pregnancies. As he offered his congratulations on their brand new babies, he was inundated with compliments on his choice of a new partner. Joshua never received such feedback when the guys of Breedville ObGyn covered for him. He was pleased they were so happy, but also felt some vague feelings of resentment. Did his patients think that Alex cared for them better than he had? He tried to push those feelings down deep where hopefully they'd disappear.

"I've got to say, you're becoming a pretty popular doc awfully quickly around here!" Joshua mentioned to Alex as they returned to the office.

"Well, it's a relief to hear that! You're so popular, I was worried that they might not take to me!" Alex replied.

When they got back to the office, each adjourned to their own consultation room to review paper work and prepare for their first patients. With both physicians in the office today, Ann had called in one of their part-time nurses to assist Joshua while Lois was scheduled to help Alex. Despite the increased volume, Ann held her own running the front desk.

Alex's first patient of the day was newly pregnant Jody Pinkham, back for the results of her biopsy. With her suspicions about gynecologic cancer confirmed, she knew that this would be a very difficult appointment.

Alex briefly examined Jody to check the biopsy site. There was no further bleeding from where she had taken the sample. The tumor mass was unchanged, and still an angry red. Alex asked Jody to redress and meet her back in her office.

"Mrs. Pinkham, sit down," Alex said as Jody entered her office. Jody hadn't looked worried when she arrived at the office that morning, but now her face was beginning to show signs of anxiety. She sat down, holding her jacket and purse in her lap, not saying a word.

"I'm afraid that you have a serious problem," Alex started to say.

"I have cancer, don't I?" Jody interrupted, her voice beginning to waver.

Alex was astounded and didn't quite know how to continue. She paused. "Yes, Mrs. Pinkham."

"I knew it! Am I going to lose my baby?" she asked, wiping the tears away with a tissue, but managing to maintain a striking level of calm.

"I'm afraid so," Alex confirmed. "You're going to need an operation to remove the cancer. The baby will not be able to survive at such an early gestation."

"Will I be able to get pregnant again?" Jody pushed on.

"No. The operation will require that your uterus be removed."

Jody gasped a bit, choking back tears. "What if I refuse to have the surgery?" she asked. "Would I still lose the baby?"

"Probably not, but I would not advise that. You need to have surgery fairly soon. We can't wait until the baby is mature enough to survive outside the uterus. You could die if you don't have the surgery in a timely manner."

"Isn't it possible that I may die even if I have the surgery?"

"It is not an impossibility. But if your tumor is confined to the cervix, as I expect that it is, you stand an excellent chance of leading a perfectly normal life. As long as we do this soon."

Jody sat there, staring off blankly for a moment. "A perfectly normal life." She paused. "A perfectly normal life would include children. If I have the surgery, I am not only aborting an innocent and healthy child, I am also eliminating any chance of becoming a natural mother." She added firmly, "I don't think I could deal with that."

These types of patient conversations were always hard, but Alex had had no clue that it would take this kind of turn.

"I think you would be making a serious mistake, Mrs. Pinkham," Alex said clearly and directly. "But let me make a suggestion. I will set up an appointment for you with a gynecologic oncologist—a specialist in this kind of cancer. Let him do the tests necessary to evaluate your tumor. This way he can give you the most accurate information on what your chances would be with and without the surgery. Leave your mind open. If you still wish to continue the pregnancy, I will be happy to provide you with prenatal care and deliver your child. But think about it. Discuss it with your husband. Listen to the oncologist and then make up your mind."

Jody nodded gratefully. "I know you must think I am crazy, to risk my life like this. But you must understand where I am coming from. My husband and I have been trying to conceive for six years. We've seen many of our friends have children, and we've anguished over our prolonged infertility. I had had a work up several years ago with Dr. Barron, and he couldn't find anything wrong. We'd just about given up when I got pregnant. I can't end this pregnancy now," Jody said, with resolution in her voice. "We look at this as our gift from heaven. We want this child too much to give it up." She gulped. "Even if it may mean my life. But I appreciate your willingness to listen to me, even if you don't agree. I will take your advice and see the oncologist, but I don't expect to change my mind."

Alex nodded. There was nothing else to say to persuade her. "I'll have my nurse make the appointment for you. You will be seeing Dr. Aaron Speiser at the regional medical center in Manchester. My office will see that he receives the information and your pathology slides prior to your visit. I would like to see you again in two weeks, unless you and Dr. Speiser have made other plans."

Jody nodded, and then a look of joy came across her face. "Could I just ask one more favor," she queried. "Could I hear my baby's heartbeat?"

"Of course you can," Alex said.

They returned to the examination room. Jody lay back on the table while Alex uncovered her stomach, spreading a clear gel on the skin's surface. She took the doptone, placing the transducer on Jody's abdomen. The clear, crisp beat of a twelve-week fetus was easily heard. At this point, there were tears welling up in Alex's eyes as well as those of her patient.

"It sounds so strong," Jody said.

"Yes," Alex agreed. "Yes it does."

While Alex was seeing Jody Pinkham, Joshua was in the examination room with Ellen Landry. Ellen had called first thing after the office opened, and Ann was able to squeeze her in before Joshua's first scheduled patient.

"So you say you've been bleeding irregularly since the delivery?" Joshua asked as he reviewed Ellen's chart.

"Yes, Dr. Barron. At first I thought it was normal. I remember bleeding irregularly after my daughter was born. It's just that it hasn't stopped. It's also making a mess out of our sex life!" Ellen confessed with a sheepish laugh. "It was actually Jack who suggested I make an appointment to see you. I probably would have let it go for a few more months."

"Well I'm glad he suggested it," Joshua said as he closed the file. "Irregular bleeding can sometimes be a symptom of a serious problem. Is there any chance that you could be pregnant again?"

"On, no! We've been very careful. Besides, there haven't been many opportunities, if you know what I mean."

Joshua had Ellen lay back on the examination table and inserted a speculum into her vagina. There was still some bleeding in the vagina In addition, a small piece of pink tissue was extruding through the opening in the cervix. Joshua teased it out, placing it in a bottle of formaldehyde. It had grape-like character to it. He removed the speculum and inserted two fingers of his gloved hand into her vagina, raising her pelvic organs for palpation by his other hand, resting on the lower portion of her abdomen. He could feel a mildly enlarged uterus, consistent with a pregnancy in its second month. He left the room, allowing Ellen to dress and join him in the office.

"Have you felt nauseous or tired recently?" Joshua asked her.

"Well, I have. But I've been so busy with the baby and my daughter on top of that. I'm exhausted, so exhausted I feel sick sometimes. But I figured that was all normal."

"Any shortness of breath, or coughing?"

"Maybe a little, but the baby has a cold." Ellen hesitated. "Why do you ask?"

"Ellen," Joshua went on, ignoring her question, "I'd like to get a blood test, a pelvic ultrasound and a chest x-ray on you. There was a little tissue in the vagina that I am sending off to the pathology department. Let's set up another appointment for early next week and see how you're doing by that time. I'll be able to help you a lot more once I have these tests back."

"Is there something wrong, Dr. Barron?" Ellen asked, detecting some heightened concern in his voice.

"I'm not sure, Ellen, but let's get these tests and give it a few more days."

Ellen seemed satisfied with Joshua's vague answers, mainly because she had so much faith in him. He had always taken care of her in the past, and she was confident that he would be able to take care of this, too. Ellen left his office, greeting Ann in the reception area who gave her a follow up appointment.

Despite keeping things vague during his talk with Ellen, Joshua already was very suspicious of the diagnosis. Her symptoms of pregnancy despite little sexual activity, combined with the tissue found in her vagina pointed towards a choriocarcinoma—an unusual malignant tumor that can occur after a pregnancy. This cancer generally developed from abnormal placental tissue, and produced the pregnancy hormone, which provided symptoms of early pregnancy such as morning sickness, breast tenderness, and fatigue. It also yielded a positive pregnancy test. Joshua decided to order the chest x-ray because this form of cancer was also known to spread to the lungs. Despite its virulent pattern, choriocarcinoma was one of the few metastatic tumors that responded very well to chemotherapy, and most women could be cured of the disease if detected early. Joshua hoped for the best for Ellen, and would simply have to wait for the test results before moving forward with a plan of action.

Due to these complex morning patients, neither Joshua nor Alex had time to step away for lunch. Ann Stremp sent out for sandwiches from the hospital coffee shop, and they each gulped down their meals between patients. Things didn't slow down until about five o'clock, when Joshua went to Alex's office to check in.

"I think we both earned our salaries today, Alex," Joshua said, running his hands through his hair. Alex gave him an empathetic smile.

"I agree with you. I'm looking forward to being off tonight."

"Hey, don't rub it in!" Joshua said, smiling at her. "By the way, I saw Jody Pinkham earlier in the day. What happened with the pathology report?"

"Well-differentiated squamous cell carcinoma of the cervix," she reported. "And you won't believe this," she continued. "She's planning's to continue the pregnancy!"

"No," Joshua exclaimed, knowing that diagnosis could easily be a death sentence. "You can't let her!"

"Joshua, I tried. I told her that she could lose her life carrying the pregnancy to term. I didn't know what else to say. I at least talked her into seeing Aaron Speiser. But somehow I don't think he'll be able to change her mind. After we finished, she wanted to go back into the exam room to hear the heartbeat."

Joshua's face became stern. "Alex, you shouldn't have. You're only making it harder for her by encouraging bonding."

"What am I supposed to do?" Alex said, throwing up her hands in defense. "Refuse to let her hear her baby's heart beat?" She shrugged. "Part of me was rooting for her."

"You can't be serious," Joshua said flatly. "She obviously feels close to you. You've got to convince her to change her mind!"

"I'm sorry Joshua, but I have to disagree with you on this one. My job is to present the facts and alternatives. Only Jody can make the decision."

"You're thinking like a woman, not like a doctor in this case," Joshua persisted. "It would be bad medicine for us to condone this kind of a decision."

"Look." Alex said. "I've made the appointment for her to see the consultant. I have a follow up appointment with her in two weeks. I agree that it would be in her best interest to go ahead with the surgery now, but I couldn't disagree with you more. The final decision has to be hers, and it is my job to do the best for her that I can, regardless of that decision."

Joshua sensed a stalemate and backed off, allowing the tension to subside. He returned to his office as Alex finished her paper work and took off for home.

On the way to the labor floor to make afternoon rounds, Joshua Barron stopped at the physicians' dictation room to see if there were any incomplete charts waiting for his signature. Joshua was one of the more compulsive physicians when it came to completing charts. Many of the physicians on staff had dozens of incomplete records waiting for signatures. It was for these doctors that the medical records department put out hot coffee and fresh doughnuts every morning in an attempt to lure them in. It was in the dictation room that Joshua found Phil Lambert slumped on one of the couches, deep in thought.

"What's happening, Phil?" asked Joshua. "You look like you've got the weight of the world on your shoulders."

"It feels that way," Phil said, looking up. "I received the final pathology report on Mark Uber. There appears to be no question that he died from sepsis secondary to a perforated gastric ulcer. The heart was clean."

"Well that shouldn't come as much of a surprise," Joshua replied, trying to sound casual. "That's what you suspected when I spoke to you the other day."

"I know. But now there appears to be another wrinkle," Phil went on. "I called Sally Uber to give her the final report and to express my condolences. Apparently the funeral was today. Anyway, when I told her about the ulcer, she said she already knew." Phil said, a befuddled look on his face.

"How did she know?" asked Joshua.

Phil shrugged. "Furthermore, she felt that if the diagnosis had been made correctly, her husband might still be alive."

"That's ridiculous Phil and you know it." Joshua could see that his friend was extremely depressed. "The guy had no chance. He was dead within an hour of arriving at the hospital. No one could have saved him!"

"Maybe you're right," Phil conceded, "but we'll never know. I can't help but think that things might have gone the other way if I had been more aggressive."

"Did she sound like she was going to speak to a lawyer?" Joshua asked.

"There was a lot of bitterness in her voice. I almost wouldn't blame her for hiring one." Phil's voice trailed off as his gaze slipped into space.

"Well, no good lawyer would take a case like that. But I'm sure she could find an ambulance chaser if she looked hard enough. Anyway, even if that happened, you'd be vindicated." Joshua leaned over to give Phil a nudge on the shoulder. "You've got to believe in yourself, Phil. You're a great doctor. You just expect too much from yourself. Remember, you're only human."

"Patients don't want their doctor to be human, Joshua," Phil said. "They expect perfection." He rubbed his eyes and stood up. "I guess I better get on home. Cindy will be wondering where I am."

"Take care, Phil. I'll see you later."

"Yeah, you take care too, Joshua."

CHAPTER SIXTEEN

PEAK WEEK WAS STRICTLY a New England phenomenon. The winters were cold and wet, the summers hot and muggy. No one could ever quite tell if a true springtime occurred, but they all agreed that autumn belonged to New England. Come late September and October, the six o'clock weathermen spent a good portion of their broadcast following the colorful changes in the landscape. The flow was gentle yet methodical, sweeping down from northern Maine through the Green Mountains of Vermont and the lakes of New Hampshire, past the Berkshires and Connecticut River valley and on into the New York metropolitan area where it died amongst the congestion and mass of humanity. Tourist season was in full swing throughout the six New England states, many towns abundant with apple picking, harvest festivals and pumpkin patches.

Breedville was no exception to this tradition. The town fathers were always looking to squeeze an extra buck out of the tourists between the summer buzz and the advent of ski season. There were crafts fairs all about town, displaying custom made furniture, quilts and candles. Endless stock of antiques and yard sales drew many hoping to cash in on an unexpected bargain or a hidden treasure. This was Breedville's most bustling since Granite Greatness of early July. With the swollen transient population admiring the foliage and buying up the local products, the stores and inns were full. The hospital, on the other hand, continued along without much change in the daily routine. It was one of the few times of the year in which a swelling populace did not provide increased business for the medical community. Whereas summer had its fireworks mishaps, boating injuries and barbecue burns, and winter its skiing trauma and holiday drunkenness, people just seemed to be safer in the fall. Of course, the maternity floor knew no seasons and babies did not wait for a special time of the year to make their entrance into the world.

Therefore, Joshua Barron and Alex Faber continued to keep busy. Not much had changed since Alex came to town. There were a few more young mouths to feed in the community, and a few less adults to pay taxes. The field of obstetrics and gynecology was generally much more involved in ushering people into the world, rather than showing them the way out. But it was not without its harder times. There was a baby, born ten weeks premature to one of Joshua's infertility patients, who died in his mother's arms shortly after birth. A couple in their mid-thirties put their newborn up for adoption, unable to cope with the reality of a child with Down's syndrome. The head of the hospital aid association succumbed to advanced metastatic ovarian cancer at the age of seventy, and one of the operating room nurses lost a breast to a malignant lump.

Ellen Landry had been one of the lucky ones. As Joshua suspected, her pregnancy test had been positive. The ultrasound showed no pregnancy in the uterus; her chest x-ray was full of metastatic disease and the pathology report on the vaginal tissue had returned choriocarcinoma. She had been referred to Aaron Speiser in Manchester, the same doctor who was treating Jody Pinkham. Ellen was now recovering uneventfully from her surgery and chemotherapy, expected to live disease-free for the rest of her life.

As for Jody, she had been found to have a cervical cancer that showed no sign of spread. As she promised Alex weeks before, she elected not to have the cancer treated with a hysterectomy, and awaited the birth of her firstborn. Dr. Speiser removed the malignant lump from her cervix, closing the resulting defect with a surgical suture, requiring Jody to deliver by cesarean section. This had been a compromise that she ultimately agreed to. Immediately following her cesarean section at term, she would undergo the radical hysterectomy originally recommended by both Drs. Faber and Speiser. Until then, the best they could do was provide Jody with excellent prenatal care, and keep their fingers crossed that the malignant tumor would not spread during the pregnancy.

Phil Lambert seemed to have recovered from the self-doubt that beset him at the time of Mark Uber's death. Although he continued to blame himself for not being more attentive, the passage of time and a large volume of patients had seemed to put the case into proper perspective for Phil. What also helped Phil's spirits was the absence of any apparent litigation on the part of the family. After his initial disturbing conversation with Sally Uber, there had been no further contact, either by the family or an attorney. Phil surmised that perhaps Joshua had been correct, that there was really no basis for malpractice and that no reasonable lawyer would take on a case that he felt destined to lose.

Julie Barron's heated July fling cooled rather quickly after her urinary tract infection. She had vehemently denied doing anything wrong when her mother spoke to her about it, but decided on her own that she and Brad had gone too far too soon. She was rather relieved when school went back into session, and the advent of football practice, homework and other activities took up most of their free time, once again. She still socialized with Brad at the occasional school dance or class party, but it was nothing like it had been over the summer.

As for Joshua and Alex, the first few months were not without their struggles. Tensions surfaced periodically as Joshua struggled to transition from solo practitioner to partner. His hands-on approach and need to be in control conflicted with the reality of shared responsibility with a junior partner. His concerns about Alex's ideas regarding patient management and petty jealousies over her popularity made for long discussions with Elizabeth, who tried to point out all of the benefits of Alex's presence. His wife found it amusing that it was Joshua who had to convince her of Alex's worth, only a few months prior. Alex's own insecurities would surface whenever Joshua felt obliged to question her clinical judgment. It was at times an uneasy peace between them, but a peace they were both willing to work hard to maintain despite their differences.

Alex's social life remained static for her first several months in Breedville, despite the best intentions of several friends and co-workers to find her a mate. She successfully managed to fend off further advances by Frank Dimento, though she was unsure how much longer she could keep him at bay. Her relationship with Ron Dorcik remained distant, due in no small part to her conversation with him that night on the labor floor. They both were also quite busy with their respective new positions. Still, Alex knew deep down that she still had feelings for Ron, and was a bit worried about how that might all play out on the stage of Breed General Hospital.

After a rocky start with Elizabeth Barron, their relationship was actually starting to blossom. Alex enjoyed Liz's company, and appreciated the fact that she was one of the very few people who had not tried to find her a date. They went shopping and antiquing together, and Liz helped decorate Alex's new home in no time. She had a standing invitation for dinner at the Barron's whenever she wished. Alex thought of Liz as an older sister. She also knew that Liz appreciated Alex's presence in her husband's professional life. Everyone could see that Joshua was more relaxed, and was able to spend much more time at home with his family now that he had a partner.

As their friendship grew, Alex also began to depend upon Liz as a confidant. She was the person in Breedville whom Alex felt closest to, and comfortable confiding in. She would talk about her upbringing, her former relationship with David Arnold and her marriage to Ron Dorcik. Elizabeth responded in kind, sharing her anxieties about Julie's summer bout with cystitis and feeling left out of her son James' new life at college.

Beyond the general ebb and flow, there was one particular disturbance of note within the Breedville community. A series of unsolved rape cases had occurred. In each instance, the perpetrator had worn a ski mask and kidnapped his victim in the vicinity of the hospital. To the town's dismay, the police were baffled and there were no suspects. The attacks began shortly after July first, and there were three victims to date. Breedville was not used to violent crime and the populace was justifiably worried. Security was beefed up at the hospital and six weeks had passed without an additional attack. The police hoped that the perpetrator was not local, and had skipped town.

CHAPTER SEVENTEEN

Amanda Perkins was becoming a fixture in Joshua Barron's office. The thirty-five year old native of Breedville and town librarian had been seeing Dr. Barron twice a month for the past six months. She was undergoing intrauterine inseminations due to a sperm antibody problem. When she first started coming to the office nearly a year ago, Amanda and her husband Todd had just celebrated their eight-year wedding anniversary. Todd was in charge of one of the production divisions at the telephone plant in town, and together with Amanda's salary, the couple had been able to put away enough money for a modest home in one of the nicer sections of Breedville. After five years of marriage, they felt comfortable enough financially to begin a family. For the first six months, Amanda was sure that she was fertile and would have no trouble getting pregnant, especially since she'd already had two elective abortions much earlier while with Todd. But as months passed into years, the reassurance faded and panic began to set in.

Joshua Barron had taken Amanda and Todd the whole nine yards when it came to searching for the cause of their infertility. Todd's sperm count had been reasonably high, the fallopian tubes were open and there had been no evidence of endometriosis on laporoscopic examination. All of her blood work was normal and a biopsy of the inside lining of her uterus showed no abnormality. The only consistently abnormal test was a Sims-Huhner examination. This evaluation consisted of removing a sample of mucus from Amanda's cervix during the preovulatory phase of her menstrual cycle, within hours of an episode of intercourse. By viewing the mucus sample under the microscope, Joshua noticed an extremely low motility of otherwise healthy looking sperm. It was as if some invisible force was cutting down these fertile missiles in mid-flight, not allowing them to reach their target. Those that were moving staggered in disjointed fashion across the microscopic field. He felt like a war correspondent, viewing the aftermath of a bloody battle from a helicopter high above the area of encounter.

These results, seen consistently on several Sims-Huhner tests over the course of her work up, led to an evaluation for anti-sperm antibodies. This is an ironic clinical situation where the female body recognizes the sperm of her partner as foreign, mounting an immunologic response to these invaders. The unfortunate result was very often the successful defense of the human body to the exclusion of conception and fetal development.

Once Joshua had accurately diagnosed the Perkins' infertility issue, they were able to plot a plan of action. Amanda was now returning frequently to Joshua's office for intrauterine inseminations. Todd supplied a semen sample, which was washed and prepared in the hospital laboratory, and then Joshua would inject the sample directly into Amanda's uterus in an attempt to bypass the antibodies found in her cervix.

On this particular Friday afternoon, Amanda Perkins was in Joshua's office to complete her bi-monthly routine. Her ovulation kit and her temperature curve predicted ovulation within the next twenty-four hours. She had brought in Todd's sperm earlier that afternoon to the hospital laboratory for preparation prior to the four o'clock insemination. After leaving the sample, she had stopped at the supermarket to pick up a few last minute items for dinner. Since the library was closed on Friday afternoons, this was always the time she had for last minute chores and errands. She returned to the physicians' office building a few minutes before four and found Joshua on time for her appointment.

"How's it going, Mrs. Perkins?" Joshua asked as he began the procedure. He had inserted the speculum and was cleaning off her cervix prior to inseminating the sperm.

"I'll let you know in a couple of weeks, Dr. Barron," Amanda said, trying to relax. Even after months of this, she still got tense every time. Amanda was not thrilled with his artificial replacement for natural fertilization, but it would have to do.

"You're going to feel a little cramp," Joshua continued, pushing down on the syringe plunger, giving rise to a true microscopic melodrama as millions of anxious sperm swam past the forbidding antibodies of the cervix. "I'll have Lois come in to tell you when to get up," he said as he inserted a plastic covered sponge into her vagina to prevent leakage of the seminal fluid from the uterus. Amanda knew from experience that the sponge was to be removed later that evening.

She lay there for several minutes, her knees up in the air, trying to provide whatever assistance she could to the endangered warriors now on maneuvers inside her uterus. Lois entered the examination room ten minutes later and told her she could get dressed. By four thirty, she was back in her car ready to head home.

With her mind still on the procedure, Amanda was oblivious to the man lying still on the floor in the back of her sedan. It was the same man who had been following her around town all afternoon on a black motorcycle—Amanda had been too distracted to notice him. She was just about to turn out of the hospital parking lot when her breath was taken away by a knife at her throat and a husky voice.

"Don't make a sound," the voice commanded. "Just do what I say and you won't get hurt." The knife blade was pressed firmly against the soft fleshy part of her neck.

"Please don't hurt me!" Amanda cried. "What do you want? I don't have much money."

"Don't turn around or I'll kill you!" her assailant snarled. "Make a left here and drive straight ahead." Amanda did as she was told, trying to place the voice of the man behind her. When she had driven several miles out of town, he had her turn off onto a dirt road for several minutes further.

"Stop here!" he ordered. "Get out of the car!"

Amanda thought of running, but her legs wouldn't move. Her mind was swirling. She left the car as ordered. The assailant also got out, and she saw for the first time that he was wearing a ski mask. Beyond that, the man was tall and muscular, with dark brown hair. He wore jeans and a tee shirt that read "Don't take New Hampshire for Granite." All she could feel was terror.

"What do you want?" she asked, her voice shaking. "Please don't hurt me!" she begged. Amanda's plea only seemed to fuel his vicious excitement.

"I'm not going to hurt you, honey," he said in a syrupy voice that made her cringe. "We're just going to have a little fun." He put his hand to her cheek, studying her features for a minute. He wet his fingers with her tears, then brought them to his lips.

"Take off your clothes, little lady," he continued. "I want to see how beautiful you are."

"Please let me go!" she continued to beg. "I'll get you money."

It was obvious that money was not on his agenda. When she hesitated to undress, he tore open her blouse with the tip of his knife, scratching her chest in the process.

"I said strip, you bitch! Don't play with me!" he yelled. "I want to see you now!" Amanda realized it was useless to fight. He was much bigger than she and he was armed. She removed her slacks and panties while her assailant watched, a grin appearing on his face under the ski mask.

"Very pretty, little lady. You were worth the wait today." He pushed her to the ground, unbuckled his jeans with his free hand and slipped them off. Now the urgency in his voice was gone—seemingly willing to let this go on as long as it could. Still holding the knife in his left hand, the tip up against her neck, he tried to enter her. Meeting the resistance of the sponge that had been inserted less than an hour earlier, he became livid.

"What the fuck do you have in here, lady?" he cursed, groping inside to remove the obstruction. "Well, what do you know," he grinned again, "The bitch keeps a plug in her hole! Hey, honey, it's going to take more than a plug to keep me out of you." Even more violently than before, he pushed himself into her. She could feel a tearing as he penetrated deep inside her vagina. He was so turned on that he quickly spent within her.

Amanda lay helpless on the ground while he got up and dressed. His knife was re-sheathed, no longer posing a threat. He knew she would not challenge him at this point. Leaving her lying on the ground, bruised and crying with her clothes scattered, the man in the ski mask returned to her car and drove away, abandoning her to fend for herself.

"Thanks a lot, honey," he said as he turned the car around. "Hope to see you again someday." She could hear his laughter as the car careened down the dirt road.

Joshua Barron was making rounds late that night when he received a call from the emergency room.

"Hi, Dr. Barron. We have a thirty-five year old woman down here who claims to have been raped. She says she's a patient of yours and would like you to see her."

"I'll be right down," he said. He finished seeing his last post-operative patient and headed down to the emergency room.

"My god! Its Amanda Perkins," Joshua gasped as he picked up the chart in the outpatient department. He moved quickly to her room.

"Dr. Barron!" Amanda cried upon the comforting sight of her doctor entering her room. "It was so horrible! Horrible! He made me undress and then he raped me." Amanda dissolved into panic-ridden tears.

"It's okay, Amanda. You're safe now. I'm going to take care of you," he said softly.

"Have you called her husband?" Joshua asked the nurse.

"He's on his way. He should be here any minute."

"Amanda," Joshua said, turning back to her. "I'm going to have to examine you. Will that be okay?"

Amanda lay quietly on the examination table. She seemed to be in another world. Slowly and gently, Joshua examined her for trauma, taking samples of hair and semen for police analysis. He was rather unfamiliar with the protocol used on rape victims—this was typically the province of the emergency room physician. Joshua had been called at the insistence of Amanda Perkins. The emergency room nurse helped guide him through the protocol, collecting all available evidence and describing his findings in detail into a tape recorder. When he was finished, he left her lying quietly, the nurse holding her hand and continuing to reassure her. He met Todd Perkins outside of the exam room.

"What happened, Dr. Barron? Is she okay? I came as soon as I was called!" Todd's face showed both worry and extreme anger.

"Physically, your wife is okay, Mr. Perkins," Joshua assured him, "but she's been through a terrible experience." He opened the door for Todd, accompanying him into the room. Todd rushed to his wife's side.

"Oh, honey!" he cried, holding his wife and rocking her. "I'm so, so sorry this happened to you. I'm here; everything's going to be OK."

Joshua left them and returned to the nurses' station. There he met with a member of the Breedville police force who had picked Amanda up on the road heading back into town and had taken her directly to the hospital.

"Do you have any leads on the guy?" Joshua asked.

"Not yet, Dr. Barron. It may be the same assailant who plagued the community over the summer. She gave me a description of her car, which he drove off in. We found it in the hospital parking lot, with the keys inside. Obviously he had some other means of transportation here at the parking lot. I understand she had just left your office when she was abducted. You didn't happen to see anyone following her from your office?"

"No. I still had several more patients to see this afternoon when she left. She came into the office by herself to the best of my knowledge. I'll be happy to ask my staff if they saw anyone else."

"We'd appreciate that, doctor. Any help you can give us. You can call me at the station if you have anything to add later."

Joshua returned to the nursing desk where he finished Amanda's chart. There was one piece of unfinished business. Normally, when a rape victim has not be using birth control, they are offered the morning after pill. This pill contained a high dose of standard birth control pills, commonly used to protect a woman from conception when she had had unprotected intercourse. This was standard operating procedure for rape cases. This pill would, however, also negate the effects of the insemination he had performed on her earlier in the day. Joshua would need to discuss this with both Amanda and Todd.

When he returned to the examination room, he found Todd sitting next to his wife, stroking her hair. She was resting more comfortably, though still sobbing. He explained to Todd the predicament regarding birth control, and encouraged him to bring Amanda into the office tomorrow when they would discuss her options. He reassured him that there would still be plenty of time for the pill to work if she decided to take it the following day. Todd was clearly distraught, and Joshua felt for him deeply. He couldn't fathom what he'd do if it were Elizabeth lying in that hospital bed right now. He surely would want to hunt down and kill his wife's rapist with his bare hands.

Seeing that his wife was in no state of mind to discuss this issue at the moment, Todd agreed to bring her back tomorrow. He thanked Joshua for his support, then went back to comforting Amanda. Joshua returned to the labor floor to check out before going home for the evening.

Phil Lambert was having a good day. Office hours were running smoothly and his three patients in the ICU would soon be discharged to the regular medical floor. He was planning to meet Cindy in town for their anniversary dinner. The kids were staying with friends for the night, and they were very much looking forward to a romantic evening together. He had seen his last patient of the day, a fifty-eight year old male with chronic hypertension. Phil was pleased to see that the medication he started him on several weeks ago was finally having an effect. He bid goodnight to his nurse and receptionist, promising to lock up for the weekend after reading his mail.

Most of the mail consisted of medical journals and offers from headhunting firms, attempting to lure him into joining some exciting practice at an unbelievable salary in a beautiful area. The journals were either filed in the "need to read" pile or thrown out, while the job opportunities were dumped immediately. There were several requests for medical records from insurance companies. At the very bottom of the stack was a small envelope with the return address "Stanislav, Victor, Ferguson and Grant." At first, he didn't make the association between the name Stanislav and the awful ambulance chaser featured on TV commercials. As he opened the letter, his stomach rose to the back of his throat.

> *Dear Dr. Lambert,*
>
> *Please be advised that the firm of Stanislav, Victor, Ferguson and Grant represents the family of the late Mark Uber in a case of litigation against you for Mr. Uber's wrongful death due to your gross medical negligence. We request from you all records pertaining to Mr. Uber's medical management and will be in touch to arrange a deposition.*
>
> *We appreciate your cooperation in this manner.*
>
> Sincerely yours,
>
> Jeffrey Stanislav, Esquire

In an instant, all of Phil's anxieties over Mark Uber's care rushed back at a screaming pace.

The following day, Joshua met Todd and Amanda Perkins in his office to discuss his concerns about pregnancy protection in light of the assault. It had been a horrible night for both of them. After her physical examination in the emergency room, Amanda spent several hours at police headquarters, giving a statement and trying to identify her assailant. When it became clear that she was too upset to be helpful, Todd took her home. The night was spent in mutual crying and reassurance, as the reality of the attack descended upon them both. By morning, both Amanda and Todd were emotionally drained and physically exhausted, but still showed up to Joshua's office at nine o'clock, as requested.

"I'm sorry to drag you back here, Amanda," Joshua apologized, "but I need to talk to you about birth control."

"Well, I'm confused," Amanda said. "Todd and I have been trying to get pregnant for three years without success. Why do I need protection from the attacker? Aren't these antibody things preventing me from getting pregnant?" She managed a sarcastic laugh. "My body's been doing a pretty good job at natural birth control. I don't need to worry about that bastard." She crossed her arms defiantly, as though to signal that she had made up her mind.

"What you say is true, Amanda. However, the antibodies that you have demonstrated may only affect Todd's sperm—we do not know how they affect anyone else's sperm. We just don't know enough about the immunological basis for infertility to tell for sure."

"But if I took these pills, wouldn't I also be affecting the insemination I went through yesterday?"

"That's true, Amanda. But we would be able to do another round of insemination soon. I think it is worth the sacrifice. I would hate to take the chance that you became pregnant as a result of the attack."

Amanda was verging on exasperated. "But what if I am pregnant, and what if the baby is Todd's? I can't take the chance of losing a pregnancy with Todd. We already had two chances for a pregnancy," she said, referring to the elective abortions many years ago. "And we gave those up. I won't take that chance again. I can't."

Joshua looked to Todd for help. He looked disturbed, yet helpless.

"I'm sorry, Dr. Barron," Todd responded, shaking his head. "This is how Amanda feels. It is her body. I can't change her mind." It was clear that Todd struggled with his wife's decision, but loved her too much to ask her to change it. "But," he added, "can't we do a paternity test early on, if she does get pregnant?"

"That's true, we can." Joshua answered. "I would just hate to have you make such a decision once a pregnancy is established."

Amanda Perkins left Dr. Barron's office that day, aware of the possibility that she could be pregnant with her rapist's child. He was quite surprised by her decision, but as her physician, it was only his job to care for her and guide her as best he knew how.

CHAPTER EIGHTEEN

B Y THE TIME ALEX arrived at the Barron's home, Liz had had the family distributed and accounted for. Joshua had long since left for the hospital to make rounds and see Todd and Amanda Perkins in his office; Julie was off to the high school football game, and Jeff was spending the day with a friend. Jim, of course, was in his first semester at Dartmouth, even though it sometimes took Elizabeth a minute to remember that her eldest no longer lived at home. It was another beautiful Saturday in autumn, the temperature was just right—a perfect day to go antiquing. Alex still needed to find some furniture for her new condo and Liz always loved the thrill of the hunt, even when she didn't need a thing. The front door was open as Alex climbed up the steps of the Barron's large colonial home.

"Liz, it's me," Alex called through the screen door.

"Come on in!" Liz called from the second floor. "I'll be down in a minute." Alex entered, heading towards the kitchen where she found the rest of the morning coffee, still hot. She poured herself a cup and sat down at the kitchen table. Liz hurried down the stairs.

"I hope you don't mind my making myself at home," Alex said.

"Not at all, Alex," Liz said and she tidied up the kitchen. "Help yourself."

"So where are we off to?" Alex asked.

"I thought we would head towards Hanover," Liz suggested. "Joshua and I found quite a few fascinating shops along the Connecticut River towns when we took Jimmy to school last month."

"Do you want to stop by to see him while we're in the neighborhood?"

"Oh no!" Liz laughed. "I couldn't do that. He would be furious if he thought I was checking up on him."

"Have you seen him since he left for school?"

"No, we haven't. Joshua talks to him every weekend, and with next week being homecoming, we're going down to visit. Joshua wasn't the least bit interested in football when he was at Dartmouth, but now he can't seem to get enough! This will actually be his first homecoming since he graduated."

Somehow, Alex could not see her sedate partner churning up excitement for a football game. She grinned as she thought of Joshua sitting up in the stands, with his face painted green and white, yelling "Go Big Green!" She finished her cup of coffee and helped Liz clean up. Soon, they were out the door.

Their trip took them through the back roads and small highways of rural New Hampshire. With the White Mountains behind them, they traveled in a westerly fashion over smaller hills and wide expanses of farmland, gradually dropping into the Connecticut River Valley. This area formed the natural boundary between New Hampshire and Vermont. There were no interstate roads in the direction they were traveling and the towns they passed through were all even smaller than Breedville. The foliage was striking. Waves of reds, oranges and yellows contrasted with the greens of the pine trees, making for one breathtaking view after another.

It took about an hour to reach their destination. They parked in front of a large open flea market on the Vermont side of the river. Most of the merchandise consisted mainly of furniture and Americana memorabilia. Writing desks and sewing machines, fountain pens, figurines and commemorative plates were every which way. It was hard to tell which items were authentic and which were just cheap knock-offs, but that was all part of the fun. Liz found an antique tea service from England that appeared to be genuine—it certainly was if the price tag gave any clue! A large wing back chair intrigued Alex. The upholstery was in good condition and the wooden frame had been refinished.

"That's a lovely piece you got there, ma'am," the antique dealer stated. He was a stout fellow with a bright yellow and black flannel shirt tucked into a pair of faded blue jeans. The pants were held up by a pair of black suspenders with brass snaps.

"It's really in excellent condition," Alex agreed. "How much are you asking for it?" The dealer took out his book, listing the prices of his inventory.

"That piece is six hundred, Ma'am. It's a fair price. I've already marked it down from eight hundred, so you're getting a great deal." Alex was never good at bargaining and was ready to pay the six hundred.

"I think that you might want to look around some more, Alex," Liz said. She was far more acquainted with this environment than her friend, and knew never to pay the first quoted price. "Besides," she continued, "I wouldn't pay more than four hundred for that, anyway." She grabbed Alex's hand, moving down the aisle towards another group of antique furniture.

"Okay ladies, you broke my arm," the antique dealer said. "I'll give it to you for four-fifty, but that's the best I can do."

At this offer, Alex turned to look at the piece again. The dealer had her. Liz was not in time to interject.

"I'll take it," Alex said triumphantly.

"You won't regret it ma'am. You've got a fine piece of furniture there."

Liz helped Alex carry the piece out to her car. The dealer entered the selling price into his inventory book, a big smile crossing his face. Liz caught his eye, assuming he'd probably only paid about one-fifty for it. But the deal was done.

"I think you could have done better," Liz told Alex as they lifted the chair into the back of the station wagon.

"I'm sure I could have, but I'm just not good at this. Besides, I probably would have spent a lot more than this at a regular furniture store, so I'm happy."

"I'm afraid you have a lot to learn about New England, Alex," Liz said, laughing out loud as they got into the car and moved on to their next destination.

The next stop was a small inn, located picturesquely by the side of a brook. There were several round tables complete with umbrellas set up on the outdoor patio. Elizabeth had frequented this inn on several antiquing trips, occasionally in the company of her husband, who looked at it as an oasis in an otherwise long day of shopping. Alex had a crabmeat sandwich on a croissant while Liz enjoyed a spinach salad. They each ordered a glass of white wine. Liz tried to teach Alex the fine art of negotiating, while Alex confessed that she was a hopeless sucker.

There was a pause in the conversation as they sat back and enjoyed the beauty and calm of the moment. The patio began to empty out as shoppers returned to their exploits. With the lull in surrounding conversations, the rushing water of the adjacent brook filled the void, creating an almost idyllic setting. The moment was broken when the check arrived. Liz reached for her pocketbook, but Alex picked it up before she had a chance.

"This one's on me, Liz," Alex said.

"But Alex, you're my guest today."

"I insist," said Alex. "After all, look how much money you saved me on the chair!" They both laughed, and Liz graciously gave in. After Alex signed the receipt and sent the waitress off, Liz took the opportunity to mention a topic that she'd been meaning to bring up.

"So, I wanted to talk to you about Julie." Liz said, adjusting her posture in her chair. "I'm concerned that she may be having sex." Alex nodded and took a sip of wine. "She denied it when I brought it up last July, but I'm not convinced she was telling the truth. Her relationship with the football player seemed to cool down a bit as the summer wore on, but it seems to be picking up again."

"Have you talked with Julie about this type of thing? Not just specifically with the football player, but about sex in general?" Alex asked.

"Well, we've certainly talked about sex, and about protection. I even offered to take her to see someone if she ever felt the need to discuss things with someone outside of the family. She knows about birth control and STDs. Of course, this was all several years ago, when the issue was moot." Liz took a breath and sighed. "Fifteen year old girls don't want to talk about these things, especially with their parents. I've tried bringing it up more recently, but I'm just meeting resistance. I feel distant from her." Liz looked up from her glass, and spoke frankly to Alex. "I was wondering if you might see her. She's been complaining recently about menstrual cramps, and maybe its time for her to see an ObGyn. Maybe she'll be able to open up to you."

"You know I'd be happy to help, Liz," Alex said. "Julie's a great girl, and I think it would be entirely appropriate for her to see a gynecologist." She paused. "I feel a little uncomfortable bringing this up with you, but Joshua and I haven't exactly been seeing eye to eye on patient care. He's been critical of the way I've handled some of the patients lately, and I'm honestly not sure how he'd feel about Julie coming to see me. Even if things were perfect between us, it might pose some potential issues, since we've also got the issue of confidentiality. If Julie were to come see me, I would have to offer her a completely safe haven, to the exclusion of you and Joshua. The only way I can help her is if she believes she can trust me. I would certainly encourage her to include you in whatever decisions were made, but you have to understand, I couldn't force her to do that."

Liz realized that her request might stir up such a conversation, and she was happy to discuss it with Alex.

"First of all," she leaned over and touched Alex's hand, "you're right that Joshua can be very critical and controlling. The transition has been difficult for him, but you need to keep in mind that it isn't personal. He was a solo practitioner for so long—it is all he knows! I know that he has so much faith in your abilities and judgment—he never would have hired you if he didn't. Just be patient. Personally, I think that he's a little jealous of just how popular you are!" Liz laughed. "But he'll come around."

"Thanks, Liz. That means a lot," Alex said. Hearing Liz's take on things was very helpful and refreshing.

"And in terms of the confidentiality," Liz went on, "I understand that it would be strictly private. Of course I'd love a full transcript of her visit," she added with a sarcastic laugh, "but seriously, the most important thing is that she sees a professional who she can be open with. I trust your judgment, and know that you'd guide her well."

"I appreciate that. I would be more than happy to see her," Alex said. "I just feel it is important that we're all on the same page. I really love my position here and would never want to do anything to jeopardize it. I feel so much like a member of your family. You've become like an older sister to me and it would be my pleasure to be an older sister to Julie."

"We're so happy to have you," Liz smiled. "Thank you."

The trip back to Breedville was slow, as Alex and Liz stopped frequently along the way at several other antique shops. But the selection they found was not as great as at the first stop, but it was a successful trip since neither was going home empty handed. No further discussions about Julie arose. Instead, the conversation drifted towards gossip about all of the various Breedville personalities whom Alex had met in her first few months in town.

"I guess Joshua told you about my connection to Ron Dorcik, the new hospital administrator," Alex said.

"He did!" Liz said, glad that Alex had broached up such an interesting topic. "That must have been quite a shock for you to see him at the reception back in July. I can only imagine."

"It was indeed!" Alex chuckled. "He was the last person I expected to see. It really is quite an odd coincidence. But we're both so busy, I've hardly seen or spoken to him since."

"Tell me if I'm prying," Liz started, "but how do you feel about it? About him?"

"It was a long time ago. I was going through a really difficult time back then. Ron and I have both moved on, and it's probably for the best." Alex tried to sound convincing. She didn't dare let on, especially not to Joshua's wife, that she still had feelings for Ron,. Luckily, Liz sensed Alex's discomfort and changed the subject.

They arrived back in Breedville around four. Liz helped Alex get her new chair into the condo, and they reveled at how well it looked in its new home. They said their goodbyes, and Liz headed back to the house.

There, she found Julie and two of her friends from the cheerleading squad in the kitchen with a plate of chocolate chip cookies and milk.

"How was the game, girls?" Liz asked brightly. "Did we win?"

"We were awesome, Mrs. Barron!" one of Julie's friends offered.

"Yeah," said the other. "Well, we lost the game, but our squad was so much better than the other team's." The girls all nodded in agreement.

"Anything on tap for tonight, Julie?" Liz asked her daughter.

"Well, there was supposed to be a victory dance down at the school gym tonight. Now it's just a regular dance, but we're still going. Can you give us a ride?"

"Sure honey. What time do you think you'll need a pick up?"

"Oh, that's OK. We'll get home all right." Julie looked to her friends. "Your mom can pick us up, right?"

"Um, yeah," Sally said. "My mom can drive Julie home."

Liz wasn't convinced, but didn't want to question Julie in front of her friends. She'd have to wait.

"Make sure you put the plate and glasses in the sink when you're done," Liz said as she headed upstairs to freshen up. When she returned, the other girls had left and Julie was in her room, listening to music on her headphones. Liz entered the room and gestured for her attention. Julie looked up and took off the headphones.

"Why do I get the feeling that there is something else planned for tonight, other than the dance?" Liz asked directly.

"Oh," Julie shrugged. "Its nothing-Sally's having a party at her house after the dance."

"Are Sally's parents going to be home?" she demanded.

Julie paused. "I don't know. I'm not sure . . . maybe? But everyone's going."

"I'm not comfortable with that arrangement, Julie," Liz said, anticipating an argument.

"Mom!" Julie wailed. "I have to go! Everyone's going! What do you think I'm going to do?" Liz felt a twinge of dread inside her. She shook it off.

"I just don't trust the situation," Liz said firmly. "You can go to the dance, but not to the party. Not unless Sally's parents will be home."

"You can't do this to me!" she exclaimed. "I already said I was going—everyone thinks I'm going to be there!" Julie was on the verge of tears.

"I don't think it's a good idea, honey. I'm sorry. I'll ask your father to see how he feels about it, but I doubt he'll disagree with me."

"Why do I always have to be the only one? You and Dad are living in the Dark Ages, Mom. Everybody's parents let them go to these parties. Everyone."

"I told you I would speak to your father, but I'm not in favor of it. We'll be happy to pick you up after the dance. You can have some friends sleep over if you'd like. We could even have a party here after a dance sometime."

"Get real, Mom." Before Liz had a chance to say anything else, Julie had returned the headphones to her ears, tears streaming down her face.

Liz left her to contemplate her new image as the most unpopular girl in school. She went to the kitchen to call Joshua.

"Of course I don't want her going to a party where there are no parents present. I wonder if Sally's parents even know there's a party at their house tonight. Doubtful."

"Well, Joshua, we have a very sad girl on our hands."

"That's okay. She'll get over it," Joshua said, seemingly unfettered. "How was the antiquing today? You and Alex have a good time?"

"It was a picture perfect day. Until I got home."

"What else is new?" Joshua asked. Liz told him about her discussion with Alex regarding Julie.

"Would you have any problems having Julie see her?" she asked him.

"Not at all," he answered nonchalantly. "Do you think she would go?"

"I think so, if I put it in a non-threatening vein." Liz sighed. "I'll wait till after this weekend to discuss it with her. Give her some time to cool off."

"Looks like I've got the easy job this weekend," Joshua chuckled. "All I have is four patients in labor!"

CHAPTER NINETEEN

I T HAD BEEN SEVERAL weeks since their antiquing trip, and Alex had all but forgotten her discussion with Liz about Julie Barron. By now, peak week's gorgeous hues were painting the New York metropolitan area, and New England was getting ready for winter. There was a nip in the evening air and the discussion around town concerned the cost of a cord of wood and whether it would be cheaper than burning oil this year. The final ski sales were winding down prior to the pre-Christmas mark-up and Halloween decorations were all around. Halloween was always highly celebrated in Breedville, though the recent community rapes put a damper on the usual festive cheer. Police were urging parents not to let children trick-or-treat alone, and lectures on personal safety were given at all schools. For teenagers, organized parties were strongly recommended over wandering the streets at night.

As fall hurdled steadily towards winter, Alex Faber's busy patient schedule barely allowed her to notice the change in season. Due to her popularity, Alex's office days were consistently booked solid. She'd come in every morning and briefly scan her patient list, pleased at how many new patients and complex cases she was getting on a regular basis. She didn't even notice it when Julie Barron's name appeared on her list one morning, and it wasn't until Lois Wilner announced the arrival of her "VIP guest" that Alex remembered her conversation with Liz.

"Hi, Julie!" Alex said as she breezed into the exam room, shutting the door behind her. "How are you?"

"Hi, Dr. Faber," Julie said timidly. "I'm good."

"So, what can I help you with today?" Alex asked as she pulled up a stool and sat down. She wasn't surprised that Julie was shy. A girl's first trip to the gynecologist was always an uncomfortable experience.

"My mom thought I should come in because of my cramps. They're really bad, and sometimes I have to miss school because of them."

"Well, Julie, your mom's right—when something is out of the ordinary, it is always a good idea to get it checked out. There are several things we can do to ease the cramps. I'd like to start by asking you a few questions first, okay?"

"Ok," Julie said with a nervous giggle.

"Great." Alex took out a pen to jot down some notes on Julie's file. "How old were you when you had your first period?"

"I was eleven," Julie answered. "But they sort of came and went for a while—I've only been getting it regularly for about two years now. And they didn't hurt at the beginning, either."

"Do you ever bleed between periods?" Alex asked.

"Not anymore. Not since they started to hurt." Julie looked down at her hands. Alex scribbled a quick note, then took a breath as she looked up.

"Have you ever had sex, Julie?"

Julie's face flushed. "No—never! Honest Dr. Faber! Did my mom ask you to ask me that?" Her face looked pained.

"I ask that question of all my patients, Julie. It has nothing to do with your mother or father. I can only do my best to take care of you if I know your sexual history." She looked Julie directly in the eyes. "Anything you say to me here is just between you and me."

Julie looked down at the floor. "One time, Dr. Faber. Only once."

"When was that?"

"Back in July, when I got my bladder infection."

"Was it before or after you had your bladder infection?" Alex asked, predicting the answer.

"It was just before," Julie answered. "Why?"

"It would be unusual for you to get a bladder infection unless you'd had sex."

"I kind of figured that that's what caused it. It felt like I was being punished."

Alex leveled her gaze on the girl and gave her a soft smile. "Bladder infections are very common, Julie. Married women get them from having sex, too. You need not feel like you were being punished. But let me ask you another question. Did you or your boyfriend use any protection?"

"You mean like a rubber or something?"

"Yes."

"Well, I don't think anything went inside of me. He pulled it out," Julie said, lowering her head.

"That isn't much protection, Julie."

"Why not? I can't get pregnant if nothing went inside me," Julie said with adolescent confidence.

"You're not alone in thinking that way, but there is nothing safe about pulling out before ejaculation." Julie winced at the word. "I have delivered countless babies to mothers who didn't intend to get pregnant. Besides, even if no sperm enter your vagina, you can still get several pretty nasty infections."

Julie was silent, and a look of fear washed over her. Alex felt she had made her point with the teenager.

"Now, I don't think your cramps are a sign of any infection. I just tell you for precautionary reasons." Alex stood up. "Let's do a quick exam, and we'll be done soon. Just lie back."

Alex began examining Julie, including her heart, lungs, throat, breasts and abdomen. When she was ready to do the pelvic exam, she explained to Julie what would happen.

"I need to have you slide your bottom down to the end of the table, Julie. Keep your knees apart, and try to relax your muscles as much as you can. This shouldn't hurt."

Alex continued to explain each step of the exam as it was being performed. Julie remained surprisingly calm, considering it was her first vaginal exam. After finishing up, Alex had Julie get dressed and meet her in the office.

"Are you going to tell my parents about last July?" Julie asked as she sat down across from Alex.

"That's between you, me and your medical chart. It might be a good idea for you to talk about these things with your mom. I am sure that she would welcome it, and you might feel better if you had open lines of communication at home. But," Alex said firmly, "she won't hear anything from me."

"Thanks, Dr. Faber," Julie said, looking relieved. "I appreciate that."

"Patient confidentially is an important part of my job. For you and for all of my patients," Alex said. "I'd like to ask you a few more questions."

"Okay."

"Do you think you're going to be having sex sometime soon? Remember, this is just between you and me."

"No, I don't think so. That bladder infection really shook me up," Julie confessed.

"I could put you on the pill, Julie." Alex continued. "Even if you aren't planning on having sex soon, you never know. In addition from preventing pregnancy, it would keep your periods regular and decrease your monthly cramps." She went on, "What it wouldn't do, however, is protect you from getting an infection down there. Only a condom can protect you from that."

"I don't know, Dr. Faber. I really don't think I need it. Is there anything else I can use for the cramps?"

"Yes, there is a medication I can give you to take when you get your period. Are you sure you don't want the pill?"

"For now, Dr. Faber. I'm pretty sure."

"Okay. But remember what I said, Julie. You can get pregnant if you do what you did before. Be smart and use a condom for protection. Don't count on your boyfriend to be responsible. You're the one who'll get stuck." Alex reached into her desk drawer and took out a small package. "Put this in your pocketbook. Having one doesn't mean you have to use it. Just call it an insurance policy." Alex smiled at her and wrote out the prescription to help with her menstrual cramps. "Try to open up to your parents a little more—it might help. And remember, I'm always here if you need me."

"Thank you so much," Julie said, putting both the prescription and the condom in her bag. The two left Alex's office and met Liz in the waiting room.

"How'd we do?" Liz asked with a smile.

"She did just fine, Liz," Alex said. "She's got a prescription that should help with the cramps."

"Thanks so much, Alex!" Liz said. "I really appreciate your fitting her in. You'll come over for dinner soon?"

Alex nodded and bade so long to her friend and her new patient.

Alex's next patient of the day was Jody Pinkham, who was now nearly six months pregnant. Jody was complaining of the usual aches and pains that go with an advancing gestation. What made her symptoms more complex, however, was the possibility that they could be the effects of a spreading malignancy. Alex examined Jody, visualizing the scarred cervix. The stitch that held the baby in the uterus was in place, and there was no obvious disease recurrence. Using her examining fingers, Alex probed the sides of the vagina, searching for the nodularity deep in the pelvis that would portend an advancing growth. Fortunately, the exam was negative. She finished by measuring Jody's abdominal size and listening to the fetal heart.

"It sounds strong, Dr. Faber!"

"It certainly does." Her reassurance lit up Jody's face. "I think it's time to schedule your next MRI." Alex was referring to a scan that used magnetic waves to visualize the inside of the body without any risk to the baby. Using this technique, it would be possible to evaluate whether there was any gross evidence of spreading cancer. The baby was now reaching the age of viability. Once viable, Jody could be delivered if necessary, and the baby would stand a decent chance of survival outside of the uterus. As long as the MRI remained normal, Jody could wait for the baby's lungs to mature before delivery would be initiated. That, however, wouldn't be for at least another two months.

The mention of the MRI did not dampen Jody's spirits. Hearing her baby's heartbeat was all the solace she needed. She left Alex, heading towards the front desk so that Ann could schedule the MRI. Ann also made an appointment for her to see Alex again in another two weeks.

A bit later on, Alex's morning was interrupted by a call from the labor floor. One of her patients was moving quickly through labor and her presence was requested upstairs immediately. Alex left in a flurry of apologies to the patients in the waiting room and hurried to the labor floor. She found her maternity patient sitting up in the birthing bed, breathing rapidly. The bed sheets had fallen to the floor and the woman was letting out loud grunts.

Alex turned to the maternity nurse. "Do I have time to change?"

"There's no head in sight yet, Dr. Faber," the nurse answered.

Alex crossed the hall to the doctors' lounge where she rapidly removed her blouse and skirt, throwing them onto the bed and slipping into her scrub suit almost in one motion. She did not see Gerald Ransom in the corner, the New England Journal of Medicine spread open in his lap.

"Well, hello there Dr. Faber. Good to see you again," Gerald said, leering at her with a grin.

Alex bolted out the door, not giving Gerald the benefit of seeing her red face. She returned to the birthing room to find her patient lying on her left side, her right leg supported by her husband. Between her legs, a bulging mass represented her child's initial descent into the world. Alex donned her gown and gloves, setting up the instruments on her table in preparation for delivery. With the next contraction, the baby's head crowned up, stretching the vaginal opening to its limits. As Alex gently delivered the remainder of the child's head, she could see the vagina drop back over its neck, awaiting the subsequent delivery of the shoulders. Alex suctioned out the baby's nose and mouth, removing as much mucus and amniotic fluid as she could in preparation for the baby's first breath.

As she prepared for the shoulder delivery, it became very clear that the largest part of the baby had not yet traversed the opening. The obstetrician's worst nightmare, a shoulder dystocia, was playing out right in front of her. If the shoulder got stuck behind the bony pelvis, the baby would be forced to remain inside its mother, doomed to asphyxiate. Alex's mind flashed to the myriad options she had when dealing with this emergency circumstance. She had seen first-hand the death of an infant whose attending obstetrician was unable to deliver the child in time. She couldn't pull too hard on the head for fear of tearing nerves in the child's shoulder, potentially leading to arm paralysis. She grabbed for the scissors, cutting a generous episiotomy to allow more room to maneuver. The nurse helped her bend the patient's thighs up onto her abdomen and the laboring woman bore down with all her might, but to no avail. She then reached inside the vagina with her finger, pushing the baby's shoulder down in a corkscrew maneuver, trying to free up the trapped child.

"Dr. Faber, we are now two minutes since delivery of the head."

Alex knew she only had another two to three minutes before irreversible brain damage would occur. Her heart thudded within her chest as her stomach began to tighten. A wave of claustrophobia came over her and her breathing became labored. Don't panic! she told herself. She knew the next opportunity might be her last chance to deliver a healthy child. She reached up inside, grasping an arm and pulling it across the baby's chest and outside the vagina. The trapped shoulder was free, and the child tumbled out into her arms. The baby began to scream almost immediately, as though complaining of its violent entrance into the world. With the apgar safely in the high single numbers, Alex clamped and cut the cord, delivered the placenta and sewed up the episiotomy. By the time she left the birthing room, her scrub suit was soaked with her own perspiration and a glop of meconium adorned her pants. She had been pooped on by the baby she had saved who had obviously given her low marks for technique!. She returned to the lounge to change.

"You definitely look better without your scrub suit than with it, Dr. Faber," cracked a grinning Gerald Ransom, looking up from his journal.

"Spare me, Gerald," she snapped. "I just had a tough shoulder dystocia. I'm not in the mood for humor." This time she was sure to change in the bathroom. She left without further acknowledgment, returning to her hectic waiting room, leaving Gerald once again to face a cold shower.

Alex arrived back at the office, surprised to see no patients waiting for her. Joshua had come back from the operating room early, hoping to get some paper work done before his afternoon office hours. Instead, he had spent the time running through Alex's remaining patients, unsure of when she would be able to return. She found her partner in his office.

"If you'll excuse my less than professional manner, Dr. Barron, you are a sweetheart!" She walked over to him and planted a kiss on the top of his head.

"You'd have done the same for me, Alex. Besides, it's bad for business to leave the customer waiting!" he said smiling at her.

"Always thinking of the bottom line, partner." She continued the sarcasm. "Come on, I owe you lunch."

While the drama was unfolding on the labor floor, Sergeant Mitchell Karas was meeting with Ron Dorcik in his office at the hospital. Sergeant Karas was a big man, clean-shaven, with a horseshoe of hair left on his head that made him look ten years older than his thirty-five years of age. His uniform was spotless, from the bright, shiny badge, down to his recently polished black shoes. Of the five detectives on the Breedville Police Force, Sergeant Karas had been assigned to the case that was now being referred to as serial rape.

"Mr. Dorcik, I don't have to tell you what a difficult time we're having with this case. We still have no good witnesses, none of the victims are able to help us with a composite sketch, and we can't find any leads on suspects." Sergeant Karas looked tired and frustrated. "The only piece of solid information we have is that the assaults all occurred on the hospital grounds or started here, all after July first. I'm going to need a list of every new employee that started work at Breed around that time."

Ron leaned forward, clasping his hands together atop his desk. "You mean besides me, Sergeant Karas?"

Sergeant Karas let out an anxious laugh. "Obviously, sir, since you are not presently a suspect in this investigation."

"Of course," Ron said with a smile, as he leaned back in his chair. "Well, I had my personnel department head review all new hires since July first. There are only three employees who began work at that time. You're welcome to speak to them."

"I would also like the opportunity to have my staff review your personnel records and perform background checks on your other employees."

"Are you including the medical staff as well?"

"Yes sir. And for completeness sake, we will ask to review your background as well."

"Very well. I have nothing to hide. I am just as anxious as you are to get to the bottom of this."

Joshua had the lab slip in hand when Todd and Amanda Perkins arrived for her one o'clock appointment.

"I'm pregnant, aren't I?" Amanda asked urgently before even taking a seat.

"Yes, you are Mrs. Perkins," Joshua acknowledged. "And as happy as I am to tell you that, I was hoping it wouldn't occur during this cycle."

"What do we do now?" Todd asked anxiously. "We have to know whose it is. As soon as possible."

"That is up to you two," Joshua answered. "If you wish, I can set you up for a chorionic villus sampling so we can tissue type the pregnancy and know for sure who the father is. The procedure is quite simple, with very little risk to the fetus. We are fortunate to have an obstetrician on staff who has been trained in this technique. His name is Dr. Ransom. We could set you up to have the procedure in about four weeks. After the results are back, you can decide how you'd like to proceed."

"I know that this is Todd's child, Dr. Barron," Amanda said. "There is no question in my mind. I would not consider aborting this pregnancy."

"I don't know how you could be so sure, Mrs. Perkins." Joshua locked eyes with her. "There really is no way of telling without this test. Would you want to take the chance that this pregnancy might be the result of your assault?"

"I know I wouldn't want to take that chance," Todd interjected. He turned to his wife. "Honey, I don't want to have any lingering doubts.

I know how much you want to be pregnant. So do I. But I want to be able to love this child and I don't know if I could, not knowing if I am the father."

"Of course you're the father, Todd!" Amanda said to her husband. "I just know that you are!"

"Fortunately, we don't have to make a decision today," Joshua told them. "We have plenty of time to decide. Why don't you two give yourselves a chance to discuss this for a while. I'd like to see you again in three weeks, and if you wish, they'll still be plenty of time to perform the exam."

The Perkins' left. Though Amanda was overjoyed with her long-awaited pregnancy, Todd was visibly troubled. This unique situation held the potential for a very painful irony, and Joshua had never in his career encountered such a case. He was not looking forward to their next meeting.

CHAPTER TWENTY

NO CELEBRATORY ANNIVERSARY DINNER ever took place the night Phil Lambert received the letter about the upcoming Mark Uber litigation. He was already running late for the dinner when he opened the letter, and lost track of time from there, blankly staring at the words on the page. Phil had never been a defendant in a malpractice case, even during his training. This status was unusual in this day and age, and much of it could be attributed to his compulsive attention to detail, an excellent grasp of the principles and practice of medicine, and the warm regard in which he was held by nearly all of his patients.

Cindy began to worry when Phil hadn't shown up at home to pick her up for dinner. She called his private number at the office, letting it ring for several minutes. When it was finally answered, she was hard pressed to recognize her husband's voice.

"Hello," said Phil with a vacant tone.

"Honey, is that you?"

"Ah-hah," he answered, the sound barely passing his lips.

"What's the matter, Phil? Are you okay?"

"I think so," Phil answered, again his voice hardly audible.

"I'll be right down, Phil. Just wait for me in your office," Cindy said.

"Sure, whatever you say," he said flatly.

Cindy hung up and headed for the car. She knew that Phil had fought bouts of depression over recent months. She didn't like the sound of his voice on the phone, and she wasn't going to take any chances. It only took her a few minutes to reach the hospital. Phil always liked the idea of living close, so that he would be available for his patients in a moment's notice. Cindy pulled into the parking lot at the doctors' building and let herself in to her husband's office.

"Phil, it's Cindy!" she called into the dark waiting room. "Where are you?"

There was no answer.

"Oh God!" Cindy wailed as she searched the office. She heard a distant voice, muttering softly. She opened a door and walked into the receptionist's area enclosed in glass windows, where the medical records were kept. There was Phil, with his back to her, sitting on a stool with a chart in his hand.

"Where did I go wrong? If only I had come right in ... why was I so careless? None of this had to happen ..."

"Honey, what's wrong?" Cindy asked softly, approaching him gently so as not to frighten him. She put a hand on his upper arm and looked over his shoulder. Her eyes spotted the name "Mark Uber" on the outside of the folder. The name sounded familiar. Then she saw an official looking letter printed on lawyerly-stationery in Phil's hand. All of those awful weeks in July came flooding back. Cindy remembered the self-doubt and loss of confidence. She had never seen her husband so down over a medical case. He had lost patients before. In his field, it was inevitable. But never had it affected him as much. She had been so relieved when he finally came out of it and everything returned to normal. But when she'd heard his voice on the phone earlier, she had a feeling this case had reared its ugly head. She was right.

"Come on, Phil. Let's go home." She reached for her husband's hand and helped him to his feet. He responded to her efforts grudgingly, without emotion. Phil left the chart and letter on the stool behind the desk and allowed his wife to help him to the car. He was in no shape to drive, so she left his car behind and drove her broken husband home.

After arriving there, Cindy called the Barrons. Liz answered the phone.

"Hi, Liz, this is Cindy. Is Joshua there?"

"Hi Cindy. No, Joshua's at the hospital. Is there something wrong?"

"I'm worried about Phil. He received a letter from a lawyer today about that horrible case back in July. He's really upset, and doesn't seem to be responding to me very well. I thought Joshua might be able to reach him."

"Cindy, let me call Joshua at the hospital. If he's freed up, I'm sure he'd want to come over and help. I'll call you right back."

"Thanks, Liz. I'd appreciate it."

Liz paged Joshua at the hospital. He returned her call from the emergency room. She relayed Cindy's concern. Joshua was dismayed that the Uber case had crept back up again, and he offered to stop at the Lambert residence on his way home. Liz called Cindy back to reassure her that Joshua would be over soon.

When Joshua arrived at the Lamberts, he found Phil sitting at the kitchen table, an untouched cup of coffee in front of him. His friend appeared to be in another world, and although he looked up when Joshua entered, there were no visible signs of recognition in his face.

"Hi Phil. Sorry to hear about the letter," Joshua said as he pulled up a chair. "Guess the family was able to find a lawyer desperate enough to take the case."

"Stanislav," was all Phil said. "Stanislav."

Cindy turned to Joshua. "What's he talking about?"

"Stanislav? I don't believe it!" said Joshua, throwing up his hands incredulously.

"Who's Stanislav?" Cindy asked again.

"Only the biggest blood sucking leech in the legal profession! Even his colleagues call him a whore. He's the smooth talker who advertises free consultations on TV if you think you've been a victim of medical malpractice." Joshua's voice was agitated. "On more than one occasion, I've been taking care of a woman in labor when that miserable excuse for an attorney comes onscreen to peddle his wares, dangling a lottery prize in front of the woman's face," Joshua said, feeling his face grow hot.

"Is he good?" Cindy asked.

"I've heard he's very good, unfortunately. However he rarely goes to trial. He uses every legal manipulation in the book to wear down his opposition into settling. He'll pester you with depositions, release information to the local newspapers, and take up valuable practice time with court shenanigans—anything to get the poor sucker to give in! Then he collects his third of the pie and takes his expenses out of the plaintiff's share. He's got a whole group of like-minded attorneys on board with him now, hungry for the fast buck. I'm afraid Phil has a real professional shark holding on to his leg."

Cindy looked sick to her stomach, and Phil continued his same emotionless stare.

"I'm pretty surprised he took on this case himself, actually" Joshua continued. "He usually seems to take on only the sure bets. There is no evidence of malpractice here. Frankly, I don't think he stands a chance and I'm sure that when the defense lawyer reviews the facts, he'll recommend not to settle to the insurance company."

"In that case, couldn't it drag on for a long time?" Cindy asked.

"It might. But Phil has nothing to fear. He did the best job he could. He knows that."

"Stanislav," Phil mumbled again. "I can't believe I've got to deal with Stanislav!"

"Phil. C'mon. Talk to me," Joshua said directly to his friend.

Phil seemed to come above water for a moment. "What am I going to do, Josh?"

"Phil, everything is going to be fine. I think Stanislav is making a big mistake this time. You know you didn't do anything wrong."

"Maybe I did, Joshua," Phil said. "The guy died from a cause I never even considered!"

"You didn't have any time to consider the other diagnosis, let alone save him. You heard what Ted Dennis said. There was no time to operate on him. He would have died on the table." Joshua was referring to a general surgeon on staff who had discussed the case with Phil and Joshua back in July.

"I hear what you're saying, Joshua. I just can't believe this thing is coming back to haunt me." Phil hung his head. Despite looking utterly dejected, Phil appeared to be back in the real world, which reassured Cindy and Joshua.

"Here's what'll happen," Joshua said, speaking with brisk confidence. "Call the insurance company on Monday to alert them to a potential suit. You comply with Stanislav's request after you talk to the insurance company's legal department. And then, you go on practicing the high quality of medical care which has kept you out of a malpractice suit for the better part of ten years."

Just then, Joshua's beeper went off. It was the labor floor. He had left the hospital with one patient in very early labor and he was sure things must be picking up.

"I've got to head out, Phil. Take it easy and don't let this ruin your anniversary. You'll take care of everything on Monday." He gave his friend a strong pat on the back and put on his coat.

"Thanks for coming over, Joshua," Cindy said giving Joshua a hug. "We appreciate it."

"Watch yourself, Joshua," Phil said, extending his hand up to his friend. "It's a dangerous world out there!"

Joshua smiled, glad to see a glimmer of the old Phil.

Despite Joshua's reassurances that night, things did not get better for Phil. He remained depressed all weekend, which scuttled most of the couple's plans for celebrating. Phil notified the insurance company on Monday, and was contacted by a member of their legal defense team later that day. He asked Phil a few questions and suggested that he comply with Jeffrey Stanislav's request for records. He also requested that a copy of Mark Uber's records be sent to his attention at the insurance company. He told Phil to keep him informed of further communication from Stanislav, or any other lawyer, about the matter.

"Frankly, Dr. Lambert," said the attorney in closing, "it doesn't sound like much of a case for the plaintiff. Try not to let it bother you. And, of course, do not discuss this case with anyone without speaking to me first."

After this conversation with his defense lawyer, Phil felt a bit better. Being that the legal system moved so slowly in litigation matters, he had no way of knowing if and when he would hear more about the case. By the end of the week, he had convinced himself that everything was going to be all right, and he returned to focusing on his priority: his patients.

It was four weeks until the persistent shark resurfaced, this time taking a more secure hold of Phil's leg. The defense attorney was contacted by Stanislav, who assured him that the plaintiff had every intention of pursuing litigation. They were asking for one million dollars and the insurance company turned him down cold. Stanislav informed him that they would be deposing Phil Lambert in the near future. He reassured Phil that he would be with him during the deposition, watching out for his and the insurance company's interests.

Once again the dark clouds gathered over Phil's mood. As he discovered the following day, the phone call had just been the tip of the iceberg. It was the front page of *the Breedville Bugle* that sunk the ship.

An article entitled "Local Cardiologist sued for malpractice in case of mistaken diagnosis" described the rapid demise of Mark Uber during the final night of Granite Greatness that past July. The plaintiff, Sally Uber, was asking for one million dollars in damages for wrongful death. There were several quotes from Mrs. Uber, who claimed she was never given a clear response regarding her husband's cause of death. She also stated that Dr. Lambert had been overheard admitting that he had made a mistake. The article cited that Dr. Lambert was unreachable for comment. This statement in particular burned Phil, because they had called his office after hours on his day off. While of course he would have relished in giving the scoundrels who wrote the article a piece of his mind, he would have been unable to make a statement anyway, upon the recommendation of his attorney.

The article rapidly circulated around the hospital, and everyone offered his or her unsolicited opinion on the case. There was universal condemnation of the legal system and an outpouring of sympathy and support for their embattled cardiologist. Phil tried to keep a low profile, not leaving his office all day except for early morning and late afternoon rounds. Almost every patient that day expressed their support for him and their rage at such careless journalism. Despite the fact that Phil was not alone in the suit (the hospital and the emergency room physicians were also listed) all he wanted to do was crawl into a hole and be left alone.

Alex was having lunch in the hospital cafeteria that day when Ron Dorcik stopped at her table.

"Mind if I join you, Alex?" he asked, holding a tray with a salad and sandwich.

"Not at all, Ron. Have a seat," she gestured for him to sit down.

Ron unwrapped his sandwich. "Poor Phil. What a horrible situation for him, especially now that it hit the newspaper," he said.

"I agree," she said, shaking her head. "I hope this doesn't turn into a trial by newspaper. I guess this is also your headache now, considering the ER staff was implicated, too."

Ron nodded, continuing to chew. "True, but for Phil it is so much more personal. So much more direct."

"It doesn't seem fair," Alex continued, picking at her salad. "He's such a compulsive doctor. From what I've seen here so far, you couldn't get better medical care anywhere." She sighed, crumpling up her napkin and tossing it into her barely touched food. "The system has to blame someone when something goes wrong. The way the legal profession is set up, people have nothing to lose by suing! It's the jerks like Stanislav that thrive off of the system's deficiencies. I can't practice medicine this way!" Alex slumped back in her chair, visibly frustrated.

Ron nodded in agreement, sorry that he'd brought up such an unsettling topic. He continued to eat as Alex took a minute to calm down. The two then concentrated on their lunch. The silence became obvious as neither party seemed to know what to say next. Finally Ron spoke.

"I was wondering if you would join me for dinner sometime? I need a break from eating with community leaders and charity organizers," Ron smiled.

Alex looked Ron straight in the eye. "Do you think that would be a good idea?"

"Can't think of a better one!" Ron said enthusiastically. "I've felt awkward about contacting you ever since we ran into each other in July. No strings attached!" he added. "I just think it would be nice for us to catch up and ease any tension."

"Okay," Alex agreed with slight hesitation. "How about this weekend?" Ron was pleasantly surprised by her quick agreement.

"Saturday night works for me," he said.

"Saturday night it is." Alex's beeper interrupted any further conversation.

"I've got to run," she said. "Call me later in the week with a time and place."

"Great. See you around."

She withdrew to the phone and then quickly left the cafeteria.

The deposition occurred two weeks later at Jeffrey Stanislav's office in Concord. It took place in an imposing set of rooms with rich woodwork and plush carpeting. Phil Lambert and his defense lawyer were ushered into the library—a large room with oak trim, bookshelves lining the walls from floor to ceiling. A long conference table with a dozen matching captain's chairs dominated the room. The defense lawyer who had been assigned to this case sat with Phil at one end of the conference table. Off to the side was a court stenographer who would be recording the deposition. On the other end was Jeffrey Stanislav, Esquire.

The attorney who evoked such fiery passion from New Hampshire physicians was actually a very plain looking man. He was a bit stocky for his five foot eight inch frame, and he combed his hair so as to cover what was obviously a paucity of follicles. He wore an expensive pinstripe suit with monogrammed shirt. A Phi Beta Kappa key chain hung from his vest pocket and a Rolex watch glistened on his left wrist. The clothes were making the man in this case, no doubt. He rose to his feet when Phil and his lawyer entered the room, offering his hand to both.

"Good to see you again, Harold," Stanislav said to the defense lawyer, and to Phil, "it is a pleasure to meet you, Dr. Lambert."

Phil merely acknowledged the greeting with a nod of his head. He felt like the condemned prisoner, being offered a few words of encouragement by the warden prior to climbing up the gallows steps. Stanislav spent no further time on pleasantries.

"Just for the record, Doctor, we will start with some basic questions."

Phil nodded.

"Please state your name, address and hospital that you are affiliated with."

"Phillip Henry Lambert. 12 Oak Place, Breedville, New Hampshire," Phil stated, his voice having trouble rising to the occasion. "I practice at Garrison Breed General Hospital."

"Please speak up, Doctor, for the stenographer's sake."

Phil nodded again.

"Could you state for the record your field of medicine and how long you have been practicing in this field?"

"I completed a residency in internal medicine and a two year fellowship in cardiology. I have been practicing for ten years."

"Are you board certified in internal medicine and cardiology?"

"Yes, I am."

"Could you tell me how you came to be responsible for the medical care of Mark Uber on July fourth of this year?"

"I received a call from the emergency room that Mr. Uber was being seen with chest pain. The emergency room physician felt that an admission was indicated. I was on call for internal medicine that night and accepted the admission."

"Was there anything unusual about the chest pain that Mr. Uber was exhibiting?" Before Phil had a chance to answer this question, the defense insurance lawyer requested a brief recess to confer with his client. Though obviously irritated, Stanislav stopped the questions and the two men disappeared into an adjoining room.

"What's the problem?" Phil asked the lawyer.

"You've got to be very careful here, Phil. He's going to try to make it look like you were relying on the emergency room physician too much and shirking your responsibilities as the attending physician. Your job is to get across that you had some questions about the diagnosis and that you came in as soon as you could to check on the patient. Do you understand?"

Again, Phil nodded. The two returned to the conference room.

"I'll repeat the question for you, Doctor. Was there anything unusual about the chest pain which Mr. Uber was exhibiting?"

"Yes there was. The electrocardiogram was normal."

"Why is this unusual?"

"If a person is exhibiting the chest pain of angina pectoris, or coronary artery disease, you would expect certain changes on the EKG."

"And these changes were not apparent?" Stanislav reiterated.

"Correct."

"Did you see this EKG yourself?"

"No. I was not in the hospital at the time."

"What did you do after you were told about the EKG?"

"I told the physician to admit the patient to the coronary care unit and that I would be in to see him."

"Did you ever ask the physician any other questions about the patient's symptoms?"

"No, I did not. He presented the case over the phone as an angina pectoris and so I admitted him to the unit for observation. He was stable at the time, and I planned to take my own history when I arrived."

"How long after you received the call from the emergency room did you arrive in the cardiac unit at the hospital?"

"About an hour, I believe."

"About an hour," Stanislav repeated, emphasizing each word. "Were you concerned that maybe there was something else going on with this patient, Doctor?"

"I wasn't sure."

"You weren't sure," Stanislav again repeating Phil's words with harsh enunciation.

"You heard him, Jeffrey," piped up the defense lawyer. Stanislav turned to the stenographer.

"That last statement was off the record."

The deposition continued with Stanislav reviewing every detail of Phil's arrival at the hospital, including his discussion with the emergency room physician and his time of arrival at the coronary care unit. Stanislav then went into complete detail of the resuscitation attempt, giving Phil a chance to recount the situation. Stanislav repeatedly referred to the "failed resuscitation" in an apparent attempt to wear Phil down.

"I would like to skip to the following day, Doctor. You attended the autopsy on Mr. Uber, did you not?"

"I did."

"And did you receive some information at the autopsy regarding Mr. Uber's cause of death?"

"Yes I did."

"And what was that, Doctor?"

"The pathologist did not see any problem with Mr. Uber's heart, although he had not yet reviewed the microscopic slides."

"Did he see something else at that time?"

"Yes, he noticed a perforated gastric ulcer with signs of sepsis."

"Thank you doctor. Now if we could skip to a little later that morning. Were you engaged in conversation with a colleague in front of the elevator of the hospital?"

At this question, Phil was slightly confused. All of the other questions had been anticipated, but not this one. Stanislav was fishing for something.

Then it hit him like a ton of bricks. Right after leaving the morgue, he had run into Joshua. He remembered feeling very depressed and down during their exchange. Phil turned to his defense lawyer and asked for a brief adjournment. Once again, Stanislav was irritated but acquiesced. The two men returned to the smaller office.

"What's the problem, Phil?" his attorney asked.

"The day after, I made some comments to my friend Joshua Barron that could be construed as admitting guilt. Someone must have overheard our conversation." Phil ran his hands through his hair, worried. "What should I do?"

"You can say that you don't recall the words of the conversation, even if you remember having one."

"Is that legal?" Phil asked.

"Do you really remember exactly what you said four months ago?"

"Well, not exactly."

"There you go," reassured the attorney. "That's the tactic you take."

Phil took a deep breath. This part of the deposition was unexpected, and his heart was racing. The two men returned again to the conference room. Stanislav continued where he had left off.

"Do you remember having a conversation with one of your colleagues around that time?"

"Yes, I do."

"Do you remember what you said to him?"

"No, I don't."

"Let me refresh your memory, Doctor. Do you remember saying, and I quote," Stanislav eyed Phil, then looked down to a typed piece of paper in his hand, "'I'm afraid I blew the diagnosis. I can't help feeling like I failed the guy somehow. Perhaps I should have been more demanding of the moonlighter's work up when he was reviewing the case with me over the phone.'" Stanislav looked up. "Unquote."

The blood drained out of Phil's head and he broke out in profuse perspiration.

"I'm afraid I don't remember exactly what I said at that time."

"Oh come on, Doctor!" Stanislav emitted a sharp laugh. "Your reaction gives you away. Isn't that what you said to your colleague, that you blew the diagnosis?" His voice had reached a crescendo.

"I object to this questioning," the defense attorney spoke up. "He's already told you that he doesn't remember. You're not supposed to badger the witness here, Jeffrey. This is only a deposition."

"I have no further questions." With that, the deposition was finished. Jeffrey Stanislav rose from the table, offering his hand to a dejected Phil.

"No hard feelings, Dr. Lambert, I hope? We're all just here to see that justice is served." Phil turned away from the self-assured attorney, rejecting the handshake and refusing to look him in the eye. He exited from the inquisition chamber, shoulders hunched.

Meanwhile, Stanislav turned to Phil's attorney, offering his hand in friendship.

"Harold," Stanislav addressed the defense attorney. "Good to see you again. I hope you can make it to the racquetball match tonight at the club."

"Jeffrey," said Phil's attorney. "You know I wouldn't miss it for the world."

CHAPTER TWENTY-ONE

T HE SODA WAS FLAT and the pizza was cold as Mitchell Karas, Senior Detective for the Breedville Police Department, pored over his files. He had information and background on each male staff member at Breed General. Mitchell was an organized man. The files were neatly arranged in three piles: new employees since July first, all other employees, and medical staff members. He was on a fishing expedition. The fact that all of the attacks originated near the hospital may have been the modus operandi for the assailant, but did not necessarily point to a hospital staff member as the perpetrator. During the last few months, he had combed the known and suspected felons in the area, only to be left empty handed. He even submitted a request to the FBI to search their records for similar unsolved crimes in the northeast. The government search had turned up two other cases: one in New York City and the other in Hartford, Connecticut. Mitchell found it laughable that the Feds could only come up with one unsolved serial rape case in New York City. Hell, he thought to himself. There must be a thousand in that piss hole! When the government files came through on the fax, Mitchell gave them a very preliminary skim, then stuffed them into yet another manila file.

His partner on the case was Walter Fallon, a ten-year member of the force and a recent addition to the detective squad. Walter was diminutive in stature, with fine, almost fragile facial features behind wire rimmed glasses. His body frame belied the fact that he was an avid exercise fanatic, running several miles a day. While it was normally pizza and soda that stocked the office on these late work nights, Walter would have preferred yogurt and fruit.

"Mitchell," Walter asked, closing up the box that housed the final piece of cardboard-like pizza. "Any luck on the hospital employees before July first?"

"Not really," his partner answered. "It's a large pile, but I haven't found any previous convictions, questionable backgrounds or even anyone who has lived in Hartford. There were several who lived in New York, but they were already up here when the crimes were committed down in the city."

"Well, I found nothing in the medical staff pile," Walter added, folding his arms across his chest. "Besides, these guys would have lost their licenses if they had any criminal background."

"Don't be so sure," his partner warned him. "I've heard of several cases of docs leaving one state under questionable circumstances and starting up fresh somewhere else. The state boards aren't as careful as they are with police applicants, you know!"

The third pile, involving only new employees and medical staff hired since July first, was much smaller. That had been the first group reviewed, again with nothing suspicious surfacing.

"You know, Walter," Mitchell said as he reopened the pizza box, snagging the last slice, "that guy Dorcik's last job was in Hartford."

"Really?" Walter asked. "What's the lowdown on this guy?"

"Well, he's thirty six years old and has been in hospital administration for the past twelve years, first in Greenwich and then in Hartford. He was divorced once a long time ago and has never remarried." Mitchell sifted through Ron Dorcik's file. "He had good letters of recommendation from his last employer and the hospital apparently was doing very well under his direction." He looked up. "Frankly, I don't understand why a single guy with a good job in a big city would leave for a similar position in a smaller hospital, in a tiny town out in the boondocks. And for less pay."

"Well, maybe there's something there," his partner offered. "Let me review the details on the assaults in Hartford from the Feds."

Walter picked up the FBI file and thumbed through the pages.

"According to these reports, the assaults all occurred around the hospital campus where our friend Dorcik was working." Walter took his feet off the desk and sat upright in his chair. "And listen to this! None of the victims could identify the assailant because he wore a ski mask." Walter looked up at Mitchell. "He never physically beat any of the victims, just threatened them with a knife and raped them. None were robbed." He closed the file and tossed it onto the desk. "And there have been no attacks since early May of this year."

Mitchell put down the file that was in his hand.

"Looks like we need to talk to Dorcik, after all. The descriptions of the attacks down in Hartford are too similar to what we've been dealing with here. Especially with the ski mask. Maybe he left because the trail down there was getting too hot."

"And maybe we're jumping to conclusions because we're so desperate," Walter admitted. "But it certainly wouldn't hurt to talk to him again."

Alex hoped that her second visit to The Tavern restaurant would be more successful than her first—the scene of her uncomfortable interview dinner last spring. Now, instead of facing the jealousies of Elizabeth Barron, she faced her ex-husband. Alex was a bit anxious about accepting Ron's invitation, but she was still intrigued by him, and hoped the night would go well.

"What are you thinking about?" Ron asked Alex from across the table as he poured her a glass of wine. "You look preoccupied."

"Do I?" Alex laughed. "I don't know. It just seems so strange to be here with you after all of these years."

"A good kind of strange—or just strange, period?" Ron asked playfully.

"A little bit of both, I guess!" Alex answered in kind. Her response was followed by a pregnant pause.

"How's practice going?" Ron asked, restarting the conversation on safer ground.

"It's really wonderful. It's everything I wanted. I feel so much a part of my patients' lives. And delivering babies—it's a high that you just can't get anywhere else."

"I am really happy for you," Ron said, raising his glass and taking a sip. "You seem so much more at ease and in control now. When I think back many years, I can see how you felt trapped. You wanted more. I'm glad things have worked out for you, Alex. I really am."

"Thanks, Ron." Alex took a sip from her glass, feeling herself relax into the evening. "How about you? How are you doing?"

"Well," he smiled, "you know how much I like being in charge. The opportunity to run an individual hospital is a real challenge. And you know what? I'm good at it. Charity Hospital in Hartford was in significantly better financial shape by the time I left." Ron buttered his roll and did the same for Alex. "There are a lot of changes going on with the business side of medicine, and I think that the bigger changes are yet to come. Doctors and hospitals have never looked at themselves the way other businesses have, and from that standpoint, the industry is still in its infancy. But as money gets tighter, and I am convinced that it will, hospitals will have to take on a whole new role in their relationship with physicians and insurance companies. I like to think that I will be able to keep pace with those changes."

"But what about the patients?" Alex asked. "Where do they fit in? When someone is sick and in need, their concerns may not go along with the bottom line."

"I agree," Ron answered. "That's what makes the health care industry unique. Wall Street only cares about the bottom line. Hospitals and physicians have never cared about the costs. The successful health care venture will have to find a happy medium."

The conversation continued to flow between Alex and Ron as each made their points regarding compassion and its place in the business world. Appetizers flowed into entrees, and then into dessert. They managed to stay within safe topics, and there was little of the awkwardness that Alex had feared. Dinner seemed to end too soon, and Ron drove Alex home.

"I had a great time, Ron," she said, her hand on the door handle of his Volvo sedan.

"So did I," he said. "I'd like to do this again—sometime soon."

"No strings, Ron. Remember?"

"No strings, Alex. Good night." Ron sat in his car as Alex walked to her door. She opened it, turned back briefly to wave, then went inside. Ron let the car idle for a few more minutes as he sat there, still trying to figure out what went wrong so many years ago. He shifted into drive and drove off. Ron didn't see Alex looking out her bedroom window, and even if he had, he wouldn't have been able to make out the tears in her eyes.

CHAPTER TWENTY TWO

Alex knew it was going to be a difficult case. Wendy Butler had come to her four months earlier, complaining of chronic pelvic pain. She was a thirty six-year-old mother of three who had been plagued by endometriosis for over twelve years. An infertility specialist in Boston had made the original diagnosis. Wendy went to him after two years of inability to conceive, and after an exhaustive work up he found the problem while performing a laparoscopy. Six months of Danazol and she became pregnant with her first.

Back in those days, Wendy had yet to experience the symptoms of endometriosis, a chronic gynecologic enigma that plagued many women. She had no painful periods, no chronic pelvic pain, no painful intercourse. The specialist had explained to her that endometriosis was a condition where tissue that was normally confined to the inside lining of the uterus would grow outside of its normal habitat. These cells, though located outside of the uterus, would still respond to the hormonal changes of the monthly cycle and bleed at the time of menstruation. He further explained that the tubes and ovaries do not necessarily need to be blocked or covered to produce an infertile state. The mere presence of these sites of misplaced endometrium could produce an environment that would be hostile to conception.

The Danazol that Wendy took had the effect of producing a reversible menopausal state. In the absence of ovulation and menstruation, the endometrial implants were absorbed by the body and disappeared. After Wendy's first pregnancy, she heeded her doctor's suggestion to have her children close together so as not to allow the endometriosis to return. Over the following few years, she was fortunate to conceive an additional two times without further therapy. Her physician said the three pregnancies were good for her, in that they appeared to have a suppressive effect on her condition. Yet he was convinced that the endometriosis would return eventually and probably make her infertile again.

He was right. After five years of conceiving, carrying and nursing, Wendy began to experience significant pain with her periods. Though she and her husband did not use any form of birth control and would have been delighted with more children, it appeared that her condition had returned, and they were happy with the three they had.

Though infertility was no longer a concern, the painful symptoms that went hand in hand with her condition began to occur. First came the menstrual cramps, then the painful sexual relations, and finally a state of chronic pelvic discomfort. Wendy survived on Tylenol, then Motrin and finally codeine. Their sex life had all but disappeared, and for four days a month Wendy was unable to function at all. By this time the family had moved to Breedville due to Bob's job transfer. She brought her medical records with her, giving them to Alex at her first visit. There wasn't a question in Alex's mind as to what the next step for Wendy would be. The specialist down in Boston had predicted it too: a complete hysterectomy with removal of the tubes and ovaries. The case was scheduled for just after Thanksgiving to give the family the opportunity to spend the holiday together, and hopefully provide Wendy with enough recuperation time prior to Christmas.

Thanksgiving came and went. On the day of her surgery, Alex met Wendy in the preoperative area. Her husband was standing by her bed.

"Hi, Mrs. Butler, Mr. Butler. Did either of you have any questions before we get started?" Bob shook his head.

"Just do a good job, Dr. Faber," Wendy answered. "I can't wait to get this behind me."

"It won't be long now," Alex reassured her. She reviewed her patient's preoperative studies, making sure everything was in order prior to surgery. The nurse who started the intravenous on Wendy began to inject a tranquilizer in preparation for general anesthesia. Her husband was politely discharged to the waiting room and Wendy Butler was wheeled down to the operating room. Ted Dennis, a general surgeon, was scheduled to assist on the case. Alex met up with him in the surgeon's lounge.

"Afternoon, Ted. I appreciate your helping me out here."

"It looks like you've been a pretty busy lady today. I don't mind telling you I'm a bit jealous."

"You know how cases run in spurts. I sometimes go weeks without an elective case. It seems that everyone wants their surgery between Thanksgiving and Christmas." Alex paused. "Frankly, I'm not expecting an easy time here. I'm glad to have your experience on the other side of the table."

"Hey, don't look to me for guidance—I'm just crew. You're the captain of the ship!" Ted said, referring to a term from the earlier days of medicine, where the primary surgeon was responsible for everything in the operating room, from the anesthesia to the counting of instruments.

In the current age, the legal system was beginning to recognize the split responsibilities of the various specialists in the confines of the operating room, so as not to saddle the primary surgeon with all of the burden.

"Well, despite your humility," Alex continued, "I'm glad to have you on board."

"Aye, aye, Captain."

The circulating nurse who would be helping on the case stuck her head through the door of the lounge.

"We're ready for you, Dr. Faber."

Alex and Ted headed down the hall for what would be a very long afternoon.

Phil Lambert had returned from the deposition feeling about as glum about the Uber case as ever. Stanislav's techniques, combined with the selected leaks to the local paper, had their desired effect. In addition to *the Breedville Bugle's* original piece on the impending lawsuit, the newspaper went on to run a review of the entire field of medical malpractice, consisting of a series of articles showing the many facets of the controversial topic. Each of the articles referenced back to the Mark Uber case to provide continuity, and also to take advantage of the hottest news to hit Breedville in quite some time.

Joshua stopped by Phil's office a few days after the deposition to see how he was doing. He had been worried about Phil ever since Thanksgiving, which the Lambert and Barron families had celebrated together. Alex had also been invited, but several deliveries that day found her eating cafeteria turkey with the staff members who had been unlucky enough to work the holiday.

At the dinner table, Phil could not stop obsessing about malpractice and the legal system. Whenever the conversation went in any other direction, Phil just sat quietly, eating little and staring out into space. After dinner, he excused himself due to a bad headache and took a nap in one of the bedrooms, leaving the kids to watch a video and the rest of the adults to clean up.

When Joshua arrived at Phil's office, the front door was open. The receptionist and nurse had left for the day.

"Hello, Phil, anybody here?" Joshua called out in the silent office.

"I'm back here, Joshua," Phil replied. Joshua found his friend sitting at his desk, a huge pile of patient charts in front of him.

"Looks like you've got a little work to do, Phil," Joshua remarked. He was no stranger to the paper work that marked a busy medical practice, a task usually relegated to the end of the day.

"Oh, I'm all finished with my work for the day," Phil said. "These are charts of patients whom I've take care of in the past several years who had pleasant outcomes. Remember Mrs. Macklin, your pregnant lady with the viral cardiomyopathy? She went into heart failure just after the delivery. I remember both of us taking turns holding her hand in the ICU. It took a lot of work, but she finally pulled through. I saw her several weeks ago and she looks great!"

"Why are you going through these now, Phil?" Joshua asked gently.

"I dunno. Just felt the need to remind myself that I'm not that horrible doctor they're writing about in the paper."

"How did the deposition go? You never told me about it."

Phil put down Mrs. Macklin's file. "He's a real shark, Josh. Everything you heard about him is true. And after chewing me up and spitting me out, he offered me his hand and tells me about justice being served."

"Well what about your lawyer? He must have stepped in to help."

"Are you kidding?" Phil laughed. "First of all, I don't have a lawyer. The insurance company has a lawyer. As I'm walking out, feeling like shit, he and Stanislav are talking about a racquetball tournament that night at the club! When a doctor and two lawyers show up together, Josh, it's always two against one. And guess who the 'one' is."

"Maybe you should get your own lawyer?" Joshua suggested.

"No, no. The best thing that can happen at this point would be a settlement. I can't prolong it. I'm just afraid the insurance company won't see it that way and will push to keep this thing going all the way to trial."

"Have you spoken to your lawyer since the deposition?"

"Yeah. He thinks this one is winnable. I agree it may very well be, but it could be over my dead body," Phil said morosely.

Joshua rose to leave. "Well, I'm heading home. I'll see you around, pal. Just wanted to stop by and say hello. Let me know if I can do anything for you. I'll speak to my brother. He's a lawyer in Boston. Maybe he'd have a suggestion for someone up here who could be on your side."

As he left Phil's office, he could hear his friend quietly mumbling to himself as he sifted through patient files, trying to recapture the confidence he once had.

A sedated Wendy Butler was more asleep than awake when her gurney was wheeled into the operating room. She was unaware of being moved from the stretcher to the table, and could not feel the various wires and plates that were attached to her near-naked body. The sterile green tile of the room, the bright circular lights beaming down on her and the glimmer of cold stainless steel instruments did not disturb her semi-conscious state. Even the masked strangers hovering over did not disturb her relaxed countenance. The medication that Dr. John Stands had ordered was clearly doing its job.

"Wendy, you will be going to sleep now," Dr. Stands said to his patient. "You may notice a garlic taste in your mouth. Everything will be just fine and we'll take good care of you." With that he injected the pentathol into the intravenous tubing, checking Wendy's conscious level by brushing her eyelashes with his finger until no reaction occurred. The succinylcholine drip began to have its effect as her whole body twitched, her nervous system discharging multiple stimulations to her musculature as the paralyzing drug turned the system off. Wendy was now fully dependent on the anesthesiologist. John Stands hyper extended her head, sliding the laryngoscope into the back of her throat to visualize her vocal cords and the all-important windpipe below. With the dexterity and confidence of years of experience, he slipped the endotracheal tube into her windpipe, blowing up the cuff to prevent its slippage while removing the laryngoscope at the same time. He connected the other end of the tube to the respirator and listened carefully over her chest for the rush of oxygen entering her lungs to confirm its correct placement.

The sheets were pulled back, exposing Wendy's lower half. Her breasts remained covered, confirming that there was still some appreciation for the patient's dignity. She was moved into a frog-legged position in order to insert a catheter into her bladder. This would keep it from interfering in the surgical field and decrease its risk of injury. The vagina was then washed out with an iodine solution and her legs repositioned on the table, a velcro strap holding them in place.

Alex would be making a pfannensteil incision for the entrance into the abdomen, necessitating the shaving of much of Wendy's pubic hair. This incision was aptly nicknamed a "bikini" incision. After a vigorous washing of her abdomen with the iodine solution, the paper drapes were placed, exposing only the field of the operation. By this time, the surgeons had entered the operating room and were scrubbed, gowned and gloved.

Alex turned to the head of the table. "May we start, Dr. Stands?"

"Any time, Dr. Faber."

With that, the surgery began.

The strong and loving support of her husband was the only thing that helped Amanda Perkins through the aftermath of her assault. The fact that the police had been unable to find a suspect did not help her psyche. Her mind replayed the horror many times, always finishing with the assailant's last words, "Hope to see you again someday." That thought alone made it difficult for Amanda to venture out on her own, and she sought the companionship of her husband on even the most minor of errands.

Throughout it all, Amanda was still quite confident that the baby she was carrying was her husband's. Todd was less convinced. After meeting with Joshua at the end of October, the two had spent many hours agonizing over the decision to check the tissue typing of the fetus to confirm paternity. Joshua had reassured them that chorionic villus sampling carried a very low chance of miscarriage, and that they were fortunate to have a local physician who had been trained in this procedure. After much persuasion, Todd was finally able to convince Amanda to have the testing done.

Joshua was happy to hear that Amanda had agreed with her husband's wishes. He was no close friend of Gerald Ransom's, but he was a practical man, and was aware of Gerald's experience in this technique due to his perinatology fellowship. He felt that Amanda would be more comfortable and better off having the test done in Breedville, rather than have to venture to a large hospital center. He had set up an appointment for both of them to see Gerald just after Thanksgiving, when she was ten weeks pregnant.

On the day of the test, the couple met Gerald in the radiology department of the hospital. The ultrasound technician had been sent to Boston over the summer at Gerald's insistence to learn chorionic villus sampling from the same people he had worked with. The technique required a close coordination between ultrasonographer and physician. They had performed nearly a dozen procedures together over the past few months and were comfortable working together.

Amanda had been instructed not to empty her bladder for at least two hours prior to the procedure, so she was feeling somewhat uncomfortable when they arrived at the hospital. Unfortunately, a full bladder was necessary to visualize the pregnancy at such an early gestation. She was placed on an examining table with her knees lying over special supports to keep them up and out of the way. The ultrasonographer took several pictures of the pregnancy, documenting the gestational age and the location of the placenta. Gerald sat at the end of the table, between Amanda's legs. He placed a speculum into her vagina, visualizing the cervix. After clearing out the mucus and painting the area with an antiseptic solution, he gently inserted a plastic catheter through the cervix and up into the placental bed. While viewing the placement of the catheter on the ultrasound screen, he applied suction to the tube, dragging the catheter over the placental site and removing a small amount of tissue. When he was satisfied that he had an adequate sample, he removed the catheter.

The parents could see the fetus bouncing around in the amniotic sac, apparently oblivious to the presence of the foreign intruder in its protected world. Amanda was relieved that the procedure had gone so quickly and painlessly, and thanked Gerald profusely, complimenting him on his expertise.

"There is no substitute for good training and experience," Gerald said to his captive audience. "It's amazing what can be done nowadays, given the level of technology and expertise in the field of obstetrics," he continued. "With my special training, I am able to bring the cutting edge of progress to Breedville and even the most uncomplicated of my obstetrical patients is able to benefit."

"I'm sure that's the case, Dr. Ransom," Amanda said. "And if I didn't think the world of Dr. Barron, which I do, I would consider having you take care of my pregnancy."

Even Gerald realized that he may have gone a bit too far.

"I appreciate the compliment, Mrs. Perkins. But I can assure you that you are in excellent hands"

"Thank you, Dr. Ransom. I appreciate it."

"I should have the report within a week and will give it to Dr. Barron. He will contact you with the results. You may notice a small amount of bleeding over the next few days—that is completely normal. If you develop heavy bleeding, bad cramps or a fever over 100.4 degrees, call my office immediately and you will be seen right away."

"Thank you again, Dr. Ransom."

"I'm glad to be of help, Mrs. Perkins, Mr. Perkins." With that, Gerald left the procedure room.

"He certainly thinks a lot of himself," Amanda said to the ultrasonographer.

"Yes he does," she agreed. "He's received excellent training and is a real asset to the hospital." She added with a smile, "They just don't have a humility course in Boston!"

Meanwhile, Alex's case in the operating room was moving as slowly as she had feared. Because this was Wendy Butler's first abdominal surgery, the opening of the abdominal wall with its many tissue layers had gone smoothly. But once the peritoneal cavity was opened, Alex could see massive adhesions and scarring from her years of endometriosis. In a normal, healthy pelvis, she would have found both ovaries and tubes hanging freely from their attachments and a clear space between the lower bowel and the back of the uterus. Likewise, the bladder would be freely dissectible off the front of the uterine wall. But twelve years of endometriosis had bound her tubes and ovaries to the side walls of her abdomen, and the bowel was connected with dense adhesions to the uterus, obliterating the usual space between the two and making the dissection far more difficult. Alex slowly dissected the bowel free from the pelvic structures, avoiding injury as she progressed. Having Ted Dennis in assistance was a great benefit, since he had the expertise to recognize and repair bowel problems, should they occur.

After a tedious hour of dissection, Alex was able to free up the uterus, left tube and ovary, and was in the process of clamping, cutting and tying off the support structures to the diseased organs. The right ovary and tube were hopelessly attached to the wall, and were left in place until the rest of the case was finished. With some difficulty, the bladder was dissected free of the uterus. By the end of the second hour, Alex had reached the top of the vagina and had removed the uterus, left tube and ovary from the surgical field.

With the bleeding under control, she focused her attention on the right tube and ovary. The paramount concern was the location of the ureter, a tubular structure that traversed below the adherent organs, transporting urine from the kidney to the bladder. Care needed to be taken to remove the tube and ovary without compromising the integrity of the ureter. Ted was impressed not only by Alex's surgical skills, but also by her grasp of anatomy. She slowly opened the space where the ureter lay, and followed this important tube down into the mass that had been Wendy's right tube and ovary. At this point the anatomy became quite distorted, but through perseverance and patience, she was able to free up the diseased organs and remove them from the field. What was left behind was a bed of bleeding and traumatized tissue. Through the use of fine suture and surgical clips, the bleeding was stopped and Alex was able to reapproximate the distorted anatomy.

Alex was concerned with a small amount of fluid leaking at the operative site. It was not bloody in nature. Fearing that she may have injured the ureter, she requested that the anesthesiologist inject a blue dye intravenously, which would be picked up by the kidneys and shuttled off to the bladder. If a ureter was cut, the blue dye would enter the operative field. John Stands injected the dye she had requested. As feared, after several minutes the operative site turned a bright blue.

Ron Dorcik couldn't get his mind off of his dinner with Alex. She was still as beautiful as the day he had met her at Columbia. Despite the years, he'd never managed to get over her. Her sudden request for a divorce had left him shocked and confused. The intervening years left his questions unanswered. He dated other women, but was never able to find the same spark and passion. Several relationships developed, but none to the point of commitment. He had moved on from Greenwich to take over a struggling Catholic hospital in Hartford. During his tenure, he turned things around as the fledgling hospital progressed to become a dominant player in the Hartford medical community. Its affiliation with the University of Connecticut Health Sciences, a move nurtured to fruition through gentle but persistent negotiation on his part, gave the hospital a status it had never enjoyed before. The board of directors wanted him to stay on indefinitely, but Ron had heard through his contacts in New York City that Alex had moved on to Breedville. As luck would have it, they were looking for a new administrator. He knew it was a step backwards in his career. There would be less money and less opportunity for advancement. But he would be close to Alex, and Ron felt a need to fill the one remaining void in his life. Of course he hadn't yet admitted this to her. He would bide his time. And even if it didn't work out, just being near her might be reward enough.

Ron was in a good mood, and whistled to himself as he arrived at his office. At first he didn't notice the two police detectives waiting in the administrative lobby.

"Mr. Dorcik," Mitchell called, crossing the lobby to catch up with Ron. "I wonder if my partner and I could have a moment with you."

"Sure, Detective," Ron answered, checking his watch. "I have a little time before my first meeting."

"Mr. Dorcik, this is my partner, Detective Walter Fallon."

"Nice to meet you, Detective," Ron put out his hand. "How's your investigation going?"

"Slowly, Mr. Dorcik," Mitchell answered. He swallowed. "Walter and I would like to ask you a few questions, if it is okay."

"Certainly. I'm looking forward to this case being closed. I don't have to tell you how the heightened security is spooking our staff and patients." The two detectives joined Ron in his office. Mitchell took out a leather notebook.

"I was wondering if you could tell us anything about the serial rapes that occurred in the vicinity of Charity Hospital in Hartford earlier this year?" Ron's countenance immediately darkened.

"Why would you be interested in that, Detective?"

"Well, we reviewed the report from the Federal Government, and there are a lot of similarities between the assaults in Hartford and what we have been experiencing up here," Mitchell answered. Walter remained quiet.

"What are you suggesting?" Ron asked.

Walter spoke up. "The facts, Mr. Dorcik, are as follows. Both series of rapes either took place on hospital campuses or the victims were kidnapped at those locations. The perpetrator raped his victims, using a knife as a threat of force. None of the victims were robbed or physically harmed except for the sexual assault. The perpetrator could not be identified by any of the victims because he was wearing a ski mask. And there have been no further rapes in the Hartford area since May of this year. The first assault in Breedville took place in July." Walter paused. "Can you tell us what happened in Hartford?"

Ron didn't know what to say. He was aghast that the police would actually consider him a suspect.

"There is nothing I can add to what you already know about the assaults in Hartford. I really have nothing to hide."

"That's good 'cause we have a search warrant with us and would like to look around your office." Ron looked at the official document.

"Go ahead," he said, his face turning red. "I had nothing to do with these crimes."

"Thank you for your cooperation, Mr. Dorcik. This won't take long."

Mitchell and Walter rose from their seats and began to scour the room. Walter started in the closet while Mitchell perused the bookshelves and the area behind the desk. It was behind a stack of files in the bottom drawer of his desk that they found a black ski mask and a hunting knife.

"Mr. Dorcik," Mitchell asked. "Do these items belong to you?"

"I've . . . I've never seen them before!" Ron stammered. "Someone must be trying to set me up!" His voice reeked of panic. Walter took out the Miranda paper.

"Mr. Dorcik, you are being arrested for suspicion of rape and assault with intent to harm. You have the right to remain silent. Anything you say may and will be used against you in a court of law. You have the right to an attorney. Should you not be able to afford counsel, a lawyer will be appointed by the court." Ron's hands were cuffed and he was led out past his speechless secretary.

With the bluish discoloration spreading over the operative field, Alex's worst fears were realized: she had injured the ureter. She would have to call in Frank DiMento for help closing the defect. Ted Dennis had come to the same conclusion, although he was unaware of Alex's feelings of discomfort having Frank joining her in the operating room.

Alex turned to the circulating nurse. "Pat, you want to see if Dr. DiMento is available? I've got a severed ureter."

"Sure thing, Dr. Faber." She left the room.

"Well Ted, I guess I've kept you here long enough. I'll be able to finish closing with Frank once the ureter is fixed. I'm sure I've got at least another hour before I'll be through. I appreciate your help."

"It was my pleasure, Alex. You've got a great pair of hands. Sorry about the ureter. I'm sure Frank will be able to help you here."

Ted broke scrub, removed his gown and left the operating room, but not before pulling the insurance information on Wendy Butler for his office.

"Dr. DiMento will be here in ten minutes, Dr. Faber," Pat said, re-entering the operating room.

Alex used the time to finish cleaning up any remaining bleeding sites. She had Pat reposition the patient with her legs in stirrups and pull out the urinary catheter so Frank would be able to visualize the bladder and slip a ureteral stent up the right side. The purpose of the stent was to keep the severed ends of the ureter approximated while he sewed them together and to provide a splint during the healing process. They were just finishing up when Frank arrived.

"Hi, Alex. Understand you've got a little problem."

"I'm afraid so," answered Alex. "I've got a severed ureter on the right side."

"No problem for old Frank DiMento!" he said, beginning to scrub. "Let me just wash up a bit." Frank scrubbed up. The nurses gowned and gloved him and he took his place opposite Alex on the right side of the patient.

"Let me get you up to date," Alex suggested. "She's a thirty six year old white female with a long history of endometriosis. I was performing a total abdominal hysterectomy with bilateral salpingo-oophorectomy. She had massive adhesions along the right sidewall and in removing the tube and ovary I must have opened into the right ureter, as amply demonstrated by the blue staining of the indigo-carmine dye."

"What about the left ureter, Alex? Any problem there?"

"I don't think so. I had very little trouble removing the left tube and ovary. All of the adhesions were on the right and between the bowel and uterus. Ted helped me with those."

As she had anticipated, Frank wanted to view the inside of the bladder and pass ureteral stents up both sides, just to make sure there was no compromise to the left ureter that had gone unnoticed. It only took a few minutes for the placement of the stents. Frank quickly saw that the left ureter had not been harmed. The two surgeons changed sides so Frank could more easily visualize the injured right ureter. Alex helped him free up the tissue surrounding the injury, making the site more accessible. Using very fine suture material with the aid of magnifying loops, Frank repaired the injured ureter. The two surgeons finished closing the abdomen without further problems and Frank left the ureteral stents in place with the intention of removing them after several days. The urinary catheter was replaced and dressings applied. Alex looked up at the clock, noting that she had been in the operating room for over three and a half hours.

She was surprised. Frank had been a total gentleman.

"That's one I owe you, Frank," she said and smiled.

"You bet, Alex," Frank said, giving her a wink.

Despite being grateful for Frank's performance, Alex regretted her comment the moment it left her lips. Frank DiMento certainly didn't need any added encouragement. The exhausted gynecologist left for the recovery room where she wrote her postoperative orders and dictated the operative note. With Wendy Butler coming out of anesthesia in the recovery room, Alex felt comfortable leaving her and went to find her husband. Bob was waiting in the lobby, and was very relieved to hear that the surgery had gone well. Alex did mention the injury to the ureter, and that it had been recognized and fixed on the spot. Wendy should, Alex predicted, have no problems from the mishap. She returned to the surgeon's lounge.

Alex took a few minutes to relax. She propped her tired feet up on the table and sipped a cup of coffee. The door opened and Frank walked in. He was still in his scrub suit with a big smile on his face.

"Thanks again, Frank. I appreciate your help," Alex said cautiously.

"No problem honey. Frank is at your service!" he said, his smile growing even brighter. Frank moved over to Alex and put his hands on her shoulders as if to initiate a massage. He leaned over slightly to peek down the front of her scrub suit. Alex sat up quickly.

"Frank, what do you think you're doing?"

"You look like you need a little massage, Alex. You spent a long time in the operating room. Must be stiff," he said slyly, keeping a firm grip on her shoulders and pushing her back down into the chair.

"Thanks anyway, Frank," Alex said, trying to sit up again. "I'm fine, really." She didn't feel like making a scene, but her blood was boiling.

"Then let's say I'm collecting the one you owe me!" he said as he swung around to face Alex, pulling her close and kissing her aggressively. Alex pulled away and clawed free from his grasp.

"Cut it out, Frank," she hissed. "Now!"

"What's the matter, Babe?" Frank said, towering over her. "First you smile at me and say you owe me and when I respond, you cut me off. I'm not a faucet. You can't just turn Frank on and off."

"Then let me just turn you off, Frank. I don't want any trouble," Alex breathed, adjusting her scrubs and putting her hair back in place.

"Well, I do," he shot back, moving in on her, backing her up to the wall. He reached for her shoulders and began kissing her neck.

"Stop it, Frank! Stop it or I swear I'll scream!"

But Frank could hear nothing at this point. His mouth was firmly secured to the base of her neck and her struggling only intensified his need to possess her. He pushed his body up against hers, sandwiching her between himself and the wall. Alex was not strong enough to push him off, but a quick knee to the groin sent him reeling backwards. With the wind knocked out of him, Alex regained her composure. She bent over the urologist who was now cringing in extreme pain.

"You're right, Frank. I do owe you." Alex whispered as she caught her breath. "I won't report you to the administration or the police. But don't you dare try this again." She fixed him with her ice blue eyes and slapped him across the face. "Now we're even." She turned and walked out of the lounge, leaving the stunned urologist to nurse his wounds.

Chapter Twenty Three

THE PEOPLE OF BREEDVILLE, New Hampshire could usually expect the first snowfall just before Thanksgiving. This year, winter was delayed. Some thought it was the doing of the much talked about Greenhouse Effect. But a close reading of the Farmer's Almanac clearly stated that winter would come late this year, so no one was surprised when a green Thanksgiving was upon them. Two weeks later, the white stuff began to fall. There wasn't much accumulation the first time. Just enough to remind everyone to check their coal and wood supplies, get the snow tires on and make room for the shovels and the sleds in the garage.

Joshua headed down Main Street in his four-wheel drive Cherokee, planning to get to the office a half hour early to prepare for his visit with Todd and Amanda Perkins. They had made an appointment to review the findings of the chorionic villus sampling one week after the procedure. Gerald called Joshua the night before to let him in on the bad news; Todd was not the father. Joshua was prepared to offer Amanda an immediate abortion. What he was not prepared for was the couple's reaction to the news.

"Frankly, Dr. Barron, I don't see how this makes much of a difference," Amanda stated. Her voice was devoid of emotion. "This is our baby. We have waited a long time for this, and Todd and I are thrilled over this pregnancy." She turned to her husband. "Isn't that right?"

Todd was slow to speak. "Amanda and I have done a lot of soul searching this past week," he finally said. "This child is only going to know us as its parents. We have a lot of love to offer and we are desperate to share it." His face looked dark and sunken. "God can work in strange ways. Despite the horror of the attack, we need to believe that it will bring something joyful into our life."

Todd swallowed. "We can live with the fact that I am not the biological father of this baby."

Joshua was speechless for a moment. He saw sadness and anger in Todd's eyes, but forced himself to believe the words he had spoken. This was the Perkins' decision, not his own. He gathered his thoughts. "I would be lying to say that I am not surprised by your reaction and your choice," Joshua told them. "But I am glad that you have been able to handle the trauma and make the very best of a difficult situation. Of course this information will remain strictly confidential and I am looking forward to providing you with your prenatal care, Amanda."

"Thank you, Dr. Barron. We appreciate your support. We know you may not agree with us, but we are very grateful to you for everything you have done. I'm looking forward to joining the ranks of your pregnant brigade!"

"In that case, why don't I have Lois set you up for a full prenatal physical examination and then we can talk further about what you can expect over the ensuing months." He picked up the test results from the chorionic villus sampling. "As far as I am concerned, these findings no longer pertain to our work here. But they do allow us to know the sex of the baby. Would you like to know?"

Amanda looked at her husband. "No, thank you, Dr. Barron. Todd and I can wait till the delivery."

Joshua looked at Todd, who nodded in grim agreement.

In Concord, four lawyers were gathered around the conference table where Phil Lambert was methodically dissected two weeks earlier. A light snow fell outside. The table was strewn with files, each representing an outstanding case. Two of the lawyers had already spoken, and now it was Jeffrey Stanislav's turn to update his partners.

"Moving on to the Uber case. The insurance company is giving me a hard time with this one. We've got the cardiologist right where we want him, though. We just need to convince them to settle."

"Do you really think they would?" asked Stan Ferguson, who was seated to Stanislav's right. "Why should they? You and I both know the case has little merit. Would *you* settle if you were them?"

"Course not," he answered with a snort. "But if I were in their shoes, I wouldn't be in this fancy office!" The partners chuckled.

"It seemed to me like this would be a straightforward 'bad result' case. And usually they're willing to settle on those. I've got a relatively young guy without any previous health problems—he shows up at the hospital and is dead within an hour and a half from a missed diagnosis. This should be open and shut."

"Has there been any further play by the press in town?" asked Stan.

"Unfortunately not. It's old news at this point. Maybe it's time to leak a little more information?" Stanislav asked, looking around for guidance.

"You're going to have to do something. Otherwise, if the cardiologist doesn't put any more pressure on the insurance company, we could be stuck going to trial on a case we can't win in court," Victor offered.

"Come on, Vic," Stanislav said to his partner. "You know very well that we don't want to go to court with this case—or any case for that matter! We just have to use pressure and strategy to get a settlement. Frankly, I can't remember the last time I went to court on a medical malpractice case!"

"What about that expert witness you deposed a few days ago?" Ed Grant asked. "Didn't he have any good ammunition?"

"Not really. Nothing the insurance company would buy. I'm afraid old Doc Kelly isn't the heavy weight expert witness he used to be. We're going to have to find someone else to put on the payroll, someone whose academic credits are a little more current. Kelly hasn't practiced medicine in ages—I don't think he could find his way through the front door of a hospital. The man needs to be put out to pasture."

"Didn't Kelly see something that could suggest a misread x-ray—something about air under the diaphragm that would suggest a perforated stomach or bowel?" Ed continued.

"Well, I thought I was on to something there," Stanislav answered. "But as it turns out, air under the diaphragm can just as easily be a stomach bubble, which is perfectly normal according to our radiology source. It wouldn't hold up." Stanislav sighed, sifting through his copies of The *Breedville* Bugle articles. "But our friends at the paper might like a little more trash for their rag!" he said, waving the newsprint in the air. "They're certainly not going to be as critical as the insurance company experts. Maybe one more article will be enough to push our little cardiologist to get them to settle. It's worth a try!"

"Indeed! Keep us posted," Stan said. "Now, what about that kid delivered in Manchester with cerebral palsy? How's that case going?"

"Now there's a case dear to my heart, gentlemen. With a little luck, we won't need to take another case for six months!" The partners laughed in unison as their meeting continued, a typical morning at Stanislav, Victor, Ferguson and Grant.

Luckily, the snow stopped early enough so the December dance at Breedville High School was still on. Julie Barron was up in her bedroom putting on the final touches before Sally's parents arrived to take them to the dance. Sally had never told them about the party she threw the weekend they were away, and Elizabeth hadn't mentioned it to them either. Despite Julie's concerns over missing Sally's party, she did not have to show up at school that Monday with a paper bag over her head, and her popularity had not dropped noticeably. Brad was as interested in her as ever, and things were back to normal.

As Julie was changing her purse to match her new sweater, she noticed the condom that Alex had given her at the office. She held it for a moment, feeling its round shape beneath the slick plastic, then put it into her bag for the evening. Just then, she heard the honk outside and ran down to greet her friend.

"I'm leaving!" Julie called out to her parents. "I should be home by 11:30!"

"Have a good time!" Liz called as Julie breezed out the door.

The December dance was not much different than the others Julie had attended earlier in the year. The music was loud, the lights were low and the chaperones were all in one corner, drinking coffee and trying to talk above the noise. The fast dances had a tendency to separate the troops into their respective sexes, while the slow dances found the kids so tightly intermingled that they appeared to dance as one. One of those interlocked couples on the dance floor was Julie and Brad. As the evening wore on, the slow dances began to outnumber the fast ones, giving the two teenagers much opportunity for close physical contact. Each dance ended with a deep kiss as their hormones rose higher and higher.

"Let's get out of here, Julie," Brad whispered.

"Where can we go?" she asked.

"Just come with me. I know where we can go," Brad reassured.

The teenagers headed down the hall, the music from the cafeteria fading as they turned several corners. Brad pushed open the door of the exercise and weight room.

"Are you sure we can be here?" Julie asked, her heart starting to race with the excitement of the moment.

"Trust me, Julie. It's fine. No one will bother us here," Brad said, walking her over to the mats on the floor.

Before she could think, he was on top of her. Brad reached up under her sweater and bra. His groin became hotter and stiffer as the two rolled around on the mat, giving and receiving the pleasure of the moment. He unbuckled his pants, slipping his jeans and underwear off. He then did the same for her.

"I don't know if we should be doing this, Brad," Julie said, though her breathy excitement didn't sound convincing.

"We love each other, Julie. That makes it right," Brad said softly as he continued to remove her clothes. The condom lay worthlessly in Julie's purse, still tucked away on the bleachers in the high school gym.

He entered her. The feeling was just as sweet as they both remembered it from the fourth of July.

"I love you," Julie moaned. Brad could not answer. It was taking all of his will power not to come quickly. But he was no match for his passion and soon he had released all of his tension within her yielding body. The two lay back, exhausted.

Their moment was interrupted by the sound of voices in the hall. They quickly dressed and slipped out the door unseen. Julie and Brad walked slowly back to the dance, her head on his shoulder, his arm around her in protective fashion.

"Where have you guys been?" It was Debbie. "My parents are ready to leave and we've been looking around all over for you."

"I'm sorry, Debbie. We just lost track of time." She turned to Brad, beaming. "I'll see you later."

"Take care, Julie." The two kissed and Julie left with her friends.

The light snow made a winter wonderland that was just right for an early evening walk. Arm in arm, Todd and Amanda Perkins covered the two miles from their home to the town green and back in just under thirty minutes. Amanda was in a wonderful mood, and her lively chatter filled the air between them as they went. Todd was, for the most part, silent.

"You're not upset that we don't know whether it's a boy or a girl, are you?" Amanda asked. "I just thought it would be such a fun surprise!" she continued, not waiting for her husband's response. "We can decorate the nursery in yellows, maybe greens—I think that would be so adorable, and less expected, you know? Maybe we can start decorating next weekend!"

The ski mask was black. The features of the malicious creature were distorted, unidentifiable. But Todd could see his eyes—hateful slits peering through the darkness. Eyeing his wife, like a piece of juicy meat for the taking.

"I'm so happy that we are going to keep this baby. I can't tell you what this means to me. I know it has been difficult, Todd, but you're going to be such a good daddy!"

"I hope so, honey."

Before those hateful snake-like eyes flashed a knife—stainless steel, glittering like a jewel. He saw it slice through the air, dancing up so close to her neck that it pressed ever so lightly into the soft white flesh. He heard the sound of a scream flying out into an answerless dark.

"Dr. Barron told me that my physical exam was completely normal," Amanda chattered. "The baby is perfect and healthy! He said that I should have no problems carrying the pregnancy." She reached down and took Todd's hand.

"That's very reassuring, Dear."

His wife lay naked and helpless in a barren, dusty ditch, legs spread open.

The creature with the black mask and the slitted eyes pierced her, again and again and again. A faint drumming sound pulsed in the background. As the grin on the creature's face grew with each thrust, the drumming in Todd's head began to beat louder.

Their walk concluded with Amanda flying high. It was just getting dark when they reached home, and after removing their coats and boots, the couple retired to the bedroom for the evening.

"Honey, you don't think I look too fat, do you?" Amanda asked as she studied herself in the full-length mirror. She was holding a pair of pink flowered pajama pants, wearing just underwear from the waist down.

The slitted eyes and glittering knife flashed wildly. The drum beat louder.

"You look beautiful, Amanda. I've never seen you look more beautiful."

She slipped on her pajama bottoms and got under the covers. "It's cold, Todd. Come cuddle up with me! You always make the bed so much warmer."

"I'll be right there, Amanda." *His wife's legs were spread wide, the creature with the slitted eyes repeatedly penetrating her.*

Todd joined her in bed. She reached over and kissed him.

"I love you, Todd"

"I love you too, Amanda." *The drumming was reaching a crescendo. The images of the ski mask, the slitted eyes, the repeated penetration of his precious wife. The drum roar was overwhelming.* He reached over to the drawer in his nightstand and took out a .38 caliber pistol. He brought the cold barrel to the side of his sleeping wife's temple.

"Please forgive me, Amanda. I love you so!"

He pulled the trigger. The sharp crack stopped the drum rolling in his head. He felt his wife's body go stiff and then limp as a curtain of blood shrouded the bed.

He then turned the gun on himself, enveloping the barrel with his mouth. He pulled the trigger again.

CHAPTER TWENTY FOUR

I T WAS THE MOST newsworthy week in the history of *The Breedville Bugle*. Normally, their stories involved local politics, fundraisers and state and national news. A local fire or town vandalism was destined for the front page. The series of rapes over the summer had been the biggest story the town had seen in decades, and the last attack had been over two months ago. But during the second week of December, the news was hot every morning, and Breedville's residents were hustling to their front lawns and newsstands to keep up.

"Local Librarian and Husband Found
Dead in Apparent Murder-Suicide"

Amanda and Todd Perkins were discovered dead in their bedroom late last night by neighbor Alfred Sutton, who heard gunshots fired at 44 Elm Street. Sutton stated to police that he heard two gunshots around 10:30 PM. Police found the body of Amanda Perkins in her bed, a single bullet

wound to the head. Her husband was found next to her, a .38 caliber pistol in his hand, victim of an apparent suicide.

The case is still under investigation by the Breedville Police Department. Murder and suicide appear to be the leading theory. No motive has been disclosed, though it has come to the attention of the Bugle that Amanda Perkins was two to three months pregnant at the time of her death. Autopsies are scheduled for later today.

Neighbors are reportedly shocked by this violent act, many who commented that Todd and Amanda Perkins appeared to be a loving couple.

The article included no mention of the attack on Amanda Perkins several months earlier, nor any further details about her pregnancy or the chorionic villus sampling test. However, Amanda had disclosed these pieces of personal information to a limited number of close friends. Word of this deeper plot must have gotten out, since it was only a matter of time until Joshua Barron was contacted by the paper for comment. Joshua had not yet seen the paper that morning.

"Dr. Barron, *The Bugle* is on line two," Ann Stremp reported to Joshua over the phone. "Shall I take a message or would you like to speak with them?" she asked.

Joshua sighed. "What could they want? I'll take it. Thanks, Ann." He clicked into line two. "This is Joshua Barron."

"Dr. Barron—this is Alan Richmond from *The Breedville Bugle* calling. I appreciate your time. I'm sorry to bother you, but I was wondering if you would care to comment on the deaths of Amanda and Todd Perkins. We understand she was a patient of yours, and had visited your office prior to her death last night."

"What?" Joshua exclaimed, feeling his stomach drop. "Amanda Perkins? Dead? Are you sure?"

"Yes, sir. She and her husband were found dead in their home last night, apparently the victims of a murder-suicide." The reporter paused, giving Joshua a moment to digest the news. "Can you think of any motivation Mr. Perkins might have to kill his wife and then himself? We understand you treated her following an assault several months ago. Could these events be related?"

"I'm sorry," Joshua sputtered, still in shock. "I don't feel that I can answer any questions at this time. Patient confidentiality bars me from disclosing any information pertaining to Mrs. Perkins' medical history or treatment under my care."

"But Dr. Barron," the reporter persisted. "Could her pregnancy have been a result of that assault?"

"I'm sorry. I can't answer any questions." With that, Joshua hung up.

Shortly thereafter, the police officer who had been at the emergency room the night of Amanda's rape arrived. Ann showed him into Joshua's office.

"Sorry to bother you, Doc," the officer apologized. "But I have a few questions to ask you about Amanda and Todd Perkins." The look of distress on Joshua's face told the officer that this news was fresh and painful. He took a seat and spoke gently. "Is there any information at all that you have that might help us with this case, Dr. Barron? I understand that Mr. and Mrs. Perkins had been here to see you yesterday. Can you tell me what was discussed at her appointment?"

Confidentiality was a moot point in light of his patient's death, though Joshua felt much more comfortable discussing it with the Breedville police than *The Bugle*. He told the officer all of the pertinent information that might have contributed to the tragedy. He disclosed details about Amanda's infertility treatments, her rape, the resulting pregnancy and even his suggestion for pregnancy termination. He concluded with the results of the chorionic villus sampling that he'd given the couple earlier the previous day.

"I probably should have been more suspicious of their reaction to such news—especially his," Joshua said, reflecting on Todd's shocking acceptance. "But they seemed so in love, so accepting of such an ironic twist in their infertility problem."

"Do you think Amanda was, you know, fooling around, and her husband had caught her at it?" the officer asked, trying to scour Joshua for any additional inkling he might have.

"No, definitely not. I believe Amanda's only sexual exposure outside of her marriage was on that dirt road several months ago." He gave a deep sigh. "Poor Todd. It must have been feeding on him all these weeks. The paternity test must have been the last straw. I can't imagine what it must have felt like. We so often forget that there are several victims involved in rape."

"Yeah, Doc," the patrolman said, matching Joshua's sigh with his own. "That's how I read it also." He stood up to leave. "I may need additional information later. Thanks for your help. I appreciate it." He left Joshua sitting at his desk, looking out the window at the snowy accumulation.

Over the following days, the paper continued to relay more details regarding the autopsies and theories on the motive for this tragic affair. But the Perkins drama was relegated to secondary status, due to further news on the continuing litigation involving Dr. Philip Lambert.

"Missed X-ray Finding May Have Led to Unnecessary Death"

Reliable sources have confirmed that a deposition taken recently by an expert witness regarding the medical malpractice case against local cardiologist, Dr. Philip Lambert, is quite damaging in its content. Allegedly, a chest x-ray obtained from the Garrison Breed General Hospital emergency room on the late Mark Uber demonstrated free air under the diaphragm. According to our medical sources, this sign points towards a perforated ulcer as the diagnosis for Mr. Uber's chest pain—not a heart attack. This finding allegedly was missed by Dr. Lambert when he reviewed the film prior to seeing Mr. Uber on the evening of July fourth. Dr. Lambert was unavailable

**for comment to confirm or deny this
latest allegation.**

Phil was home on his day off when the paper arrived with this latest lead article. Cindy, returning with the children from an afternoon of ice skating, found her husband asleep on his favorite chair in the study, a half empty bottle of scotch at his side and *The Breedville Bugle* on his lap.

"Go upstairs and start your homework," she told her brood. "I'll call you when dinner is ready."

After the kids disappeared upstairs, Cindy entered the study. Her eyes caught the latest headline, staring up at her defiantly from its perch on her husband's lap.

"Oh no!" she moaned, "Dear God, no more!" Cindy felt her heart sink as tears began to well up in her eyes. The smell of alcohol was pervasive and she had to shake her spouse several times to rouse him.

"Phil, wake up dear."

"Huh . . ." Phil sputtered, barely opening his eyes.

"Oh honey, I saw the article. I'm so sorry! Why can't they just leave you alone?" Phil's eyes were now open as his wife's tearful face came into focus.

"It's okay, hun. They can't do too much more to me." He reached up to stroke her hair. "I spoke to the lawyer at the insurance company and pleaded again to have them settle. But they're convinced they can win and plan on sticking it out. He was surprised how much information *The Bugle* got their hands on—he actually thought it was me feeding it to them!" Phil laughed, and pointed to the scotch bottle on the table. "My little friend here has made me realize that I'm just going to have to take control of my life and let the cards fall where they will. I still seem to have a few patients who want to see me. There is nothing more to do."

"Oh Phil," Cindy said, wrapping her arms around her husband. "I love you so much. I just hate to see you go through this pain."

He looked lovingly into her eyes. "It's okay, Cindy," Phil said with an expression of finality. "They can't hurt us anymore."

The week of news continued with photos from Todd and Amanda Perkins' funerals, as well as eulogies and updates on the on-going investigation. These stories disclosed information about Amanda's rape, her subsequent pregnancy and even the results of the chorionic villus biopsy. The press had been to see Gerald Ransom. Although he refused to discuss details of the Perkins' case, he went into a lengthy description of the procedure and the benefits to be derived from it, not failing to include that he was the only physician in the area capable of performing it.

Fortunately for Phil, there were no further articles on the Uber litigation case. Regardless, Breed General couldn't seem to keep its name out of the news, when a new astonishing headline appeared towards the end of the week.

"Hospital President Arrested On Serial Rape Charges"

Police have arrested Garrison Breed General Hospital President Ronald Dorcik on suspicion of rape. According to reports, a pattern of similar assaults occurred in Hartford,

Connecticut, where Mr. Dorcik previously held a similar position at Charity Hospital. These Hartford-based attacks have not recurred since Mr. Dorcik's departure from Charity Hospital and his subsequent arrival at Breed General this past July. After obtaining a search warrant, police found a ski mask and knife similar to those described by the victims in Mr. Dorcik's hospital office. Mr. Dorcik was released on $100,000 bail, pending his arraignment. The hospital released a statement from the Board of Trustees, stating full support of their President and expected acquittal of all charges. Regardless, Mr. Dorcik was temporarily suspended from his position with pay, pending the police investigation.

Alex was on her day off when the article hit. She sat at the kitchen table with her morning coffee in a state of utter disbelief. She kept reading the words, over and over, trying to sort out in her head how this could have happened. She was so wrapped up that she didn't hear the doorbell until the third ring. She finally opened the front door to find Ron Dorcik waiting for her.

"Alex, please let me in," he pleaded. "You're the only one I could think of coming to."

"Come in, come in," Alex beckoned, a million questions swirling in her head. Ron's eyes looked sunken, as though he hadn't slept. She led him to the kitchen. "What is this all about?"

"That's just it!" Ron cried, slumping into a chair. "I don't know!" he confessed. "A couple of weeks ago a Detective Karas met with me to review the assault cases. He was interested in seeing the hospital personnel files. The next thing I know, he and his partner are questioning me in my office. They had a search warrant and everything—and they go and find a ski mask and knife in my desk drawer!" Ron's eyes were red and his voice was filled with angry disbelief.

"I don't have the slightest idea how they got there. I was arrested immediately, and spent the night in jail before the hospital attorney could come and post bail. I didn't know where else to turn and so I came here. I'm sorry to drag you into this. But I'm innocent and I'm being set up. I just don't know by who or why."

Alex breathed a deep sigh. Up until six months ago, Ron Dorcik was out of her life. All of a sudden, he was back in it—and with a bang. She brought him a cup of coffee and sat down with him at the table.

"Do you want to work with the hospital attorney, or do you need to get your own? It sounds like that has to be your first decision here."

Ron looked up and extended his hand. "Do you believe me, Alex? That is the most important thing to me right now."

Alex looked at his kind, tired eyes. "I have no reason to believe otherwise. I just don't understand who would want to do this to you." Ron's shoulders visibly became more relaxed the moment Alex spoke. He took a sip of coffee. "Let me call Joshua and ask for his advice," Alex said. "He knows this community best and would probably have a recommendation for a good lawyer. I will get hold of him this morning.

Why don't you head on home—there's really nothing more you can do at this point. I will call you after I speak to Joshua."

"Thanks, Alex. You have no idea what your support means to me." A pause. "I should probably call my parents and try to explain this whole mess. My dad might know someone who can help me, too." His composure regained, Ron left Alex and returned home to take a hot shower.

The police investigation into the Perkins murder-suicide was just winding down. It was clear from the autopsies, ballistic tests and fingerprints that it was indeed Todd who had pulled the trigger both times. The facts relating to Amanda's rape, subsequent pregnancy and identification of paternity appeared to convince the authorities of motivation. A statement by a colleague of Todd's tied up any loose ends and completed the case. He said that Todd had been depressed at work recently and often discussed his difficulty coping with his wife's assault. The inability of the police to find a suspect only served to prolong Todd's agony, and without a target for his anger, all of his emotions were directed at his wife. Todd tried to suppress it all under a veil of support and understanding, but his true feelings were never far from the surface. He expressed his encouragement for Amanda to abort at Joshua Barron's suggestion, but backed off when she made it clear that she wanted to carry the pregnancy. Todd had further confided to his colleague that Amanda was having this special test to determine paternity and wasn't sure if he could deal with an adverse outcome.

Phil Lambert was feeling better than he had in months. His afternoon with the scotch bottle had opened up his eyes to what he had to do next. For several months his wife and children had been subjected to innumerable comments, suspicions and innuendoes over Phil's competence. The insurance company was making no effort to resolve the dispute that was threatening to drag on for some time. It had affected his self-confidence, causing him to question his medical judgment on many occasions. The newspaper seemed to be holding a public trial without benefit of due process. The case was damaging his relationship with his wife and children, occupying a significant portion of their waking hours as well as his sleep. He had felt powerless to stop the progression of events, but the scotch made him realize that he still had some control over the course of his life.

That Saturday afternoon, following the hectic week in Breedville, Cindy took the children Christmas shopping. They would return by dinnertime. Phil prepared his note of explanation and calmly went down into the garage. Leaving the door shut, he climbed into the driver's seat of his BMW, inserted his favorite Franz Liszt tape and turned on the engine. He listened peacefully to the strains of the Second Hungarian Rhapsody. As the composition moved to its exciting climax, the level of carbon monoxide in the garage reached a critical point and Phil Lambert went off to sleep.

CHAPTER TWENTY FIVE

"You know, Josh, Breedville is getting to be pretty well-known down here in Boston. Both the Perkins tragedy and the Dorcik case made the front section of the Boston Globe!" Stephen Barron said into the phone as he reached into the fridge to grab a Corona beer. He popped it open and settled into a soft leather easy chair in his living room.

Stephen Barron looked just like his older brother. Despite their age gap, Joshua's exercise regimen and proper eating habits had kept him looking younger, longer than his baby brother. These days, the two could nearly pass as twins. Stephen left the confines of Breedville for a post-graduate education in Boston, following in the footsteps of his older brother. But unlike Joshua, who he always kidded for having taken the easy way out, Stephen pursued a legal career and was now a litigation attorney for a large Boston-based firm. He swore to his brother that he would leave medical malpractice cases to his colleagues, spending most of his time doing corporate work. Never comfortable with the constraints of marriage, he moved from one long term affair to another, enjoying the city life from his high rise condominium overlooking Boston Harbor.

Joshua called Stephen several weeks ago to ask for advice on behalf of the beleaguered Phil. When Stephen heard that Jeffrey Stanislav was the plaintiff's attorney, he was more than willing to help out. Stephen was not alone in his dislike for Stanislav, feeling that his ambulance chasing tactics and megabucks mentality advertising was bringing disgrace to the entire profession of law. After getting Phil's consent, Stephen had been able to obtain copies of Mark Uber's medical records from the hospital, as well as the depositions which had been taken. Upon reviewing them, he found a case with absolutely no merits. He ran the facts by several of his partners who were involved in medical malpractice work and they agreed with his findings.

What disturbed Stephen most were the questionable sources that *The Breedville Bugle* continually quoted and the lackluster deposition of Dr. Kelly as an expert witness. He was able to pursue these two entities through his contacts with the American Medical Association and the Boston Globe, and much to his delight, found that Dr. Kelly was on the payroll of Stanislav's law firm as was an assistant editor for *The Breedville Bugle*. He was confident that Stanislav could be brought up on ethics charges by the New Hampshire Bar Association. One letter to the Chief Justice of the New Hampshire Supreme Court would probably take care of Stanislav's legal career, and Stephen was confident that with additional effort, other damaging facts would probably become available.

After spending some time putting together all of this information on the Uber case, Stephen was excited to call his brother with the update on his findings.

He felt strongly that if Stanislav were approached with this information, he would probably drop the charges and see that *The Bugle* set the record straight. Joshua was delighted with the news and told him to wait until he had spoken to Phil before making his next move.

After getting off the phone with his brother, Joshua hopped into his car and drove to Phil's house. For the first time in a while, Joshua felt incredibly positive and upbeat about the state of this whole mess. He was not prepared for what he found.

The door to the Lambert's house was unlocked, but no one answered when he called out. As he walked back to his jeep, Joshua heard the sound of a car engine in the garage, and saw a small amount of exhaust fumes escaping from beneath the garage door.

"Oh no, Phil!" Joshua cried. "God, no!" Joshua ran to the garage door, raising it as quickly as he could. The BMW engine was still running, the Liszt tape now on The Mephisto Waltz. He opened the driver's door to find his friend slumped down over the wheel. Joshua pulled Phil out of the car, dragging him out on to the driveway. He yelled to a passing neighbor to call for an ambulance and then evaluated his friend's medical status.

Phil's face was ashen, his lips blue. He was not breathing and he did not rouse when Joshua slapped his face with his hand. Joshua could feel a faint, thready pulse on the side of his neck and began mouth-to-mouth resuscitation. After several minutes, the pulse grew stronger, though Phil was still unresponsive and continued to require resuscitation. Joshua maintained the basic life saving maneuvers until the ambulance arrived. He quickly briefed the first EMT on the scene, who slipped an endotracheal tube into Phil's windpipe and began to bag him with oxygen. He was then taken to the hospital.

By the time they arrived, Phil was breathing on his own and beginning to wake up, fighting the endotracheal tube that was still in place. An intravenous line had been started in the ambulance. Blood gases were drawn in the emergency room, the breathing tube was pulled, and he was whisked up to the intensive care unit.

Sam Fellows was the internist accepting admissions from the emergency room when Phil was brought in. Joshua arrived at the intensive care unit just as Phil was being put into his bed. He briefed Sam.

"It sounds like you got there just in time, Joshua. He's a lucky guy, though he may not look at it that way when he's fully conscious, considering what he was trying to do."

"I know what you mean, Sam," Joshua shook his head, still a bit unnerved. "But suicide is no answer. Hopefully I'll be able to make him realize that once he's out of the woods. How does he look to you?"

"His blood gases were good and he's waking up. He never lost his pulse according to your report, so I would expect that he'll be fine. We'll just have to see once he's conscious enough to speak. I'll also have Joe Ryan from psychiatry stop by to see him in the morning."

"Thanks, Sam."

Joshua left his friend's side to call Liz and apprise her of the situation. Liz said she would go to the Lambert's home and wait for Cindy and the children. She expected them back soon, since the two couples had originally planned to go to the movies that evening. Instead, they would spend it at the hospital.

It was not until the following morning that Joshua was able to bring Phil up to date on the information from Stephen. Joshua found him sitting up in bed number one of the intensive care unit.

"What's a nice guy like you doing in a place like this?" Joshua said as he strolled in. The irony was not lost on Phil.

Phil smiled. "Joshua, I really can't thank you enough for what you did. Yesterday, suicide seemed like the perfect answer, the only answer."

He sighed. "But today really feels like a 'bonus' day. I think I'm going to be looking at every day of the rest of my life as a bonus. Seeing Cindy and the kids this morning made me realize how lucky I am that you came around when you did. I can't believe I did what I did. I can't believe choosing to never see them again." Phil's eyes watered slightly—he looked tired, but at peace. "I'm just going to have to learn to deal with my problems."

"Let me tell you why I came over yesterday." Joshua then gave Phil the complete update on all of Stephen's findings, as well as the plan to get Stanislav to drop charges.

"Does he really think it will work?" Phil asked, astonished to hear what Joshua had to tell him.

"He feels quite confident that it will, and frankly, he's looking forward to pulling the plug on Jeffrey Stanislav."

"With all due respect to your brother," Phil laughed, "I guess you need a shark to get a shark!"

"Only another shark knows the rules of the water! Certainly, we don't know them. So, do I have your permission to turn him loose?"

"Aye, aye Captain!" Phil saluted. "Full speed ahead." It was a bonus day for Phil Lambert, indeed.

Although he would not return to his practice for several weeks, Phil was stable enough to go home the following day. By Thursday, he received a letter from the defense attorney at the insurance company.

Dear Dr. Lambert:

I am delighted to inform you that all charges of medical malpractice against you in regard to the case of Mark Uber have been dropped. No settlement was made except the request that you agree not to counter-sue in this matter. I would advise you to sign the enclosed agreement and return it to me promptly. My recommendation to refuse settlement has been vindicated, and I hope that I may serve you in the future.

Sincerely yours,

Harold Sandman, Esq.

On Friday, *The Breedville Bugle* published a front page story and editorial:

"Suit Dropped Against Local Cardiologist"

The Breedville Bugle has previously covered the medical malpractice litigation between local cardiologist Philip Lambert and the family of the late Mark Uber. We have learned that the suit has been withdrawn for lack of sufficient evidence against Dr. Lambert.

Note from the Editor: As members of the press and citizens of Breedville, we at The Bugle are pleased that Dr. Lambert has been vindicated. He is held in the highest esteem by this community and we are privileged to have him on the medical staff at our

local hospital. The Bugle has made no effort to try Dr. Lambert in a public forum for these allegations without due process. Rather we are committed to providing a free press to the community of Breedville. We congratulate Dr. Lambert on his vindication and are grateful to the public for allowing us to carry out our sacred duty.

It was not until after the first of the year that *The Breedville Bugle* printed a story that was also found on the front page of other major newspapers in the state and even made the front section of *The Globe*:

"Attorney Stanislav Brought Up On Ethics Charges"

Attorney Jeffrey Stanislav appeared before the New Hampshire Bar Ethics Committee today to answer charges of influence peddling and illegal payoffs. Mr. Stanislav is represented by his partner Jay Victor. The proceedings are expected to last at least two weeks. Mr. Stanislav was unavailable for comment but his attorney stated that he fully expected his partner to

be cleared of all charges and that
these legal proceedings would occur
in the ethics committee chamber and
not in the newspaper.

CHAPTER TWENTY SIX

WHILE JOSHUA WAS RUSHING Phil to the hospital, Alex was enjoying an unusually quiet on call day at home. She made early morning rounds, and with no obstetrical patients to attend, went home to catch up on her reading and await the first call from the service. It always made her feel a little naughty when she took call from home, like a child playing hooky from school. But experience had taught Alex to enjoy the precious free time while it lasted—since it rarely lasted long. Her solitude was interrupted by the phone.

"It's Ron. I hope I'm not disturbing you."

"Not at all," Alex said, glad to hear from him. "How is everything going?"

"Well, I spoke to my parents and they suggested a lawyer from Concord. I've been in touch with him and he agreed to take my case. I'm supposed to meet with him on Monday." Ron paused. "I just wanted you to know how much I appreciate your support the other day. I'm sure I must have sounded like a crazy man. Your belief in my innocence is very important to me. You have no idea."

"Of course I believe you, Ron." she said. "I just still don't understand who would try to set you up like this! I really hope this guy can help you out."

"I was wondering if it would be okay if I came over for a while. I really don't have anyone here other than you, and I feel like a leper ever since the story got out."

"Of course you're welcome here," Alex said warmly. "I'm on call, so I'm not sure how much longer I'll be home—but please, come over."

"Great," he said. "I have a few errands and then I'll stop by. If you're not there, I'll understand. See you later."

It was only twenty minutes later when the doorbell rang.

He must not have had many errands! Alex thought as she went to the door. Swinging it open with a smile, it was not Ron, but David Arnold on her doorstep.

"David!" Alex exclaimed. "What the hell are you doing here?"

"Now that's a nice hello!" he said, taking a step forward. "It's good to see you too, Alex."

"I'm sorry, David. It's just that I was expecting somebody else . . . besides, I thought you were joining an HMO in California?" David was standing so close that Alex couldn't think to do anything but lean in and peck him on the cheek.

"Come on, Alex. I know you can do better than that!" He reached out to draw her close, but she stepped back.

"What's the matter?" he asked. "You weren't this shy in the city. I remember those nights. Has the country life cooled you off?"

"David, that's long over now. We haven't spoken in over six months!" Alex said, feeling her face grow hot. "Besides, there's someone else."

"Is it Ron Dorcik, Alex? Is he back in your life?"

Alex stepped back. "How do you know about Ron? I never talked about him with you."

"Let's just say I made it my business to find out about him, and any other competition for that matter." David's tone was no longer light. A scowl appeared on his face. Alex could feel a shiver traverse her spine.

"I don't understand why you're acting like this, David. We broke up last spring. We knew we couldn't be together—we went our separate ways. It was never more than a physical relationship. You know that."

"I could live with a physical relationship now, Alex. Sex alone will be just fine." He grabbed her shoulders, pulling her towards him. "Let's see if you still know how to turn me on."

"David, no!" Alex screamed. She struggled, but he was too strong. He pressed his lips to hers, his arms squeezing her tight so she could barely breathe.

"Let me go!" she hollered, writhing out of his grasp and turning from him.

"You think you can carry on with me and then just toss me out? I'm the one who makes that decision, girl. I've been keeping an eye on you for months up here. I've been doing other chicks, but now is the time to get you back. And I'm not going to let Mr. Dorcik get in my way. Besides, he's got his own problems now." David laughed. "A rapist, Alex? Really? You really want to get involved with old Rapist Ron?"

"He's being framed, David," Alex crossed her arms. "Ron isn't capable of assaulting anyone." David stepped in closer, once again.

"Are you saying that I am, Alex? Is that what you think? Those other women wanted me. They really did. And they didn't leave me high and dry like you did. I left them."

"Did you attack those women, David?" Alex asked her eyes wide.

"I didn't attack anybody, Alex. They all wanted me. They couldn't get enough of me. I had to push them off." He grabbed her again. This time, Alex managed to struggle out of his grasp and ran out of the room. David followed, catching up to her in the kitchen. He grabbed her wrists hard, pulling her arms behind her, avoiding her struggling legs. He held both of her arms with his right hand, reaching up under her sweatshirt from behind her with his left.

"No bra," David sneered. "That's my girl."

Feeling his muscular control, Alex realized that it was fruitless to struggle further. Perhaps if she played along, she wouldn't get hurt. She calmed her attempts to break free.

"I'm sorry, David," Alex said, panting from the exertion. "I never should have broken it off. You're right—I really did enjoy the sex. You were terrific in bed." She felt David's grip relax; he turned her to face him.

"I thought you'd come around, baby," he said confidently. "I never should have doubted that you'd come around."

"You put the knife and ski mask in Ron's desk, didn't you?" she asked quietly, placing her arms around David's neck. She noticed that the front door had been left open. She hoped Ron would get here soon.

"It was the last piece of the puzzle, Alex. It was so easy, duplicating those Hartford rapes," he said, breathing into her ear. "Find some chicks near the hospital; get a knife and a ski mask . . . child's play, really." His breath was hot. "It was just dumb luck that the Hartford rapes trailed off around the same time I started here in Breedville—lucky me. I knew it was only a matter of time before the police would suspect him. Getting the mask and knife in his desk was too easy. Sure don't have great security up here in the boonies!" David looked down at her; a glazed look had come across his features. He continued his story.

"I needed to get Ron out of your life, and this seemed like the way to do it. I needed him to go away for a long time. Now that I see you still want me after all," he shrugged, "I guess I didn't need to put in so much work." He pressed his lips to hers, sweeping her off the floor.

"You're still the best, Alex. I've got to give you that. We would have been great together." His face suddenly became dark. "But I can't let you live with all that information that I've given you. You understand, don't you?" He lowered her to the ground, moving his hands from her back to her neck.

"Please David, you don't need to do this," Alex pleaded. "I won't tell anyone! I swear!" But she could see that David was in another world, and he wasn't listening to a word she said. His eyes were dull and unfocused, his fingers slowly tightening around her throat. Alex could feel her airway closing up as her hands reached for his face. His arms were too long. He pulled her down on to the floor, his weight pinning her under him.

"I'm sorry, Alex. You were a great lay. I'm going to miss those times together." He pressed his thumbs tighter against her throat.

A chair came down with tremendous force, delivering a damaging blow to David's head. His grip on her neck loosened in an instant as his hands went to protect himself. Ron brought the chair down again, knocking David off of Alex. He rolled off to the right, blood running down the side of his face as he lost consciousness on the rug.

"Ron! Oh Ron!" Alex gasped as she burst into tears. "It was David! He did it! He's the rapist!" She buried her face in his arms.

"It's okay, honey," Ron reassured her. "Shhhh. You're safe now." There was nothing more to say. He held her gently as she sobbed on his shoulder.

When the police arrived, David Arnold was moaning on the floor, his hands tied behind him with duct tape. Alex was sitting in a chair, nursing a cup of tea, a streak of red around her neck. Ron answered the door.

"Detective Karas," Ron said, "I am actually very glad to see you today!"

"Mr. Dorcik," Mitchell nodded, "it looks like we're going to need some explanations here."

"Dr. Faber will be able to help you. She's recovering in the kitchen. For the time being, I think you'll find the man you're looking for just inside." Ron pointed the way. "He's your assailant."

The police took David Arnold away while Alex and Ron followed in Ron's car. When they arrived at the station, she was still shaking. Her voice was raspy, but Alex was able to give the police a statement. She returned home with Ron, refusing the suggestion to be seen in the emergency room.

The whole story came out during the interrogation. David confessed to everything. He had undergone long-standing treatment for manic—depression, a condition that had been well-controlled with medication throughout residency. Unbeknownst to Alex, their break-up the previous year had delivered a tremendous blow to David, and he stopped his medication soon after her departure from City Hospital. He followed Alex up to Breedville, balking on his contract with an HMO on the West Coast. He became obsessed with her, taking a temporary position in Concord and traveling to Breedville often. He became aware of her previous marriage, and was nothing short of panicked when he saw her romance with Ron beginning to blossom all over again. He was the last obstacle in David's way. David confessed to the rape attacks as well as the framing of Ron Dorcik by placing the knife and ski mask in his office. By the end of the interrogation, police felt comfortable dropping Ron Dorcik as a suspect on the case.

Alex was fast asleep on the couch while Ron just sat there and looked at her. He refused to leave her alone, and besides, there was nowhere else where he wanted to be. Her breathing had returned to normal and the red marks on her neck were the only noticeable evidence of the attack. Her eyes flickered open as she smiled, gazing upon the man who'd saved her.

"Hi," she said, smiling. "You know I've never been rescued before."

Ron smiled back. "Well, I've never rescued anybody before. This is a whole new scene for me." His hand reached for hers. "How are you feeling?"

"Much better, thanks." she answered, taking it. "This heroic stuff is not something I knew about you. I kind of like it."

"Well, don't get used to it. I prefer a more boring existence. Would you like some more tea?" he asked.

"No, I just want you to hold my hand."

"Whatever you want."

Alex drifted back to sleep for another hour. Ron sat, continuing to hold her hand, his thoughts returning to the happier days of their courtship. Alex had been so driven back then—yet vulnerable. She had encouraged him to take over, to protect her, needing to know that he loved her. And yet there were times of fierce independence, when all she seemed to want was to stand on her own. It had grown clear to Ron that Alex had something to prove—to herself, to her father, to the world? He wasn't quite sure. This internal struggle of hers was something he always found hard to anticipate, or even understand. But he loved her so. When she left, he never saw it coming. One moment she was there, and the next she was gone. No argument, no explanation. He wished he knew why.

Ron stared down at the beautiful, sleeping Alex. Her eyes opened again, a warm smile dawning on her face.

"Alex, what happened that day you left?" The warmth of the smile faded in an instant.

"Don't ask me, Ron," she said. "It was a long time ago."

"I need to know," he persisted softly. "I've been needing to know for ten years." Her face turned from his, tears beginning to appear.

"Don't go there, Ron," she warned. "Remember, no strings."

"But I want to start over again with you. There has never been anyone else. I moved to Breedville, just to be near you. But I need to know what happened. What did I do wrong?"

"You didn't do anything wrong." Alex said, continuing to look away. "I got pregnant." She paused. "I never told you. I was feeling trapped and desperate, so terribly desperate. I was losing my identity. I needed an out. And then," she hesitated for a moment, "I had an abortion."

There was nothing further to say. Alex turned her face back to Ron's, tears blurring her vision of his reaction. He was silent. His eyes lost their sparkle. His head turned from hers. Instinctively, he let go of her hand.

"I don't know if you can forgive me," Alex continued. "I don't know if I can forgive myself."

Ron got up from the sofa, as if in a trance He looked back at her briefly. The love in his eyes was gone. She could see the change.

"I told you not to go there!" she cried. "I told you not to go there!" But Ron couldn't hear her. As he left, the door closed behind him with a heavy sense of finality.

CHAPTER TWENTY SEVEN

According to the directions on the box, Julie Barron administered two drops of chemical agent into the plastic cylinder and waited. After about a minute, the control dot on the side of the container turned blue. Her eyes continued to focus on the middle of the cup, looking for the development of a comparable blue dot. She felt her life hanging in the balance. As the last few grains of sand fell from the three minute hour glass included in the home pregnancy test, a faint blue dot appeared in the center of the container. It wasn't as dark as it was supposed to be, but it was there, staring up at Julie like an unblinking eye.

"Shit!" she cried. "Oh God, how could this happen to me?" Julie was five days late for her period. Ever since the night of the school dance, she had been thinking about this, worrying about this. This time she wasn't so lucky to end up with a bladder infection. This time she might be pregnant, and antibiotics wouldn't cure the problem. She couldn't imagine telling her mother. And her father was undoubtedly out of the question. As panic-ridden thoughts raced through her head, one message from Dr. Faber rang clear: "I'm always here if you need me."

It was the Saturday after Christmas. Julie's older brother Jim was home for the holidays and had taken their younger brother to a hockey game. Her parents were out returning presents and picking up things for the upcoming New Year's Eve party. Since her dad was not at work, she knew there was a good chance that Alex was at the hospital. Julie picked up the phone and dialed.

"Breed General Hospital," the operator answered.

"Could you page Dr. Faber, please?" A few moments later Alex picked up the page.

"This is Dr. Faber. How can I help you?" Upon hearing Alex's voice, Julie burst into tears.

"Dr. Faber, this is Julie Barron," she sobbed, trying to control her voice.

"Julie, what's the matter?"

"I think I'm pregnant. My period is late so I bought a pregnancy test, and it came back blue." Saying those words out loud frightened Julie even more than before.

"Julie, have you told anyone about this yet?"

"No!" she cried. "I called you right away. I don't know what to do!" Julie dissolved into incoherent heaves of tears.

"Are you alone, Julie? Is anyone else at home?"

"No, I'm by myself. I don't want anyone else to know! I thought you could help me."

"I'll be over in about a half hour and we'll go to the office and talk this thing out. When will your family be back?"

"No one will be home until dinner. I told my parents I needed to stay home to work on a term paper." Alex looked at her watch. It was only ten thirty in the morning.

"I'll see you by eleven o'clock, Julie. Be ready to leave. We'll have to come right back here."

"Thank you! I'll be ready," Julie said through her sobs.

Alex had finished rounds and was attending to a woman in early labor when Julie paged. She excused herself from the labor floor, reassuring the nurses that her beeper was on and she would be back in about an hour. She changed out of her scrubs and drove towards the Barron's home.

As she rode, Alex took some time to turn this dilemma over in her head a few times. By taking Julie on as a patient, she knew that she entered potentially-sticky territory. Still, she remembered making things clear when Liz had broached the subject during their antiquing trip several months before. If she were to take Julie on, their relationship within the confines of the medical setting would be strictly confidential—even to the exclusion of her parents. She remembered Liz's words: "I understand that it would be strictly private . . . I trust your judgment, and know that you'd guide her well." While in some respects Alex still worried that she was entering a lose-lose scenario, she had to adhere to her values of doing what was best for her patient. She arrived at the Barron's house to find the anxious teenager waiting outside.

"Thank you for coming!" Julie said as she opened the door and got in.

"Of course. When I said I would be there for you, I meant it." Julie closed the door and Alex shifted the car into gear and headed back to the hospital. "Julie," Alex continued gently, "what happened to the condom I gave you last time? If you needed more, you could have certainly asked for some."

Julie's eyes dropped to the floor. "I never used it. I only had sex one time since I saw you—one time! Everything happened so quickly. I left it in my pocketbook."

Alex nodded. "Julie, once we sort out the current situation, you should really go on the pill. And," she added gently, "I think you should try to have some communication about this with your mother."

Julie snapped her head to look at Alex. "I can't do that! I'm not going to have sex anymore, and I'm not going to tell her!"

"Julie, I think your mother was concerned that you were having unprotected sex. That's why she wanted you to come in."

"I thought it was because of my cramps," Julie answered.

"I think your safety is of her utmost concern. Mind you, I'm sure she would rather you wait till you're older to become sexually active, and I don't disagree. But ultimately, if you are going to have sex, all she wants is for you to be safe. You should give her a chance. And your father, too. He sees teenagers with problems like this all the time. He just wants to protect you from all the hurt and pain that he sees at work."

They drove the rest of the way in silence. When they arrived at the office, Alex called the labor floor to let them know she was back and available. Then she turned to her young patient.

"Now tell me again, when did your last period begin? And when was it over?"

"My last period was on Thanksgiving. I remember because I was out of tampons and the drug store was closed. My cycles have been really regular—every 26 days exactly. By the way, that medicine you gave me really helped my cramps."

"Good. Now when did you have sex? You mentioned in the car that it was only one additional time."

"Yes—just once! I swear. It was the night of the school dance, that day that it snowed for the first time."

Alex looked up at the calendar over her desk. Julie had been directly mid-cycle on the night of the dance—her most fertile time. If she had actually been trying to get pregnant, she couldn't have timed it better. By calculation, her period should have started five days ago.

"What did the pregnancy test look like?" Alex asked.

"It was pale blue, not as dark as the test said it should be if it were positive. But it definitely was not negative."

These clues told Alex that what Julie Barron had likely seen were the results of an equivocal pregnancy test. With the history she provided, the test would almost definitely turn positive in a few days.

She turned to Julie. "Suppose you are pregnant. What would you want to do?" Although she anticipated her patient's response, Alex felt obligated to ask her the question. One thing she had learned was never to assume anything. In this case, her assumption was correct.

"I can't have a baby, Dr. Faber," Julie answered. "I'm only sixteen. I know I've made a big mistake, and I really don't want to have sex again for a long time. But I'll still go on the pill—I promise! But I need to have an abortion. When can you tell me for sure if I am?"

"Well," Alex answered, "it is still too early to tell for sure. But certainly it is reasonable to think that you might be pregnant. If you are, the test will give a definitive result in a few more days. But sometimes a woman can get her period one or two weeks late—if that were the case, you would have a borderline result like today but go on to not be pregnant." Alex did not mention that in many cases, these situations represented very early miscarriages, and these women were in fact pregnant for a very short time.

Julie looked anxious and a little sick. "Well, what am I supposed to do now? I can't wait two more days! I would die!"

"You have several choices, Julie," Alex answered. "You can wait several days to see if you get your period. If you don't and the pregnancy test becomes positive, you could have an abortion. Or you could have a menstrual extraction today." Alex paused. "I think you should discuss the options with your parents before deciding."

"What's a menstrual extraction?" Julie asked, ignoring Alex's suggestion.

"It's kind of a mini-abortion. It is a small operation that we do here in the office. If you are pregnant, it will usually terminate the pregnancy. And if you aren't, you'll get your period."

"Does it hurt?"

"You would get bad cramps. But I can give you some medicine so that it wouldn't be too bad."

"Can we just do that, then? I really don't want to tell my parents that I got pregnant—I can't. But I promise to talk with them about birth control, after this is done. Do I need their permission to get this done?"

"No, you don't," Alex conceded. She felt like she was setting herself up for a bad scene with Liz and Joshua if they were to find out, but Julie was within her rights to have a menstrual extraction without parental consent. Alex had to admit that having the procedure done today was the best way to go, given the circumstances. She just wished that Julie would open up to her parents instead of leaving her in such a difficult situation.

"Then that's what I want to do," Julie said resolutely. Alex gave a short nod of acceptance.

Alex showed Julie to the exam room where she gave her two Advil tablets for the cramping and had her undress from the waist down. Alex gathered the necessary instruments for the procedure.

When Julie was ready, she examined her with her two hands, elevating the uterus and feeling her abdomen. Julie's uterus felt normal size, as would be expected, and the two ovaries were normal as well. She then inserted a speculum into the vagina, visualizing the cervix. She injected a local anesthetic all around the cervical opening to decrease the pain of dilatation. While holding the cervix with one instrument, she inserted a second tubular structure through the cervical canal and up into the body of the uterus. She connected the other end of the tube to a suction machine. As she flipped the switch, a whining sound emanated from the machine. She began to move the tubular instrument gently back and forth and in a circular motion, suctioning out the lining of the uterus that may or may not have held an implanted fertilized egg. The suctioned tissue was collected in a cotton bag and would be discarded after the procedure.

As Alex continued to move the instrument around the uterus, Julie suddenly jerked her body in response to an unexpected cramp. Alex felt a break in the resistance, the plastic tubular instrument plunging deep inside the uterus. She felt her heart sink into her stomach as she realized that she had just perforated Julie's uterus. She quickly removed the instrument from the vagina, so as not to severely damage the other closely related internal organs.

"Owww!" Julie cried, writhing in pain. She was unable to lie still on the table. Alex checked her vital signs, which were stable, then gave her time to recover.

A uterine perforation was a complication that every gynecologist was faced with several times in their career. Fortunately, the damage was usually self-limited and observation was all that was necessary. However, depending on the extent of internal bleeding and possible damage to other organs, further surgery was sometimes indicated. Alex knew that she had to exercise every precaution—she would do this with any patient, but with Julie Barron, she felt an even deeper sense of urgency.

With Julie resting in the exam room, Alex called the labor floor to check on the progress of her patient. She was doing well, and had progressed only slightly in Alex's absence. Alex breathed a small sigh of relief. At least she would not have to be in two places at once. She returned to her young patient.

"What's wrong?" Julie asked, still wincing in pain.

"You have a complication, Julie," Alex explained briskly. "The instrument I was using went through the wall of your uterus when you made that sudden move earlier."

"Is that real bad?" Will I be able to go home soon?"

"Usually it's not that bad," Alex answered, "But I'm going to have to watch you for a while."

Over the next several hours, Julie lay on the table and Alex continued to monitor her. Her pain continued, and she began to show clinical signs of internal bleeding. Alex decided she needed a laparoscopy to evaluate the bleeding. It was now about four o'clock. She knew she had to call Liz and Joshua.

"I'm going to have to call your parents, Julie. It looks like you're going to need an operation." As Alex said the words, Julie began to cry—as much out of fear as from the increasing pain. She gave a nod of submission.

Alex dialed the Barron home. Liz answered.

"Hi, Liz—its Alex."

"Hi, Alex! How are you? It's been a while since we've spoken! How was your Christmas?"

"It was lovely—but unfortunately, this isn't a social call. I have Julie here with me in my office. She is okay—but she is going to need an operation. Is Joshua there?"

"What? Julie's there with you? What's wrong?" Liz's voice was swept with panic.

"You'll get all of the details soon, Liz—but I really need to speak with Joshua right now."

"Ok, hold on!" Alex could hear Liz emergently bellowing for her husband to pick up the phone.

"What's wrong, Alex?" Joshua said as he picked up. Liz was still on the line.

"Julie has a perforated uterus. She's showing signs of internal bleeding and I'm going to need to look inside. Hopefully it can be handled through the laparoscope. I just wanted to let you know what was going on before I proceed."

"Julie's with you? How did this happen, Alex?" Joshua demanded, though from her description of the situation, he already had a pretty good idea.

"We'll talk later. Just come to the hospital if you can. I also have a patient in labor and could use your help."

"What's happened?" Joshua insisted again.

"We'll talk later. I'll see you in the pre-op area." Alex hung up.

Liz left a note for the boys and they hurriedly left for the hospital. By the time they arrived, Alex had the operating team and anesthesiologist assembled. Julie was in a bed with an intravenous in her arm and oxygen flowing into her nostrils.

"Mommy, Daddy!" she cried as Liz and Joshua entered the room. At this point, Julie had succumbed to the fact that her parents were going to find out about the pregnancy. She was frightened, and just happy to have them with her.

"It's okay, honey," Liz reassured her, smoothing back her hair. "We're here and everything is going to be all right."

Joshua's jaw was tense. His resentment of Alex's actions was obvious, but knew that this was not the place to make a scene. Julie's health was the only focus right now. There would be plenty of time for recrimination and accusation later.

"What do you need me to do?" he asked his partner. Alex could see the upset in Joshua's eyes.

"I expect that I have an active bleeding site on the outside wall of the uterus. Hopefully I'll be able to cauterize it through the scope and suction out the blood. I have a patient in labor who is pushing and I would appreciate your covering me upstairs." Joshua was reluctant to leave.

"Take care of my baby, Alex."

"I will, Joshua. I will."

Joshua took Liz with him upstairs, nearly having to pry her hands off Julie's bedrails as she was wheeled into the operating room. He knew there was nothing for Liz to do down there but worry. This way, Joshua could keep an eye on the laboring patient while they kept each other company in the lounge. After a short while, it became clear that a birth was near at hand, and Joshua prepared to head into the birthing room for the delivery.

"Can I come in with you?" Liz asked as her husband suited up in his scrubs. "I really don't want to be left alone right now and I'd love to watch you deliver a baby."

After obtaining the patient's permission, Liz changed into a scrub suit and entered the birthing room with her husband. Joshua assumed his position at the foot of the birthing bed while Liz stood in a corner, watching intently. In all the years she had been with Joshua, she had never witnessed him delivering a baby. As the head crowned up and Joshua gently delivered it, Liz temporarily forgot her daughter's plight downstairs. He suctioned out the nose and mouth and then with gentle guidance, maneuvered the shoulders through the pelvic bones, delivering an active baby girl. Joshua wiped off the blood and secretions from the child's face and handed her to the new mother. The cord was clamped and cut, the placenta delivered and no stitches were necessary. After congratulating the new parents, he joined his wife in the corner, where they shared the loving moment with the others in the birthing room. Liz took his hand, tears streaming down her face.

"I love you, Joshua Barron," she whispered to her husband. He squeezed her hand in response.

"I love you too, Liz."

The two extended their congratulations to the new parents and left the birthing room to see how their own daughter was faring in the operating room.

Julie Baron lay on the operating table. A tube down her throat was connected to the ventilator; her legs were supported by stirrups and her body was tipped precariously with her legs up above the level of her head.

Having pierced the navel with the long metal trocar, Alex was now viewing the damage to Julie's uterus through the laparoscope. As she suspected, there was over a pint of fresh blood in her abdomen, the source of which was a bleeding vessel in the upper wall of the uterus. With Julie's body steeply tipped, the pool of blood settled in the upper portion of her abdomen. Alex was able to isolate the bleeding source and cauterize it effectively with a special instrument through a second puncture site in the abdominal wall. She then suctioned out the blood and reviewed the bleeding site to make sure it was no longer active. Satisfied with her findings, she gently scraped the inside lining of the uterus to complete the menstrual extraction she had abandoned in the office earlier. She removed the surgical instruments and left the operating room to find Joshua and Liz, who were back from the delivery and nervously waiting in the recovery room.

Alex took a deep breath. She knew that this was the best time to talk with the Barrons and tell them the events of the day. She told them that she had received a call from Julie that morning, and how she'd immediately picked her up and brought her to the office.

"She was desperate and very scared. I tried to convince her to include you both in this information and decision, but she made it clear that she did not want you to know. I explained her options, and a menstrual extraction seemed to be the most reasonable alternative."

Liz's face looked tired and sad. "I'm glad she felt she could call you, Alex. But I feel like I failed in some way. I wish she felt comfortable coming to me with such a frightening situation." She put her head in her hands.

"Don't be so hard on yourself, Liz," Alex said—reaching out to touch Liz's arm. "These things are always hard between parents and teenagers. When I think of my own relationship with my parents, my blood curdles—they never would have wanted to deal with it, even if I had reached out. You were open and willing to listen. In the end, this may make you and Julie closer."

Joshua remained strangely silent during this exchange. Alex could see disapproval in his eyes. At that moment, John Stands and the circulating nurse rolled Julie's bed into the recovery room. She was only semi-conscious and had a pallid, washed-out look that was typical of a fresh postoperative patient. Joshua and Liz moved quickly to their daughter's side.

"Julie, honey," Liz said softly to her daughter. "It's Mom and Dad. You're safe now. It is all over." Julie opened her eyes to see both of her parents looking down at her. Their faces showed love and concern—but no anger. She was still too sedated to respond, so she just looked up at them for a moment, then closed her eyes. Her hands reached for her abdomen and she groaned.

"She's going to be out of it for a while, Liz," John Stands told her. "But you're certainly welcome to stay here with her while she wakes up. She did real well and Dr. Faber took good care of her."

Alex felt like an intruder in the recovery room. She gave the family some time alone, and left for the surgeons' lounge to write her postoperative orders and dictate an operative note. After several more minutes, Joshua left his daughter's side and went to find Alex.

"I'm sorry, Joshua," Alex said, looking up from the desk as he entered. "I really tried to get Julie to discuss this with you, but she was adamant. So I did what I felt was the right thing at the time—what I felt was best for her." She paused. "As for the perforation, I feel very badly that it had to happen with Julie. But I think you know better than I that those things just can't always be controlled." She looked back to her note. "And thanks so much for covering me on the labor floor—I really appreciate it."

Joshua could contain himself no further.

"What were you thinking?" he said angrily, standing over her with his arms crossed. "What in hell were you thinking? Why didn't you contact us? This is not your daughter, or your decision. She's sixteen, for god's sake! She can't make these kinds of decisions on her own. And perhaps, if you hadn't been so rushed, the perforation might not have occurred." He stopped for a moment, his voice becoming tight and controlled, his manner cold and furious. "I think you exercised poor medical judgment today, and I resent your coming between us and our daughter."

Alex let Joshua finish, but she could feel her blood boiling as he spoke. "I'm sorry, Joshua," she shook her head. "I can't accept this criticism. I'm confident you would have done the same if the situation were reversed. Maybe you should speak to your wife before you stick your foot further into your mouth." Alex knew her words were harsh, but she stood behind them. "Liz understands this issue at home better than you seem to, and she came to me for help. I certainly did not want to involve myself in your family's affairs, and I made that very clear to Liz when she broached the subject. We had an understanding. I think you're making a big mistake by trying to turn me into the bad guy here, and to accuse me of poor medical judgment?"

"Well, Joshua replied, "maybe I've made several mistakes in this past year!"

Alex was too upset to respond rationally. She turned and left her partner to consider the ramifications of his remarks.

CHAPTER TWENTY EIGHT

JODY PINKHAM LAY VERY still in the long cylindrical compartment of the magnetic resonance imager. It was a tight fit, made even tighter by her protruding abdomen. Although the technicians had told her to try to sleep, her anxiety level made the suggestion nearly impossible. Why don't they try getting crammed in here for forty-five minutes, she thought to herself, and then try telling me to relax!

Jody heard the banging noise of the machine as it rapidly took multiple images of the lower portion of her abdomen. Thankfully her fetus was cooperating this time, taking a break from its usual activity to catch a few winks. Being that it was Jody's third MRI this pregnancy, she was handling the procedure far better than she had before. For her first go-around, she had to receive a hefty dose of Valium to calm her down and prevent the inevitable claustrophobia. While it had the desired effect on her, the medication seemed to cause the baby to go into overdrive, much to the consternation of the technicians and radiologists.

From what could be determined without operating, Jody's cancer had been confined to date. No enlarged lymph nodes or abnormally thickened tissues had been seen emanating from the uterus in the first two MRIs. With her due date creeping closer, Jody was beginning to breathe a few sighs of relief. Dr. Faber had even scheduled her for an amniocentesis in two weeks, hoping to find a baby with mature lungs. If that were the case, Jody would deliver via cesarean section and then have the necessary definitive surgery to cure her of this malignant scourge.

As Jody lay there, Dr. Aaron Speiser watched the screen with his radiologist colleagues. He had been uncomfortable with the plan to wait on the cervical cancer until the baby was mature, but Jody was adamant. The compromise was to follow her with MRI and pelvic exams until lung maturity. He had reluctantly removed the local malignant growth last July, a medical decision that went against everything he had learned in his training and eight years in practice. But Dr. Speiser had been so impressed by Jody's faith and resolve that he had felt obligated to be more flexible. Of course he had her sign all kinds of forms, acknowledging the unorthodox nature of the plan and the risks she was taking. Yet somehow, despite his extreme reservation, this woman's steadfast belief in her pregnancy had rubbed off on his orthodox views and he found himself cheering her on to fight the odds. He was looking forward to the delivery almost as much as his patient.

He was also looking forward to meeting her obstetrician. Dr. Speiser had spoken to Alex on several occasions over the past six months, as they continued to watch over this premium pregnancy. Arrangements had been made to have Alex perform the cesarean section at New Hampshire Medical Center in Manchester, with Dr. Speiser himself assisting. She would also remain scrubbed to assist in the radical hysterectomy that would follow. It had been a long time since Dr. Speiser had been involved in a delivery. Gynecologic oncologists put in many long years of training in order to distance themselves from the labor floor. Most were quite satisfied with this distance, and accepted the depressing though more predictable environment of tumor surgery.

Dr. Speiser was an exception to that rule, having sorely missed obstetrics in the pursuit of his specialized career. As he let his mind briefly wander back to his training and those long nights of deliveries, his thoughts were interrupted by a disturbing image on the screen.

"You see that, John?" he asked the radiologist, who was viewing the images as the computer spit them out. He pointed to an asymmetric thickening of the broad ligament, the structure that supported the uterus. This was the most common area for initial spread of a cervical malignancy once it passed through the uterine wall.

"Yeah," the radiologist answered, looking intently at the spot. "I don't know . . . let's take a closer look." He called to the technician to rescan the isolated section. Upon closer review, it was clear that one side of the uterus was significantly thicker than the other, indirect evidence that Jody's tumor was breaking out of the uterus. This was a sign they'd been on watch for all these months. And with Jody Pinkham finishing her thirty-fourth week of pregnancy, the fetus was viable. Dr. Speiser knew immediately that Alex would not have the luxury of demonstrating pulmonary maturity before delivery. Ready or not, this baby would have to be delivered as soon as possible.

Thirty minutes later, Dr. Speiser was able to reach Alex from his office.

"Hello, Dr. Faber," he said. "This is Dr. Speiser calling from Manchester."

"Hi Dr. Speiser," Alex answered. "Please, call me Alex—we've been working together for months now. How did Jody's MRI come out?"

"Not so good this time," Aaron answered. "There is an asymmetric thickening in her left broad ligament that may constitute tumor spread. I think we better move quickly. There were no enlarged lymph nodes, but the chances of nodal involvement at this point would be quite high, as you are aware." He was referring to the lymphatic system, a group of vessels and nodes that paralleled the circulatory system in the body, responsible for defense from invaders such as bacteria and cancer. If the lymph system were involved with Jody's tumor, there was a much higher likelihood that the malignancy was now spreading throughout her body, making it much less likely that she could be cured.

"I was hoping for a little more time, but the baby should do well at thirty four weeks. We should at least be grateful for the time that we had," Alex responded, gearing up for a sooner than expected delivery.

"My thoughts exactly," Aaron agreed.

"When did you have in mind to operate?" she asked.

"This week."

"Well, I'm off tomorrow. Could you get her on the schedule that quickly?"

"We will if we have to. I'll have my secretary call your office back to let you know what time we can start. Do you still want to hang around for the entire case?"

"I wouldn't miss it!" Alex said. "I must admit, I'm a bit of a frustrated oncologist at heart. I loved the big time surgeries. Just couldn't deal with the poor outcomes."

"I'll be seeing Ms. Pinkham in my office over the next hour and will give her the MRI results. I would just as soon keep her here overnight to prep her for surgery. She's been pretty strong in her opinions, but I hope I can convince her to stay."

"I'll be happy to talk to her if you have any problems. I don't think she'll have any objections. She's just as anxious to get this thing over with as we are."

"Looking forward to seeing you, Alex, and please call me Aaron."

"Looking forward to meeting you, Aaron."

Aaron Speiser wasn't aware just how anxious Alex was to get out of Breedville for a while. It had been only two days since her blow-up with Joshua, and time was weighing heavily on her. She had been hurt by his comments, and was trying to convince herself that he didn't really mean it. He had reacted as an anxious father, not an objective professional. But as she completed her weekend on call, he had made no effort to contact her to apologize. In fact, she had not heard from or seen either Joshua or Liz since storming out of the surgeons lounge on Saturday evening. Julie left the hospital on Sunday morning. She was feeling significantly better and thanked Alex profusely for her help. Julie remained completely unaware of the aftermath between Alex and Joshua, and Alex was glad for that. But she was surprised when neither Liz nor Joshua contacted her when they picked their daughter up. She had finished rounds, and when she passed by Julie's room for the second time that morning, she was gone. The floor nurses had said the Barrons had wasted no time in taking their daughter home.

While Alex was on the phone with Dr. Speiser, Joshua was in the operating room. He wasn't scheduled for patients until the afternoon. Alex was set to wrap up her office schedule by noon, so there would be little opportunity for them to interact that day.

Alex leaned back and stared out the window into the gray winter sky. Her relationship with Ron was another thing on her mind lately. It had been over a week since her attack and her confession about the abortion. She had not heard from Ron at all, and felt awkward about calling. His sudden departure from her home that day leant a sense of finality to a relationship that was just beginning to blossom again after so many years of dormancy.

As expected, Dr. Speiser's office called to tell Alex that the surgery was scheduled for 10 AM the following morning and that Jody Pinkham would be spending the night in Manchester. Alex finished her last patient and left for the day.

The trip to Manchester was only an hour and a half, but in light of New England's unpredictable winter weather, Alex elected to leave that afternoon. She booked a room at the Ramada Inn next to the medical center. Since she was not on call for several days, she had had Ann reschedule her Wednesday morning patients. This would give her plenty of time to get back to Breedville, and also the opportunity to stay two nights in Manchester if she wished. Alex recognized this as a juvenile way of running from her local problems, but she just didn't feel like handling this in particularly grown-up fashion. Besides, it would give her more time before she had to face Joshua.

Upon arriving in Manchester, Alex went to a movie in town and got to bed early, anticipating a long day in the operating room. What she did not anticipate, however, was her reaction to Dr. Speiser when she finally met him the next morning.

"Alex, it is indeed a pleasure to meet you," Aaron greeted her outside of the operating room.

"You as well!" Dr. Speiser was not the bookish oncologist that Alex had foolishly expected. He was tall, dark haired and athletic. His broad shoulders and narrow waist seemed more apropos for the movie screen than the operating room. His sharp angled features gave him a serious appearance that changed dramatically when he smiled. Alex could almost feel the warmth of his personality as he shook her hand.

"Why don't I take you to see Jody before we get started? She refused to take her preoperative medications until she saw you. You know, Alex, she has a lot of faith in you. I only hope she has half as much faith in me!"

"You came very highly recommended, Aaron," Alex said, hoping he didn't catch her blush. "Jody told me many times how comfortable she has become with your care." They walked into the preoperative area. Jody Pinkham was in bed with an intravenous in one hand, her husband Charles holding the other.

"Dr. Faber! It is so good to see you!"

"This is the day we've all been waiting for, isn't it?" Alex said brightly as she approached the bed.

"The baby's real active today. He must know it's his birthday," Jody smiled. She'd found out the baby's sex at a recent ultrasound, and was excited to meet her new son.

"Guess so! Well, the nurses are going to give you some medication now in anticipation of your surgery. We'll make sure Charles gets to see the baby just after he's born. He'll stay with him in the nursery until you get to the recovery room." Jody looked calm as Alex explained everything.

Dr. Speiser nodded to the nurses to begin the preoperative sedation. He then showed Alex to the locker room. In short order, the two physicians were facing each other over Jody's pregnant figure. To decrease the amount of time that the baby would be exposed to the gases, there would be a rapid sequence induction of anesthesia. Jody was prepped and draped while awake, a catheter placed into her bladder. As soon as the anesthesiologist gave the word, Alex made a vertical incision into the abdomen with Aaron assisting. She rapidly entered the uterus, delivering a screaming little boy. Alex cut the cord and the baby was handed over to the obstetrical nurse and pediatrician who were in attendance for the first part of the surgery. She then put a running suture into the uterine incision to decrease the bleeding in the field, and handed the instruments over to Dr. Speiser.

"Your turn, doctor," she said, feeling like she was on the set of a soap opera with this handsome leading man who was only pretending to be a surgeon.

Out of the corner of her eye, Alex could see the baby being brought out to his anxious father. Charles picked up the child in his arms, his expression under the mask showing an incredible mix of emotions that only a scenario like this one could evoke. As the obstetrical nurse guided Charles away, the more serious part of the surgery began.

Aaron removed Jody's uterus to allow for greater exposure of the operative field. It was clear that there had been tumor invasion into the broad ligament on the left, but there was no obvious spread through the other abdominal organs. He methodically removed the lymph nodes from around the aorta and continued the dissection deep into the pelvis. With a surgical skill that impressed Alex, he dissected free the remainder of the broad ligament on both sides of the absent uterus, aggressively freeing up the ureters so as to leave no possible tumor growth behind. As he deftly cut around these tubular structures that connected the kidneys to the bladder below, Alex couldn't help but wish he had been with her during her difficult hysterectomy on Wendy Butler several weeks earlier.

Four hours in the operating room passed quickly for Alex. After the two surgeons put Jody's abdominal wall back together, they left for the lounge to dictate the case and write postoperative orders. After he finished a complex dictation, Aaron turned to Alex.

"I just hope we got the tumor out in time. Some of those lymph nodes looked a little enlarged. But I feel that we were able to get around the tumor mass on the left. It's now up to pathology to tell us how she's going to do."

"Well", Alex responded, "I don't think we had a whole lot of choice here, given the circumstances. It would be nice if we could borrow a little bit of Jody's faith on this one. But it was a great case—I was really impressed. You certainly know your way around the female anatomy!"

Aaron blushed a bright crimson before Alex realized what she had said, then shared in the embarrassment.

"There is not much I can say to follow that remark," he quipped.

"Well, I think maybe it's time for me to head up to the nursery and see how baby boy Pinkham is doing," Alex said, the flush in her face not yet clearing.

"Mind if I join you?"

"Not at all."

Upon their arrival in the nursery, they found the infant had taken a turn for the worse. Charles Pinkham was peering through the nursery window, his eyes affixed on his newborn son. The baby was beginning to experience the difficult breathing that was common in premature infants, and had been placed in a baby warmer, his head surrounded by one hundred percent oxygen.

"How's he doing?" Alex asked Charles.

"The pediatrician said that he expected this, but that doesn't make it any easier." He looked up. "How's Jody?"

"She's in the recovery room. I'll be happy to take you down to her."

"I'd appreciate that. This is even tougher than I thought it would be," Charles admitted. He looked back at his son in the warmer. "Having the two most precious things in your life in danger at the same time . . ." Alex nodded and put her hand on his shoulder. She and Aaron took the distraught man to the recovery room where he was able to spend a few minutes with his wife. They decided to give the couple some time alone, and headed down to the hospital coffee shop to get Charles a muffin and juice, since he hadn't eaten all day.

"Will you be going back to Breedville right away?" Aaron asked as they headed back to the operating room.

"Well, I'm not due back till tomorrow afternoon, so I'm not sure what my plans are," Alex replied.

"I know this is forward," Aaron said, "but would you like to have dinner with me tonight? To celebrate what will hopefully be a successful case! We could make it early so you don't have to travel late at night."

"Actually," Alex laughed, "I booked a room at the Ramada for tonight—I thought I would leave in the morning. Hopefully I can check in on Jody and the baby then, and leave them in better shape. So," she went on, "I'd love to take you up on your invitation."

"Great!" he replied with a nearly adolescent enthusiasm. "Why don't I pick you up at your hotel at seven?"

"Sounds good to me. I hope dinner will be informal. I didn't bring any dress clothes along," Alex smiled.

"No problem. There's a great place in town and the dress is strictly casual."

"See you then!" Alex watched him turn, heading towards the men's locker room. She could even hear his whistling faintly as he went.

It was a little too noisy for Alex's taste, but the corner booth sheltered them from most of the rowdy environment. The restaurant was rather nice: a combination of polished wood and brass and soft leather, giving the impression that you'd left the east coast for some small town in Texas. The only thing this place needed was a mechanical bull. But the atmosphere was relaxed and the food was greasy and good. After David

Arnold's attack, her falling out with Ron, the ordeal with the Barron family and Jody's surgery to cap it off, Aaron could have taken her to McDonald's and she would have been happy.

Alex found her unexpected date to be as charming as he was good-looking. Considering his position as head of gynecologic oncology at the medical center, Aaron was very down-to-earth, and even a little shy. His personality was in stark contrast to the typical arrogant New York City surgeon, so it came as a surprise when she learned that it was Manhattan's Sloan-Kettering Cancer Institute where he had completed his fellowship. His medical school and residency had been completed at the University of Pennsylvania, a natural step from his childhood years on the main line in suburban Philadelphia.

Their backgrounds were very different. Aaron grew up amongst the Jewish affluent in southeastern Pennsylvania. She was from a working class Catholic family in Queens. But their enthusiasm for their work with a deep commitment to patient care bridged the chasm between their backgrounds. Their respective fields of medicine were the main topics of conversation that night.

"You know, your partner has a very high opinion of you," Aaron said. Indeed, he had gotten some details from Joshua about his new partner.

When they spoke, Joshua spent most of his time discussing Alex's natural transition to private practice and her extremely caring attitude, but he did not neglect to mention that his new partner was very attractive and single. "I must admit, with our many conversations over the past six months, my curiosity was piqued and I asked Joshua to fill me in on all the details."

Alex giggled, and blushed all over again. "And what did he have to say?" She was a bit nervous to hear how Joshua might describe her.

"Well," he continued, "first he said you were single."

"Now there's a compliment if I ever heard one!" Alex said sarcastically.

"I think he led with that to hook me in to the rest of the description," Aaron grinned. "He also told me about your interview, and how he expected you to be a man!"

Alex laughed out loud, remembering fondly the scene of a stammering Joshua trying to remain in control under such shock.

"He then told me, as objectively as a happily married man can, just how attractive you are and how well you carry yourself amongst your peers. But really, he spent most of the time talking about your keen medical judgment and how he was convinced that no one could feel as strongly about patient care as he did, until you came along. Your presence has been a salvation for him."

As Aaron relayed the story, Alex realized how desperate she was to hear these words. In light of recent events, it felt good to know how her partner had talked about her behind closed doors.

"Did Joshua ever say anything to you about me?" he asked.

"Honestly, I hadn't asked," Alex admitted. "My social life in Breedville has been less than torrid I must admit, but I've gotten used to the slower pace, and my practice has filled most of my vacant moments." Her mind wandered. She could see Ron's face set aglow when he saw her at the president's reception in July. She felt the tenderness with which he held her hand after the attack. Heard the finality of the door closing behind him as he left her. "Why don't you tell me about yourself, where you're from, where you did your training, that sort of thing.," she said, trying to refocus on the conversation at hand.

"There's not a whole lot to talk about," Aaron said, taking a sip of beer. "I've been a workaholic for most of my life. I've dated around, but never seriously. As a single Jewish doctor, I've had more than my share of pressure to find someone and get married." He laughed. "When I went from Philly to New York, it was going from the frying pan into the fire! New Hampshire has been a really nice respite from it all. But around my fortieth birthday last year, I started to think more seriously about starting a family . . . regretting not doing it sooner." He sighed. "After eight years up here, it's easy to get into a routine—let yourself work too hard, and not have to commit to anything else." He reached for her hand, but Alex withdrew. "But I wouldn't mind spending a little time in Breedville now and then," he said, looking into her eyes hopefully. Alex averted her gaze.

"Frankly, Aaron, I'm not sure how much time I'm going to be there."

"What do you mean?" He looked confused.

"Well, Joshua and I have had a recent falling out over a personal matter."

Aaron's look of confusion deepened. Alex shook her head. "It's not what you think. There has just been some tension between us for a while now. I don't know if it's a fear of loss of control, or if I'm being too aggressive. But something happened recently, and I think it might have been damaging to our professional relationship. Also," she continued, her eyes suddenly unable to meet his, "there is someone else in my life. I don't know what will happen there."

Alex looked up for a moment, staring beyond her dinner date out into open space. Aaron could see the fire leaving her eyes as Alex seemed to be contemplating her next move. The pause in the conversation became uncomfortably long.

"Who knows," she finally tried to joke. "Maybe you could use an additional OBGYN down here? After all, Manchester is a good sized town."

"That's a major change, Alex. You certainly could find a place here in Manchester. But I can't believe that whatever has caused this schism between you and Joshua can't be righted. I've known him for over five years. He's a great guy. I'd hate to see you two part, knowing how much your presence has meant to him."

"Well, we'll see," Alex said in a tone that sounded defeated. Aaron paid the bill and took Alex back to her hotel. The silence in his car was deafening.

"Will I see you tomorrow?" he asked.

"I'm planning to stop by to see Jody and the baby early, just after breakfast. Then I'm going to have to hurry back to Breedville. I've got patients scheduled for one o'clock."

"Oh," he said, the disappointment obvious in his voice.

"I had a wonderful time tonight, Aaron," Alex said, trying to keep the moment on a lighter note. "Good night! I'll see you at the hospital tomorrow." She opened the car door and exited.

"Good night, Alex." He watched her walk away.

Chapter Twenty Nine

Betty Palmer was having contractions every three minutes. Her membranes were ruptured and the fluid was clear. She had only arrived on the labor floor thirty minutes ago and was already feeling the urge to push. Mona Brent's contractions were five minutes apart. Her last baby had delivered in two hours and she arrived at the hospital eight centimeters dilated.

Carol Hingham had already undergone one cesarean section with her first child. Joshua had spoken with her about the possibility of a vaginal birth despite her previous operation. Carol had decided to wait on scheduling an elective section, hoping that an active and successful vaginal birth would intervene. Although she was not due for another three weeks, she found herself with painful contractions and a four centimeter dilated cervix. She was Joshua's third admission to the labor floor in the past two hours.

Joshua was down in his office trying to see a few of his scheduled patients when the phone rang. He had long since exchanged his dress shirt and slacks for the comfort and convenience of a scrub suit. Ann Stremp took the call and paged him in the exam room.

"Dr. Barron, the labor floor needs to speak to you right away."

"I'll take it in here, Ann." He hated being interrupted during an examination, but had no choice with such an active labor floor.

"I'm sorry, Mrs. Jerrell, but I'm going to have to take this call."

Mrs. Jerrell was in the middle of receiving a pap smear. Joshua quickly scraped the cells from her cervix, wiping them onto a slide. He sprayed the specimen and hastily removed the speculum from her vagina. He grabbed the phone, leaving the poor woman with her knees still splayed to the side.

"This is Dr. Barron. What's happening?"

"Mrs. Palmer feels like pushing and Mrs. Brent is eight centimeters. Her first labor only lasted two hours . . . we need you up here right away."

"I'll be there in a few minutes," Joshua answered. He turned to his hapless patient and rapidly finished the exam. Excusing himself from the room, he left for the labor floor. Having an office attached to the hospital gave Joshua the convenience of proximity, but also often a false sense of security that he could manage two jobs at once.

"Dr. Barron," Ann asked as Joshua sped past her desk, "do you want me to see if Dr. Faber is available to help you out?"

"No, Ann," he snapped. "I can handle this. Just apologize to Mrs. Jerrell for me. Tell her I will call her tonight. Leave her chart on my desk."

When he arrived upstairs, he found both of his patients fully dilated and pushing. Although he could usually count on a first-time mother having to push for several hours, Mrs. Palmer was matching Mrs. Brent push for push and both babies were clearly in sight. As luck would have it, Carol Hingham was experiencing severe pain in her abdomen and the monitor tracing was showing a fetal tachycardia of 180 beats per minute. Barbara Harrod, the nurse attending Carol's labor, suspected a possible ruptured uterus. She ran for Dr. Barron, who was delivering Betty Palmer.

"Dr. Barron, Carol Hingham is having a lot of pain and the fetal heart is in the 180's. Would you like me to call for help? Perhaps, Dr. Faber is home and can come in and give you a hand."

"Why does everybody think I need help?" Joshua grumbled loudly to no one in particular. "I'll be right there, Barbara," he shouted. With the head delivered, he suctioned out the nose and mouth, gently assisted the shoulders, revealing the Palmers' little girl. He cut the cord and handed her over to the nurse. Then he left for the second delivery, leaving the placenta and remaining umbilical cord still inside. Not moments after he arrived, Mrs. Brent's baby's head was crowning. In the midst of the action, Barbara opened the door.

"Dr. Barron," she called. "I don't think we can wait. The monitor strip on Mrs. Hingham is showing deep decelerations. Her fundus is soft and her pulse is up. I'm going to see if anyone is available at Breedville ObGyn."

"Barbara, you'll wait for me!" Joshua told an anxious nurse and refocused on delivering the head. "Call the anesthesiologist and move her to the section room. I'll be there shortly."

Despite the rapidity of her labor, Mona Brent's baby was taking his time coming out. Joshua expedited things by cutting a large episiotomy and applying firm traction on the neck. He felt a snap as the remainder of the baby slid out from under the pubic bone. He clamped and cut the cord, handed the screaming new male to the nurse, then flew out the door.

Joshua caught up to his third patient in the cesarean section room. Anesthesiologist Richard Brown was putting a second IV site into Mrs. Hingham in preparation for a possible transfusion and induction of general anesthesia. The fetal heart rate was in the forties, while the mother's was close to two hundred. It was clear that Mrs. Hingham's previous C-section scar had separated and she was now bleeding into her abdomen. The washing of his hands was perfunctory and the abdominal prep was minimal. Within minutes, Carol was asleep and Joshua was breaking skin. He was not surprised to find her abdomen full of blood. The old uterine incision was wide open and the baby was floating outside of the uterus. He clamped and cut the cord, handing the baby over to Arthur Hill from pediatrics, who had been called to the floor. Joshua rapidly removed the placenta from the open uterus and closed the defect with a running suture. Although blood continued to ooze from the perforation site, the bleeding was now under control, allowing Dr. Brown to stabilize Mrs. Hingham with intravenous fluids and packed red cells. Joshua called over to Arthur.

"How's the baby, Art?"

"Not good, Joshua. I've got an apgar of 2 at one and five minutes. He's being vented and I've got bicarb going through the umbilical vein. The cord pH was 7.15. How's the mom?"

"I think we're okay here," Joshua answered. He looked up at the anesthesiologist who nodded in agreement. "The bleeding seems to be under control and the main vessels are still intact," Joshua continued.

By this time, Bill Cronin had joined Joshua in the operating room to help him finish up the case. Soon, the two obstetricians had Carol Hingham put back together. Dr. Brown woke Mrs. Hingham and extubated her, then she was whisked into the recovery room. Her husband, who had been completely abandoned in the labor room during the emergency, now followed Art Hill to the nursery with his newborn son.

Joshua returned to Mrs. Palmer's labor room. The placenta had delivered spontaneously, and she and her baby girl were resting comfortably. In the Brent labor room, Mona's placenta had also delivered, and the attending nurse had packed the episiotomy site with gauze to decrease the blood loss. Joshua sewed up the episiotomy, congratulated the new parents and returned to the recovery room to check on Mrs. Hingham. At this point he was sweating profusely and nearly out of breath. Carol was now fully awake and asking for her baby.

"Where's the baby? Is he okay? Where's my husband?"

"He's in the nursery with Dr. Hill from pediatrics. Your uterus ruptured, Carolyn. That's what all the pain was from and why the baby's heart rate was so high. We got him out as quickly as we could," he reassured her. "Dr. Hill is working with him now. You rest. I'll find out how he is doing."

Joshua left the recovery room to find Bob Hingham standing outside the nursery, watching through the window as Art Hill continued to minister to the newborn.

"Bob," Joshua said, "Why don't you go down to the recovery room to be with Carolyn. I'll check in with Dr. Hill and get back to both of you shortly." The emotionally exhausted man went to his wife's side while Joshua joined Art Hill. The baby was looking better. The endotracheal tube was out and he was breathing on his own inside an oxygen hood. His color looked good and he was screaming healthily.

"I think we're going to be okay, Joshua," Art said as the beleaguered obstetrician entered the nursery. "It was close, but the ten minute Apgar was eight and we seem to be out of the woods. I don't think we had more than a few more minutes."

"I agree," Joshua said. "It was close with Mom as well. I really dodged a bullet this time."

"You did all you could, Joshua," Art insisted as they looked down at the newborn. "Considering the circumstances, things went remarkably well. The Brent baby has a broken clavicle—probably due to the difficult shoulder delivery. But overall, you've got three healthy babies, and three healthy moms. And all within a forty-five minute period!" He smiled.

"Thanks for the vote of confidence, Art. It's undeserved but appreciated."

Joshua left for the lounge. He met up with Bill Cronin, who was just changing out of his scrub suit.

"Thanks for the help, Bill," Joshua said. "I appreciate it."

"Looks like you put out quite a fire, my friend."

"Not really," Joshua said as he slumped into a chair. "I was damned lucky. Everyone kept asking me if I needed help, but I kept insisting that I could handle it. Things got out of control. I don't know why I couldn't just admit I needed backup."

"Aw, don't be too rough on yourself," Bill said as he buttoned up his shirt. "You did your best, and everything worked out fine." He shut his locker and headed towards the door. "Anytime I can help, Joshua, don't hesitate to ask." With his hand on the knob, he turned back. "Of course, with Alex around, you probably won't need us too much . . . but still, never hesitate to ask. Take it easy." The door closed behind him, leaving Joshua with increasing self-doubt.

I should have left the office earlier. Hingham should have been the number one priority. I was forced to rush the Brent delivery, leading to a broken collarbone. I should have called for back up. I don't know what I was thinking. Alex would have called for help. Alex. What have I done? I've been driving her away as long as she's been here. Am I that insecure after all these years, that I can't share responsibility with a colleague? What's the matter with me? I need to get her back. I just hope it isn't too late.

Joshua changed out of his scrubs and stopped by the recovery room. The Hinghams were all accounted for there, with the newest arrival still breathing 100% oxygen but looking pink and well.

Bob Hingham extended his hand.

"Dr. Barron, you're a life saver. I don't know how we could ever thank you for all you did for us today."

"So glad I could help," Joshua said warmly. He turned away, heading towards the labor rooms of his other two deliveries. He congratulated Betty Palmer and her husband, then walked into Mona Brent's room. The little girl was still in the warmer; her left arm lay limply at her side.

"Hi, Dr. Barron," Mona greeted him. "We certainly put you through the ringer today! Dr. Hill said there's a break in her collarbone, but it sounds like that should heal up just fine. Thank you so much for everything."

"I'm sorry about the fracture, Mona. Sometimes these things happen."

"It's okay. Dr. Hill said everything is going to be okay. I've got a healthy little girl, thanks to you!" Joshua smiled and left without further comment, happy that Mrs. Brent was not upset. His mind still swimming with self-doubt, he headed back towards his office. Ron Dorcik caught up with him in the hall.

"Hi, Joshua!"

"Hey, Ron," Joshua answered wearily.

"I hear you had a little excitement on the labor floor."

"News sure does travel fast around here," Joshua said, trying to insert some enthusiasm into his voice. Sometimes he wished news didn't travel quite so fast.

"It's a small hospital. By the way, Joshua, do you know where I could find Alex? Is she off today?"

"Yes, she's off. She'll be in tomorrow afternoon. Can I help you?"

"No thanks, I just need to speak to her. She's not answering at home. I just hope it's not too late."

"Too late for what? Is something wrong?"

Ron shook his head. "I just need to speak to her, that's all." He turned away and headed back to his office. Joshua wondered what Ron was referring to, but couldn't help experiencing a similar fear. When it came to Alex, he, too, hoped it wasn't too late.

The next morning was as hectic as Alex expected. After grabbing a quick coffee and pastry at a local Manchester coffee shop, Alex headed to the nursery where the Pinkham baby was still receiving oxygen. The general consensus amongst the pediatric staff was that he was doing as well as could be expected and should recover uneventfully after about a week. Alex found Jody awake and sitting up in bed.

"Hi, Dr. Faber! Did you get a chance to see Charlie this morning?"

"Yes, Jody. He's adorable. How are you doing?"

"Well, I'm pretty sore and I can't move around much with all of this tubing, but Dr. Speiser says I'm doing well!" Jody looked exhausted, but elated. The topic of her pathology report and prognosis did not come up—neither woman wanted to spoil the happiness of the short visit.

"Well, I hope to come back to see you this weekend, Jody," Alex told her. Jody looked directly at Alex.

"Are you coming to see me or Dr. Speiser?" she smiled playfully. The blush went up in Alex's face.

"Why do you ask?"

"Dr. Speiser couldn't say enough nice things about my doctor from Breedville on morning rounds today!" Jody said with a broad smile. "I think he's got a little crush on you!" Alex was completely flustered, and certainly did not want to discuss such a topic with her patient, so quickly changed the subject.

"Well, I'm looking forward to seeing you and little Charlie on Saturday. Take care, Jody."

"Thanks again, Dr. Faber."

The trip back to Breedville did not take nearly as long as Alex wanted it to. She was pleased to hear from Aaron that Joshua had spoken so highly of her, but she was still hurt by his biting comments on Saturday afternoon and his lack of communication with her since. And, of course, she had still not heard from Ron. She stopped home briefly to change and unpack. When she finally entered her office at 12:30, she was greeted by a vase with a dozen red roses, standing at attention on her desk.

A smile instantly crept across Alex's face, and she walked over to her desk. There was a small card nestled into the buds. *I've let you down. Give me a second chance and I promise to never disappoint you again. Love, Ron.* It was a beautiful display and Alex's heart soared. She picked up the heavy vase and set it on the credenza behind her desk. When she turned back, she noticed yet another flower—a single pink rose resting on the desk with a note attached. It had obviously been hidden by the more impressive floral display. The note was simple: *Dear Alex, You are a great partner. Please forgive me. Joshua.*

Alex bounced out of her chair and headed straight for her partner's office. She peeked in to find Joshua sitting with a pile of charts in front of him, his eyes staring off into the winter landscape.

"Hi partner!" she said, her voice light. "How's Julie?"

Joshua turned from the window and looked at Alex. "She and her parents are all doing well." He nodded, his lips twisting upwards into a small smile. "Thanks to you."

"I'm glad I could be of help." Alex turned and left. They both knew there was no need to say anything more.

EPILOGUE

IT WAS FEBRUARY AGAIN in Breedville. The lack of snow at Thanksgiving was more than made up for by the New Year's Eve blizzard—no one would be seeing the ground again till April. The plows were keeping the streets clean and the citizens in their four wheel drives were not hampered in the slightest by anything that Mother Nature was throwing at them. George Washington's fluffy white cap had appeared once again on the statue on the mall.

Jody Pinkham had long since returned from Manchester. Her baby boy had put on four pounds since his birth just before the New Year. Jody's pathology report revealed that her malignant tumor had been completely resected, with the margins of the surgical specimen free of cancer. Dr. Speiser had removed nearly twenty lymph nodes, and despite his clinical suspicion, they were all found to be tumor-free. There was nothing left to do except follow Jody with frequent exams and scans, but her prognosis was guardedly optimistic.

Gerald Ranson continued to consider himself a divine gift to the field of obstetrics and gynecology. Fortunately for him, his training and competence made up for his lack of humility and bedside manner and he provided a needed addition to Breedville OB GYN.

After her frightening experience over Christmas vacation, Julie Barron put her sex life on hold, preferring the less intimate moments of crowded class parties. Besides, her interest in football was waning, while a certain member of the high school math team had caught her eye.

Phil Lambert had returned to his active cardiology practice. His compulsive and dedicated management of his patients was unchanged, while a psychotherapist was helping him put a new perspective on his practice and his life.

Alex was once again distracting Ron Dorcik in the same manner that she had so many years ago, while Aaron Speiser had to remain content to merely provide oncology consults for Alex as her practice grew.

Joshua lay in bed staring up at the ceiling. Liz was fast asleep beside him. He was thinking about the family's upcoming trip to the west coast later that month. Among other things, Joshua was excited to trade the golf games of his dreams for an actual round at the famed Pebble Beach in Monterey. It probably wouldn't be a flawless game, but Joshua couldn't imagine anything more perfect.

The phone rang. It was the hospital.

"Sorry to bother you, Dr. Barron," Sandy said, "but Mrs. Lukken has arrived and she's very active. Would you like me to examine her?"

"That won't be necessary, Sandy," the sleepy obstetrician answered. "I'll be there in about twenty minutes."